T0157082

THE STAR SERIES

BOOK ONE OF SEVEN

VINCENT HAVELUND

iUniverse, Inc.
Bloomington

The Star Series
Book One of Seven

iUniverse books may be ordered through booksellers or by contacting:

iUniverse
1663 Liberty Drive
Bloomington, IN 47403
www.iuniverse.com
1-800-Authors (1-800-288-4677)

ISBN: 978-1-4697-4597-8 (sc)
ISBN: 978-1-4697-4598-5 (hc)
ISBN: 978-1-4697-4599-2 (e)

Library of Congress Control Number: 2012900895

Printed in the United States of America

iUniverse rev. date: 1/16/2012

Contents

INTRODUCTION

The theme of this series of seven books is about highly developed planets, and one major planet Orbsey finding planet Earth, in their search for extra terrestrial life. The series starts in the year 1 AD and concludes in the 24th century, the different planets and their advanced cultures, as well as Earths backward culture and its development over the entire period is the central theme to the books.

There is one planet that is far more advanced than the others and uses its massive resources to coordinate them all into an integrated system for, military security, trade, technological development, financial integration and health.

This major planet Orbsey has also found the secret of long distance travel by the use of the fourth dimension, and in this way beaten the tyranny of distance throughout the Cosmos.

Any wars of defense are fought with Nuclear Missiles or Robots, but major battles are rare and Orbsey is pledged to a policy of defense only within thweikr own and other planets.

CHAPTER 1/

NEW BEGINNINGS

It was the beginning of the new calendar in the year 1AD and in a small village in China a young girl named Sun Li was coming to maturity. She was fourteen YOA and appeared to be a girl who would be attractive in a few years time. She was the youngest of ten siblings and her parents were very proud of her; not only was she starting to show her physical looks, but she was by nature just as pleasing. Li for so she was called, was a dreamer and one night she had a dream she would never forget, during her long life of 'two hundred and eighty five years', lived mostly on a distant planet. She would always remember that dream which proved to be so accurate in every part of her future life.

When she was eighteen YOA she was destined to meet the 'love of her life', theirs would be a great life together working for the State and the people, and in her final years would rise to be a 'judge on her adopted countries Supreme Court'

In one of her dreams Li had gone fishing with three of her brothers and father, but her job was as the spotter. She was to swim around the area and signal wherever she could find a shoal of fish, a job she really loved doing; because she was such a good swimmer. The men had two boats, and the fish that day was very abundant, it wasn't long before by working the nets together both boats were fully loaded, and they could fish for no more. It wasn't long after they reached shore that most of the fish had been sold, to people who had been lining the river bank, and watching them hauling in fish. The men were happy because they had made a good profit for their days work, but they kept some of the fish to take back to their village to be shared with everyone.

They were on their way home when they met an old man who owned a small herd of pigs, and they were able to barter two pigs in return for some of the fish they still had left.

In the dream they were continuing their journey home when Li suddenly found herself floating off in the air, hard as she struggled to land she couldn't, and so she floated off never again was she to see her family, when she finally returned many years later they had all passed away.

When she awoke the next morning she was very distressed, but she told no one else about her dream she kept it to herself; and tried to figure out what it all meant if anything. Finally she went to her old Grandmother who was bent with age, and asked her what her dream meant. The wise old woman who was well known in the village for her wisdom fondled Li's head, and then as if in a dream began to speak, gradually the full meaning became evident, but Li was incredulous of the message her Granny gave her and doubted it was true.

The fish she had helped her family to catch and sell; meant Li would in the future feed and sustain many people, and she would live to a great age, not in China, but in some far off new home where life would be very different. The pigs meant a family of her own, but there would be only two, and they would grow up healthy and happy just as Li and her husband would be, and the entire family would travel far and wide throughout the universe. Sadly when Li finally left her home it would be under difficult circumstances, and she would never return while any of her immediate family were still alive.

The old lady finished what she had been saying and then seemed to come out of the trance she had gone into. When Li asked her what she had meant she had no memory of anything she had said, it was because of this she told Li that what she had heard was true. Everything would happen, and nothing could change what had been forecasted for Li's future life, because the 'Gods had spoken'.

Everything the old women had prophesied that day came true over Li's lifetime spent mainly living on a far away planet, and Li would often in her travels over vast distances remember with a lot of love her old Granny, who had that day predicted her life so clearly and accurately.

This is a fictional story of ten planets occupied by different types of beings living in different solar systems to Earth; they are all dominated by one planet that is far more advanced than the others. This leading planet named Orbsey has defeated the tyranny of distance in space travel, they are able to enter the fourth dimension and even with their huge space ships move immediately from one galaxy to another. There are many ways in which Orbsey is way ahead of all of the other planets; especially in technology and medical services.

Many years in the future when the main people in this story are due to retire they sat back to talk for a little about their careers, "It's been too long and now we are too tired for any more pleasure in life. There has never been the time to even spend with our children, we could go on for many years of living and the doctors could keep us alive, but I prefer to die with dignity now?" the husband said.

"Yes I too am very tired and just want to pass on, it's been a good exciting life, but the govt; kept us working for too long, now there is no pleasure left. I am 285, and you are 300 YOA; we are both so frail we can do nothing! As you say it's better to die with dignity than tarry any longer, let us go to bed and die peacefully in our sleep?" his wife said with a sweet smile at her dearly loved husband for so many years.

The next morning their daughter Lisa and son Kauri found them, they both had smiles on their faces; they had died together in dignity happy at last. The smiles reflected their many memories together, through a long and turbulent but happy life.

The biggest development on Orbsey is the age for retirement which is 260 YOA and, the average age lived is three hundred years, but it is the highly advanced medical technology that keeps people alive, and able to work that long. Many would prefer to die, but that's not allowed the doctors can and do keep everyone alive, by govt; decree.

Meantime the state has had the people working to their maximum capability, until they are allowed because of their age to retire; they may not by law retire earlier, and they cannot refuse the medical treatment that ensures they are fit for work at all stages of their five different work periods.

Earth was the first planet found, but is considered too far behind the others in every way to qualify as a member of the Federation of Planets; when it is formed rather Earth is given the status of being a protectorate of the leading planet Orbsey, and has its own special place within the group. The integration of the peoples of Earth and Orbsey are good, and any problems are overcome over the years.

We need to discern the similarities between the reality of the highly advanced planets, and the actuality of life on Earth in the 20th century; by comparing the differences which are clear. Earth at the time of Christ's birth was gradually emerging as an agricultural economy, owned and controlled in the main by the wealthy few, and the manual work all done by the peasant classes. The planets discovered by Orbsey are at different stages of development, meaning the same as Orbsey had once been but all were ahead of Earth. In other words there were only two levels of economic reality, the very wealthy and the very poor.

In the modern age on Earth during the 20th century, the people are in bondage to debt in many guises, but it's still a class struggle that goes on daily. The bankers represent the wealthy classes, and control the monetary flows by lending significantly to the middle class. The govts; in theory look after everyone, but depending on the political financial persuasion one can see different ideas, being pursued.

The series is based on the discovery of the new Planets by Orbseyn Scientists, and the interaction between the new comers, and the Orbseyn population. The beings who occupy the various planets are herein called 'people from which Orbsey is setting up small colonies' within their own territory.

This account is fast moving often funny, sometimes tragic, and other times just a difference between the citizens of ten different planets plus Earth. Naturally all have different ways, but the ones this story is about are the colonies set up on Orbsey for observation purposes, and the work that had to be done to create strong integration. When the colonies are complete they are a very diverse lot, all with different ideas and ideals, planet Earth is the most backward of them all, but in many ways the most aggressive. The 'main characters' is an Earthling and her Orbseyn husband, and the Earth colonies are favored for this and for other reasons, the main one being that 'Earth was the first planet discovered'.

CHAPTER 2/

ORBSEY A STAR IN THE HEAVENS

The discovery of planet Earth was announced by the leading scientist to the Presidium of their planet Orbsey and it was received with caution, of what interest is such a backward planet to us they had asked?

Before the discovery was released to the general public, the scientists who had discovered the new planet, were told to appear before a board of enquiry to explain what they were doing and why? The politicians conducting the enquiry were questioning the scientists by cyber space; and the scientists were in the studio of a media network, answering the questions live.

"What is the reason for this discovery; is it of any benefit to our planet?" The chairman asked.

"The want is for knowledge of the universe and to know better what is out there beside's ourselves. The need is to look forward to our own planets security, in the future there will be many planets discovered, and some will be hostiles. We have the need to know so we can protect ourselves".

"How is the knowing all about other planets going to protect us please explain what you mean in some detail, so we politicians can understand?"

"We have one very advanced planet here, but we are self centered, one day another planet will come along and want to occupy us, and we won't know how to resist. We need to get to know other planets with the view of cooperation together in some way for security purposes, and in this if we are successful we will be able to form a group working together with common goals."

"How long do you anticipate this entire program will take to put in place? And how many trained people will we need to run the program you are proposing?"

"It will take at least two hundred years maybe more, but it will be a well worthwhile investment in our planets future, and the staff will be in the thousands".

"Very well we will let you know in a week our decision thank you gentlemen, until then do nothing more please."

A week later the scientists received full support for their work, and told they could carry on, and disclose what they were doing so the entire planets population could understand. The hope was the people would be in full support of the program as outlined, by the scientists.

There had been an excited rush of applicants from all over Orbsey, of many citizens who wanted to travel to the new planet that had been found. Citizens from every country on the planet, wanted to be among the first two thousand who were to be selected to be the planets first 'interplanetary explorers'. Over one million enquiries had been received within the first week; of the announced intention to send out a space fleet with up to two thousand citizens aboard, who were to explore, and try to set up a colony on the new found planet Earth.

Every country on the planet Orbsey had set up offices, and staff to receive applications, and they had been quickly swamped with citizens; who wanted to be among the first to be going as pioneer's to a new world.

Over 2,000 years previously at about the time of the birth of Christ in a distant galaxy, on a planet "Orbsey" which was very much bigger than Earth, but whose people were in many respects similar. The scientists had started sending out probes, searching for a planet in a solar system that was capable of maintaining life similar to their own.

Their own planet was peaceful all wars had been stopped or forcefully cancelled out many years ago, but their ambitions had extended far, and now they wanted to know, are there others out there like us? If there are can we communicate with any of them?

Many unmanned probes had been sent out, but none had been successful, then on behalf of a radio based quest, a famous scientist reported a solar system had been found; from which definite signs of life had been heard. The site from where the 'radio signals' were sent were not too far distant in an adjacent galaxy, and research was being pursued to get confirmation of its existence, and whether the radio signals had been deliberately sent; by intelligent beings capable of understanding they were sending the messages. The big question was where they also trying to find any sign of intelligent life, because if they were there must be an advanced intelligence involved.

From the time of Earth's discovery many years had gone by during which more probes were sent out, and had reported back the information the scientists wanted, but now it was time to decide what they wanted to do about colonizing this new planet. It had been found that the planet was in many respects a complete replica of the Planet Orbsey except there was only one sun and one moon. On the contrary Orbsey moved in a planetary system that had three suns? Orbsey itself had several moons.

The Orbseyn population had been controlled for many years, and peace had also been normal for a long time. The people had millennia before settled all differences, and the countries of planet Orbsey lived in harmony, controlled by one big central govt; and with six different almost equal (numerically) groups all represented within the central Govt. There had been a serious overpopulation on Orbsey until they had begun to increase the natural life span of its peoples, and then control the rate of birth, the results had been spectacular, and now with the life span greatly expanded there was no aging or population problems

All aggressive wars between the various Orbseyn countries had ceased thousands of years ago, when a method had been found that nullified all weapons of war, even hand guns had been abolished. Only pistols for sporting purposes were still allowed, but they were not allowed to fire bullets, that type of weapon was confined to none destructive laser beams (Stun Guns). Laws had been legislated and enforced whereby no weapons of any level of destruction could be used for any purpose, and the police used stun guns only against known criminals.

The people are much the same in appearance as the people from Earth, but the method of communication had many centuries before changed to thought only, the only thing they had to do was think of someone and they were in instant touch. All food was ingested by simply thinking of what they wanted to eat, and the food intake was immediate through the thought process, as a result over many centuries they had gradually lost their mouths and were now quite comfortable without them, they really had no use for them except perhaps to make a noise at sporting events, but they did that well enough without mouths.

Any serious illnesses could be corrected by the simple process of replacement of the parts that were sick or weak; their heads were a little bigger than Earthlings, but they had no ears they weren't needed so again had been lost over the centuries. All other parts were still the same as earthlings, legs, arms, hands, torso etc.

It had never been general knowledge what the scientific Community had been trying to achieve, because they had wanted to keep the discovery secret, until they could be certain about what they had found. At the early stage the only contact had been by radio, but now more information had been confirmed, by way of a huge new telescope system in orbit over Orbsey, all of their scientific hopes had been confirmed and they were jubilant. When the news finally broke there was great excitement, they had even found an area on this Earth that was only lightly inhabited, within a huge area of sea and comprising several Islands, one that was very large and another with two Islands but quite small, and lots of smaller islands on the outer peripheral.

There was great excitement and expectations, finally they had found a land mass similar to Orbsey but a lot smaller, inhabited by people that looked similar to their own, but very backward in dress and development. For example the only mode of transport was horse drawn. There was much laughter among the Orbseyns about the horse mode of transport; gosh they said we left that all behind thousands of years ago they must be really backward.

The commission had decided to send enough spaceships to carry about two thousand settlers to this world, which from the scientists had learned was named Earth by the local peoples. There were no problems expected and certainly the new settler's would have more than adequate knowledge, to be quite safe in this new environment.

They would carry no weapons for any type of destruction, but they did carry the technology to neutralize all explosive war machines sent against them, for their society it was simple to cancel out the power of any explosive weapons of any type or caliber, including small nuclear devices up to a certain size. The space freighters would carry landing vehicles for use by the Orbseyn settlers, and the transport fleet would be put into permanent orbit around Earth so that the settlers could return

home at any time they wanted, the only condition being there must be at least a minimum load for a space freighter

Orbsey the Planet is twice the size of Planet Earth and located in an adjacent Solar System! The Planet has a surface area of 1.2 Billion Square Kms, within which there are twelve continents with close to one billion populations each, and another 30 independent small countries dotted around the Orbseyn globe. Within the continents there are over 300 independent small countries each with their own national integrity, but dependent on central associations.

Orbseys Great Parliament is the controlling body situated in the 'Country of Cordiance, in the State of Cordiance' and with final say over a fixed agenda. 'All Medical, Food, Homes, Transport, Clothing and Footwear, White Goods' etc; are govt; controlled. The intent was that there were to be no homeless or hungry Orbseyns that are unable to support themselves, any unfortunates that fall through the cracks must be helped, and supported by their own countries, and cared for at the cost of the central parliament.

The Law including ' Police, Lawyers and Courts' are very pro active and move very fast, there are no jails, but there is a tightly administrated system of control if convicted of any criminal offence. There are capital offences that means quick death if found guilty, and the police ability to find guilty parties is very high, if a person has been executed for false evidence and that is subsequently proved, all guilty parties are quickly executed. We need to explain here that capital or the death sentence normally means a period of forced sleep. A death sentence normally means up to two hundred years of enforced sleep in govt; controlled sleep centers, all references herein to execution refers to sleep for a court approved period.

Capital offences are Murder, Rape, Pedophilia, and all sexual aberrations. If mistakes are made the person condemned to sleep is revived and retrial held, if found innocent compensation is paid pro rata to the time having been asleep. The reason the punishment is so severe is because all such crimes are committed by persons who have the responsibility to declare their various problems, and can be medically corrected without cost quickly and easily; with very little interruption in their lives.

All other crimes the punishment is to be put on a special watch machine, and criminals are forced to make recompense to the state for all court costs, and accumulated extra costs. This also involves the working off of the debts, and repayment to the victims of such crime. When the payments are completed the criminal is fully restored to society, and regains all of the beneficial rights of a citizen of Orbsey. For Social Welfare there is none, any citizens unable to work must present for medical rehabilitation, and they will be fully fit again within a week, there is no unemployment.

Deterioration in health through age is also curable, but stops at the approved age limit. Cure at any age can still be acquired but only through private resources, the govt has completed its mandate after a citizen has reached retirement age, and by ensuring every citizen reaches that average age limit in physically good health.

Normally after retiring there's another fifty years of living if you have been a saver, and can pay for all of the luxuries you might like in old age, there is no pension for support, but there is a type of superannuation.

There is no direct tax but all consumer goods have a consumer tax added, this includes all material to produce everything that is controlled by the Central Parliament for processing etc.

The flora and Fauna suffered badly in the very early period, but has mostly been restored by the Scientists many centuries ago, and the original growth had been restored. The forests had also all been restored with native trees being forbidden to be cut down except with a govt approval; only soft quick growing trees are allowed to be cut and milled. Any exotic fined grain hard timbers are used only on the houses of the wealthy; that type of material is very expensive.

White goods are available also through the two systems, with only the wealthy being able to afford the architecturally designed products, the entire govt; guarantee product range is mass produced in enormous quantities as are all common govt; consumer goods. All of the lower demand products are left to the private industry to produce and sell, because those types of products are consumed in smaller quantities, and are unable to be mass produced economically by the govt.

The ideas behind the govt; controls is to ensure that all are fed clothed and housed to a minimum level they may rise above that level, but they may not become slaves to debt. All may have a commonly produced car, but again that's the norm for all, any may rise above that and enjoy the fruits of their labor. The reality being they are limited as to how much they can leave to individual beneficiaries etc; in their final estate.

Orbsey had several millennia ago been a world of wars and killing on an enormous scale, the death and cost of wars had been crazy, and the countries on the planet couldn't develop. They first got to a very high technical achievement, that threatened to destroy the planet, and that's when changes started. The scientists discovered ways to nullify explosive materials of all types, and this controlled the fear of total destruction. Then small weapons were banned, and scale of production was lost so again these were stopped. Then laws were legislated that unilaterally condemned certain crimes, these were universally implemented, and many draconian punishments were imposed the intent being used to stop rising serious crime.

When then the Central Parliament increased the credits repayment system of punishment for small crime gradually, even petty crime was on the wane. Then the quick police response and legal conviction was sped up so much, and the greater success was what forced criminals to change their lifestyles. There is still a lot of blue and white collar crime in Orbsey, but is very much on the wane, and they are still trying to control crime, by better police efficiency. They have robot police, but don't use them against the general populace; they actually haven't been deployed for hundreds of years.

The new settlers going to Earth had been treated so that they all had a mouth and ears, there was only one thing they were all quite brown by skin color, but they soon found there were many skin colors on earth. They could now talk and eat like Earthlings, but their heads were just a little bigger. Looked at casually it was difficult to tell the difference between Earthlings and Orbseyns.

The govt; had found it necessary to use a type of lottery to choose the citizens who would be going on the exciting trip. The launch off day had arrived and, the chosen settlers for the new world had been taken aboard, and prepared for the flight. This procedure wasn't difficult because for years daily intergalactic flights had been available, at quite nominal costs, there were many people quite used to being prepared for these flights, although never before had there been specific destinations to visit another planet. It wasn't unusual for private flights to visit one of the moons, and to the private citizens this was a thrilling experience.

As well as the passenger craft a huge cargo vessel had been loaded, with all of the necessary equipment to set up the new colony. A site had been chosen in the middle of the huge Island, which in the future would be named Australia. It was known that gold was highly valued by the Earthlings, and therefore big quantities of gold and other precious metals were on board, the intent was that they could buy any land they wanted. Australia was the chosen site, but if they were rejected they could easily return home, aboard their vessels that hovering in the stratosphere.

Although the distance between the planets was vast, sometimes millions of light years, the tyranny of distance had been conquered many years ago, and the travel time to Earth would be no longer than 168 hours. The space freighters would enter the fourth dimension and leave it at the predestinated point closest to Earth. On arrival the fleet would go into high orbit above Earth, while an advance party would land in a cruiser, and if they could set up negotiations to buy land, in the vast unoccupied desert.

It had been a wonderful trip all of the passengers were excited and full of hope, and anticipation that they were off to find a new life. There was no liquor or drugs allowed on the craft, but they had several big parties anyhow, and the goodwill towards one another was wonderful, many lifelong friendships were established during that expedition. The passengers were about 60% married couples, and the rest young men and women who were unattached, but many of these had had become attached by the time they arrived on Earth.

Once negotiations to buy had been completed another advance group would be allowed to land using the smaller transfer vessels, and unload the modules that would make their living conditions quite normal; on the desert sands. They would also land the equipment that would close down any weapons, big or small that may be aimed at them and their new homes.

The home materials were to be unloaded, but the control of the colony, once they had been constructed it would be up to the leaders of the new colonists, they would have complete control including behavior, anyone misbehaving would be held with laser shackles on board the craft circling above. There was lots of excitement aboard the fleet which was now in orbit, because soon they expected reports back from the advance parties, to advise that they could now land on their new purchase, but they were in for a rude shock.

It was after their scouts arrived in the deserts of Australia, and they had made the first contact only then did they begin to understand, what it was like to be back in an ancient culture. The first meeting was with a group of Australian Aborigines, and it was easy to communicate, all they had to do was listen and their thoughts translated immediately, then to talk back they had the natural ability to be able to converse in any language, that they heard being spoken.

They found the people very friendly and nice but extremely backward and natural! Because the climate was so hot they wore few clothes, and had no knowledge of the outside world. Although they seemed to live a happy and carefree life, it was clear they must be short lived and had to keep moving; to gather food, with women doing much of the work, and the men moving always out front hunting for food, and in charge of the community.

There was no objection to the newcomers setting up a colony, but the natives weren't interested in gold, they didn't see any use for something they couldn't eat or wear. On the other hand any articles they could wear, or at least things with a practical use would be welcomed.

When asked 'who owned the land they seemed to be at a loss to understand the word owned', they had no conception of any one belonging to the tribe owning anything, the colonists were welcome to come live and enjoy at any time.

The fleet floating above was well aware of what was happening at all times because of their level of communication being so good, and all of the colonists were in agreement they wanted to land, and set up a temporary home, and they wanted to use some time to search the world for a place they could buy, and settle down permanently.

The colonists had small craft that could be used to search the entire new planet if they wanted, but it seemed best to start where they were accepted. This would allow them to acclimatize themselves, and then seek to spread out if they indeed wanted to, if the new environment wasn't to their liking they could just pack up and go home, without any regrets. It was certain that when they got home they would be welcomed as heroes, who had visited a new world; all would be well they would all have homes again, even though not the ones they had left behind.

The transfer to the Earth was easy; they had a fleet of small craft which were used to land first the Colonists and then the equipment. The leaders of the group then set out to raise up the homes, and a dome was set up over the entire encampment to protect them from any strange phenomena that they may find. Food supplies were available in over abundance, and the desert sands would quickly be made viable for growing their needs, then immediately processing them to the Orbseyn method of sustenance.

Within two weeks there was a flourishing Colony, but the Aborigines could not be found they obviously had neither interest nor curiosity about the visitors. This was not the case with the newcomers, they were intensely interested in their new neighbors, and had hoped they would come and visit. It was to be almost six months before the same group of earth people once again appeared, but still showed little interest in what was going on, in the new encampment. The leaders of the new colony had to chase up the Aborigines, to try and at least strike up some type of acceptance. It was the children that first got together, the colony had about fifty youngsters aged from five to ten YOA they soon met up with and created the first integration something their parents had been unable to achieve.

In the meantime 'the small craft had been being used to investigate the new world, but they had done so without revealing themselves'. Firstly they found this world was very sparsely inhabited and was extremely warlike. They found all manner of differences, there were some even darker skinned than themselves, others that had different shaped eyes and a yellowish skin, others that were light skinned in color and with multi colored hair, still others that seemed to be the same color as themselves, it was a multi everything world!

The one thing they all had in common was the ease in which they killed each other, 'the men seemed to take a savage delight in death, but this was anathema to the Orbseyns', in their eyes these people were extremely barbaric, and not the type they would want to live with at this stage, or at least without in some way quietening them down. It was within the power of the new arrivals to easily subdue the local populace, and they could frighten them but there was no intent to do either. Since there was no taste for killing among themselves, this aspect of the local peoples were considered very negatively, and sadly from the beginning was prejudicial to hopes of setting up a colony

They all decided that some of the men among the new colonists would spend time in differing countries to get a real understanding of this new world, only by actually living among earthlings did the leaders think they could find out if it was possible to integrate among the earth's population. The following teams went out: China a team of six, Rome six, India six, German Barbarians six, The Americas six, New Zealand two, Australia four, Europe six, Russia six and the Pacific Rim countries six.

The hopeful colonists wanted to help modernize this world and introduce a new advanced culture gradually, but they didn't want to have to fight a war to achieve what their Planet wanted. All of the exploring groups had left at once; but the Orbseyns had the technology to change their appearance to whatever was needed. It was automatic that when the groups arrived at their destinations they would take on the characteristics of the people they were with, but they could change to whatever they wanted at any time.

All of the groups had been left off at their various destinations, and they had to be picked up again from wherever they were in six months, only then at a general meeting would the decision be made where they would live, or in fact if they would even stay.

The group to check out China had arrived, and quickly settled down in their new society, they soon found it was one in which the common people had little or no rights, and life was very cheap. The leaders could kill the commoners with little reason, it only required some small mistake to be made, and one could be decapitated instantly without any recourse for the victim's family. It didn't take the Orbseyns long to decide this wasn't a place for them to settle, because the type of warfare being waged couldn't be controlled by their anti war devices. They were horrified at what they were seeing but were stuck there for the six months period.

They decided to spend the entire time travelling throughout the country, they needed no food because they were still linked to their food supply at the colonist base in the Australian desert, all they had to do was think of food and it was there direct into their feeding system. As they travelled throughout China they found out just how big the country was, although they had several just as big pr bigger back in Orbsey. The peasants had to work hard, and most of what was produced was taken by the elite for their own use. There were no discernable rights allocated to the peasants and if they were wanted for the military they were simply taken and training started immediately. The better or middle classes if they could be assessed as so, were taken for the cavalry and the peasants were simply drafted into the infantry.

CHAPTER 3

A VILLAGE IN CENTRAL CHINA

Li had just turned eighteen YOA when her parents Wang and Sui had serious financial problems; together with an old man they had known for many years, invested in a project far more heavily than was wise. It was when the project failed they were in trouble, and their main creditor was the old man who until that time the entire family thought of as close friend. It was quite quickly after the disaster had been occurred that their supposed friend; issued a legal order that his account must be paid immediately, or action would be taken to enforce payment. This would have serious consequences for the entire family; their reputation would be ruined, and Li's Father would be a pariah in their village.

Li's father had gone to see the man and pleaded for time to get the money so he could pay, but after discussions with him an alternative had been offered. Li the family's youngest daughter was to be pledged in marriage to the old man, and in return the debt would be forgiven, and a large cash payment would be made to her father. Her father had accepted the offer, but when he returned to his home and informed his family what was to be done; it set up a storm of protest from his wife and children.

The old man whose name was Lei, had been married several times, and had many off-spring the eldest son was older than Li's father. The old fellow was very old about sixty YOA, and very ugly with a long beard, and hairs growing in profusion out of both his ears and nostrils. His eyes were always watering and he smelt really bad, from the lack of bathing, this was the man Li was now pledged to marry?

Li had been devastated she had wailed, "Do you really want me to sleep with that ugly old man, he is older than you are father and he already has at least twelve wives, I would rather kill myself than that. Oh my dearest father how can you be so cruel, he has at least fifty children older than me and they are all as ugly as he is?"

Two of Li's sisters had come to her bed in the night and in whispers had told her their mother and father were having a big argument, and their mother had said through her tears, "Do you love our daughter? If you do how can you make such an agreement! I feel inclined to take Li and leave you to sort out the mess, this is going to ruin her life, and she will always hate us for what you have done. How can you be so selfish and hateful our daughters were not born so they could pay our debts, it is in my thoughts to leave you, and take all of our unmarried daughters so they will be safe from you, you are just an animal,"

Li because she had loved her parents had gone to them the next morning and agreed that if there was no other way she would go through with the marriage, but they had to try and find some way out of the disaster, because she would never be able to forgive them if in the end she did really have to marry the ugly old fellow.

Li's father had flown into a rage and said, "You will obey our will, I have made an agreement and you will marry who ever we tell you too, who ever thought of a daughter telling a father who she would or not marry, your mother has no say in this matter. I am the head of this family and my wife and our children will obey me and none of my family are to defy my will, how dare you! Li the marriage will be held in three months, after I have made all of the arrangements!"

"That may be so but it's me that has to sleep with that ugly fellow not you, I am telling you that to me you will never be forgiven, and that old monster will have very cold woman in his bed that is my promise," Li said.

"You will do as I say this is going to be a big wedding and I have to pay all of the costs, this is the only way our family can regain its position in our village, and it is all agreed that you will marry this man that I have chosen for you. For me not to be obeyed by you would forever blight our position, and all of our family would be a joke, none of my unmarried Sons and Daughters would ever be able to marry into decent family's in our village, and the ones who are already married would be ridiculed".

"You have made a bad deal and it's me that is being used to pay your debts, I will hate you until the day I die, and as you lay me in my grave, know this I will have died hating you with all of my being, so think of that my so loving father."

"If we don't carry on the entire village would treat us as a joke and forever more we will be known as the family over whom their father had no control, your mother and myself would be better off dead. Goodnight my daughter and remember your only rights come through me, what I say is law," her father said in anger, but tinged with sorrow.

That night the four unmarried daughters met together again, but none of them could suggest a way the problem could be corrected, that would restore their family's prestige, so it was up to Li, but it seemed she had no choice, marry the ugly old man she must, and she must bear him a child as quickly as she could.

Li was in tears and that same night her mother came to her and said, "Oh my darling Daughter let us go to ask your old Grandmother; maybe she can give us good advice she is the one in the family who understands so much, she will tell us what to do and she will be right"?

So all of the women mother and daughters went to see the family Matriarch and after she had listened to their tale of woe she as usual seemed to go into a trance and started to speak her words of advice, "Li you must not worry all of the problems will be fixed, but it's not in my wisdom to tell you who you will marry, but I am allowed to tell you that your life will be long and happy married to a man you will love for your entire long life. As for your parents their debts will be paid, but you fathers prestige will suffer for a few months then he will prove his worth, and all will be forgotten and forgiven, by those who would drag him down. Now don't suffer any more before the marriage day all of the problems will be solved, and it is right that your parents should suffer for a while, they must bear the pain of their own mistakes".

As she stopped speaking the old women opened her eyes and with a smile she hugged them all one by one and then bid them leave her in peace, but the Gods had spoken, and whatever they had said would come true.

The women were all delighted but their mother said, "Let us take heart from what we have heard but we must not tell your father, because he will tell us we are just being silly and to prepare for Li's wedding."

At one village in which the group from Orbsey stayed there was an extremely beautiful young girl of 18 YOA, and one of the Orbseyns a young man of some thirty YOA was very attracted to her, from the moment he had first seen her. The age difference was irrelevant since the average age for the Orbseyn race was well in excess of 250 years; they only reached breeding aged when they 120 years old, and were restricted to two children for each couple. The young man's name as spoken on Earth was Orlos; he was single and had his parents and one brother back in Orbsey. Orlos was falling in love with the Chinese girl Sun Li, but his team was trying to keep them apart because they thought, there could be a tragedy in the making. The arrival and attentions of a handsome young man though well received by the girl; was rejected by her parents. They had no idea how young or old Orlos really was, but he looked in Earth terms to be about 20 YOA; whereas the man she was committed to was in his sixties, a grand old age on earth, at that time.

There was no reason the young couple couldn't be matched up, but the group was well aware they may not be staying, and although Sun Li could be taken with them it didn't seem wise to encourage the two especially Orlos, since he was aware of the problem. The group had been there a week, and the young couple was becoming more and more enamored of each other much to the annoyance of the girl's parents and her old paramour, things were getting decidedly hostile. The group Leader then decided it was time to move on, but the young couple took matters into their own hands and ran away together.

Of course Orlos couldn't get away he was tied to his group through thought connection, but the girl was lost to her parents and her husband to be, she would never be accepted in marriage, it was a cultural stalemate. A very substantial dowry had been paid, and that money now all had to be repaid immediately, but much of the funds had been used up for the wedding. It was a very dangerous situation until the group leader stepped in and paid the frustrated groom in full. The group left, and were joined by the young couple, but now Sun Li had to be told the truth which wasn't easy, because she now understood she had pledged herself to an Alien not one of the planet Earths men as she had thought Orlos to be. She was at first terrified, but Orlos reassured her he would never leave her and if they went back to Orbsey she would be able to go with them. Many centuries previously the marriage ceremony had been forsaken on Orbsey, the procedure now was simple a couple claimed a mate and they were together for as long as they were happy.

The rate of marital breakup was very low, and most stayed together for their very long lifetimes, there were many rules however before a young couple could be accepted by Orbseyn society as a pair. Because the young couple had eloped together as far as the group was concerned they were committed to each other, no real thought had yet been given of what would happen, if the Colony never eventuated and they all went home. The leader of the China group now decided belatedly they would split up and travel in pairs, with Orlos and a team mate making up a three some with Sun Li present.

Sun Li one night after they had left the village told Orlos she had had a dream the previous night and described it in detail. The dreams were so strange; in one 'I was in a chariot being drawn by a team of four horses, and the chariot seemed to shine in the sunlight like polished gold. There was a group of men calling to us as we left, and Orlos who was driving the chariot kept urging the horses to greater speed; until gradually our vehicle started to leave the ground, and we were rising to the heavens. The group on the ground started to cheer as we left the ground, and they were waving to us in excitement until we finally vanished from their view, it was all so exciting'.

I could see Orlos he was waving to me and shouting, "Hi Darling don't be afraid we are going home, and you will like it so much. It won't be long and we will be together forever, and we will have children that are as beautiful as you are?"

"As we rose higher the horses seemed to go faster until quite closely up ahead I could see a huge covered in vehicle that looked like some sort of building in the sky, there was a team of ten horses hitched onto the front, and looked as if they were impatient to be leaving. The horses were far bigger than any I had ever seen before and they were rearing on their hind legs; obviously ready to leave for wherever it was they were going".

I thought this big carriage must have been our transport to the home of Orlos the group had been telling me about; the closer we got the more excited I became' but Orlos was saying, "no this is wrong we must go back and start again, oh my darling I am so sorry, but this is the wrong carriage, it is going to a different planet".

"Suddenly we were at the door of the carriage and Orlos was helping me to climb into it; there was a group of people at the door shouting a greeting or so it seemed to me, but Orlos now started to shout in apparent anger. It seemed we were trying to get onto the wrong carriage, and we were being told to go away, but finally we got on board, but 'oh my and what a strange vehicle it was'. The interior was all draped out in red and black, and there were white marble statues of what must have been their Gods in every nook and cranny of the carriage. Orlos by the time we were on board was very angry and insisting a special place be set aside for me, to my surprise he was speaking in my language and the others began to do the same".

There were an equal number of men and women; the women were all in colorful flowing gowns, and each one had a peaked hat on her head. The men were dressed in flowing white robes such as I had seen Arabs wearing and they had a type of shawl on their heads, I remember thinking it must be hot where we are going! There were over two hundred adults and an equal number of children in that one huge room; it was no wonder ten horses were needed to pull this carriage.

"Now all of the people were so friendly because Orlos had been insisting we were entitled to be on board the carriage, quite suddenly there was a shout and they all broke into song in their own language. It was then I noticed they all had no mouths or ears; so how could they be making all of that noise? It was all so strange and now I was beginning to get frightened! Orlos noticed me shivering and started to reassure me that everything was fine, these people strange as they seemed were all from his own country and we were all going home, but it would take us a week to get there".

One of the women took my arm and led me to a type of locker from which she took out and gave me one of the same gowns they were all wearing plus one of the hats. When Orlos came for me he was changed into the same garb as the men had on; it was all so weird. The chariot we had left outside now turned around and headed back to earth, and our carriage started to move forward; it was getting faster ever faster until we seemed to be moving faster than the wind. Now Orlos was telling me we would be home in five days time, but it would be a very tiring journey, "and where do we change horses it's obviously too far for one team to travel?" I asked.

At this he started to laugh, "No we don't change horses, but when we arrive this team will have a week's holiday before they have to come down to Earth again.

Now let's join in the fun because it will be one long party until we arrive, come my darling now you are one of us!"

The passengers were now absorbed in all sorts of games and the children were trying to join in, but the adults soon got bored with such young games; they began to drift off and leave the children alone. All of the time there was a consistent noise until Li decided she would try to settle the children down, and set up games for them to play; this idea the parents loved in that way they could have peace and quiet for some rest while Li kept their young ones happy.

It wasn't long before the children were delighted, and asking to play some of their games with Li, "come on lady one of the bigger boys said, join in with us it will, be lots of fun, you are better than our parents, they are so boring all they ever do is sit down and say no, or that's not allowed, but you are real fun?"

Li loved children and for her the journey was turning out to be quite enjoyable, Orlos spent his time with the adult's playing cards and other gambling games, but only for nominal amounts of money, high stakes gambling was forbidden on Orbsey. Whenever Li looked outside to see how the horses were getting on they seemed to be flying they were running that fast, and the men who were driving them, seemed not to have to do anything.

The games Li played with the children were ones she had learned at home when she was but a child, and they loved them, they especially loved it when Li dressed up as a witch and pretended to chase them; throughout the cabin. The main problem was that there was no night the daylight was continuous, so the children would want to play until they fell asleep exhausted, but when the first ones who fell asleep awoke the last ones were just dozing off. For the first two days Li had no break at all, but finally she fell into a very deep sleep, and try as they might the kids couldn't wake her, so the parents had to look after their own children while Li slept.

All of a sudden Li awoke from her dream and found she was still on earth with her Orbseyn group and Orlos, the horse carriage was gone and they were waiting for the cruiser to take them back to Australia. Li began to tell Orlos all about her dream and asked him what sort of horses they were she had seen; she also said the carriage seemed so big, but the ten big horses could run as fast as the wind.

Orlos had started to laugh, "There will be no horses pulling us through space, on our planet we don't have the same horses as there is here on Earth. When our cruiser arrives you will see what I mean horse power is a thing of the past, and your first ride on a cruiser will be very fast beyond anything you could imagine, you will be the first Earthling to have such an experience.

Quite suddenly to Li's astonishment a strange looking craft landed besides their camp, and as Orlos had said there were no horses in sight, just a strange whirring noise. A door opened in the side of the craft and the group all started to board with Li being escorted by Orlos. Li's knees were shaking with fright but she managed by holding on to Orlos to board the craft just as the others had done. When she was aboard she whispered to Orlos, "Gosh this thing is huge we could get lost just walking around inside here."

Orlos laughed and said, "My darling this is just a very small vessel used for short trips and meant to carry only up to one hundred passengers, the big ones that travel to the planets can; when fully loaded carry over fifteen hundred passengers, but I hope we won't have to travel on one of them for many years."

When the cruiser took off Li hardly felt anything, but as she looked outside she could see they were traveling at a high speed. Much to her surprise she wasn't frightened, but Orlos was beside her, and held her hand for the entire journey. It was when they arrived the real test on Li's nerves began.

Orlos was thinking when we left Orbsey I had no thoughts of meeting a girl and falling in love, but the minute I first laid eyes on Li I knew she was the girl I wanted. It was unfair wrong to take too much interest in her because we might not be staying, and I knew that from what we had seen so far this most probably wouldn't be a suitable planet for us to settle in, they were way too backward a civilization for us to live in permanently. The total lack of any decent level of sophistication was way below what we were used to, and the lack of respect for life was to us appalling, already most of my companions were expressing real reservation about this strange planet.

The first day I had the chance to speak to Li it was like listening to a beautiful bird. I could only manage a smile and a simple "hello how are you today?" and only stuttered that out like a child".

Li also was very shy and could barely stutter out a "Hello I am well thank you" Gradually as we were able to see each other even if only out of the corners of our eyes we managed to sneak a smile at each other, and whenever we did I felt giddy all over, she was so gorgeous and petite, all I had ever dreamed of for my mate. I had never seen a woman that looked in my eyes to be so gorgeous. I just wanted to sit and talk to her to tell her how I felt; but that was impossible.

For the first few days I completely forgot we were on a strange planet, and when I remembered I was devastated. It was obvious we both wanted to talk together, but how was the problem to be resolved, one day we were lucky and accidentally met in the pergola on the outside of her home, that was the first chance for a real conversation.

I spoke first and said, "I have so wanted to be able to talk to you alone, how you are getting on please?" in the friendliest manner I could.

"I am quite well thanks and how long will you and your friends be staying in our village?" she asked.

I had no time to be backward so I said, "not very long sadly, but it would be nice to get to know you is that possible? I am very attracted to you and have you in my thoughts all of the time." I said with as friendly a smile as I could.

"Yes I would so love to talk to you, I also haven't been able to get you out of my thoughts since I first saw you, but I am pledged to be wedded to another, and my parents have already got the dowry so it's very difficult, but I would still like to talk alone with you, my intended husband is older than my father, and I am terrified for my future," Li Said with a wistful look on her face.

We agreed to meet that night at midnight when everyone would be asleep, and when I left her I was so excited the several hours of waiting seemed like years to me.

On the dot of midnight I was waiting for Li, she was a little late and it was getting so that she may not even show, when suddenly out of the dark she slipped into the pergola and we were together alone at last.

We were both very nervous and I was the first to regain my composure, so I said to her, "Hello Li I was getting worried thinking you couldn't come now you are here I am delighted".

"If I could have I would have been here hours ago, but my Father is suspicious, and has put a guardian to watch me, I had to wait for her to go asleep I am here now, but if they catch me there will be real trouble. My father has betrothed me to a man older than he is, and we are to be married within a fortnight, but I am terrified and really feel it's best for me to run away?"

"Is there nothing else you can do because for me it is love at first sight, may I step in and ask for your hand in marriage?" I asked.

"No my father would be furious and there has been a big dowry paid, he has spent most of it on the wedding and would be in trouble if the marriage didn't go ahead," Li said with a sad smile.

"That's not a problem my group could pay off your fathers debt would that fix it for us?" Orlos asked earnestly.

"No it wouldn't!" said a saddened Li, "the honor of my Father would be compromised, and he would be furious," Li said with a gentle smile.

"Well" said Orlos, "I am in love with you and if it comes to the final reckoning will you elope with me, and we will make our way back to my people. But you must be careful because with my people we have to be sure of what we are doing and there are difficulties which I will tell you about later. Perhaps it's best if we meet again tomorrow night, and I will check things out with my group leader is that alright?" I asked her.

"That will be fine yes I will be here at the same time tomorrow, but we must be quick because the marriage is to be soon then it will be too late, I shall be taken away and locked up until the first baby is born," Li said with a sad look because of her own thoughts.

'We parted with a quick hug, and both of us promised to meet the next night at the same time.'

'The next evening we met as agreed and this time Li was there first, but I was very soon after and we started to talk seriously immediately.'

"I have spoken to our group leader and your father will be paid the dowry money immediately, but our leader isn't so pleased with the idea, because we don't really know each other, and they think it's too quick. They have also reminded me that we are very different and you may not like to come to our country which is far, far away?" But I hope he is wrong! I knew that if she realized we were really aliens from another world she would be very frightened, and might change her mind, but I had reasoned that her situation marrying a man to her, who was so old; would be worse than with us. My love for Li I knew was strong it was obvious to me, we 'Orbseyns are known for being very quick at making these types of decisions, but then sticking to it for life.'

Li was shaking a bit but said with a determined lift of her head, "I love you and have done since the first time we shared a look from across the room with your party. It would be nice to go with you no matter where or how far away we will be going. I know it's unusual to feel so strongly at first glance, but know my love for you is real, what is important is to know if you feel the same for me?"

"I have no doubt at all that what I feel for you is true love and we will live our entire life together, there will be hard times but that's usual and shouldn't stop us!" I said with deep feeling of relief in my words.

'Li had remembered the words of her old granny, and was under no illusions now that what she had said while in her trance; was coming true?'

We made arrangements that the following night we would meet again, but this time we would elope. We also agreed that we would not make love until we had really been blessed in a marriage type ceremony acceptable to my own people. The following night we met as agreed and left immediately, we were both nervous, but certain of our feelings for each other, and so our journey into a long tumultuous life had begun. But we never wavered from that very first night on Earth when we met, and talked then ran away together.

The Colonists had quickly realized the sheer size of Australia was such that it needed a team of six not four, the size plus the apparent small population meant a lot of work, and the party would split up into pairs, and be picked up from where ever they were at the end of six months. The first party was landed in the North to what in the future would become the Northern Territory. They would then turn East and travel down to future Brisbane. The other was dropped off in the South and headed down to Sth Australia, and then would travel up to the Western area, the last two were left in the South which one day be Melbourne and would travel North up to the future Sydney.

The ones that went up to the North were staggered by the size of everything, the landscape was unblemished except for a few Aboriginal camps, the locals were not particularly unfriendly just indifferent, they didn't seem to care one way or the other what the visitors did on their land. Once the group did get caught in the big wet, but with the facilities they had available there was little problem, what the visitors did on the land to keep themselves safe. They came across a big rock (Uluru) but apart from a quick look around kept going, they had no concept of danger or getting lost in dangerous situations. Their navigational systems were so far advanced even on what earth would have in the future, that there was no danger.

They travelled up to Darwin and then started down to Cairns and Townsville on the East Coast heading towards Brisbane; they were having a great trip and were impressed that there seemed to be no fighting amongst the Aborigines. The various Colonist teams were in constant communication via thought processes; this kept them aware of the savagery being witnessed by the other teams; that were on the other side of the world.

The team that had headed west had seen and was interested in the topography, they were aware of the rich deposits of Iron Ore etc; and other minerals as they travelled, this country they knew would be a wealthy one, even if it had been on the Planet Orbsey, the natural resources were obviously immense.

The team that was travelling up the East Coast of the country became aware that this area seemed to be agriculturally the richest in the country and in time would probably be the most densely populated. If they allowed for the dryness of the continent it was a beautiful area, but would need some very hard work to develop the Continent, into an agricultural one around the East coasts then mineral mining in the arid West and Central areas.

It was obvious the present inhabitants couldn't develop the country; they lacked the drive necessary to use the opportunities that were there to be taken, but also there were only a very few of them. It had been quickly obvious the coastal areas were fertile, and would be productive at some time in the distant future, but the center of the country would lag far behind, until the real value of Australia's heart land could be understood and capitalized on. The big difference the colonists, saw and respected was the Aboriginals of Australia were not killing and murdering each other, as they had found in other parts of this to them, new world.

The team that went to Rome shared out the Roman Empire, and the various areas of Europe one pair started in Spain and travelled across through future countries such as Germany, France and the Lowlands, the other pair started in India and travelled up into Egypt as their final goal.

In Rome there was turmoil its leader Julius Caesar had just been murdered, and his adopted Son had taken his place. The Orbseyns had spent time in Rome before splitting up into three groups; their impression of this supreme western Capital was poor in the extreme. The city of Rome was host to many different travelers, and permanent residents most of whom were in some way involved with the military.

They witnessed an event in the main stadium with Gladiators fighting to the death, which to some degree was acceptable, but the feeding of criminals to hungry lions etc they found totally barbaric. The very poor living conditions, and the infanticide of baby girls was intolerable, the fact that so many men were killed in battle which made girls if they are all kept alive, becoming too high a ratio of the population.

The housing was poor and the sanitary system only really catered to the wealthy people, these fortunate's they found enjoyed a very luxurious standard of living. The only mode of transport was by horse drawn vehicles, horseback or just by walking, but they were to find the conditions in Rome were far better than some of the countries that were part on the Roman Empire. They then split up two going off to Egypt, another two went to Spain and the final two went to Constantinople, all travelled on horseback and thought of it as great fun.

Egypt they found as quite advanced compared to standards they had seen so far, but they were still unimpressed. The wealthy lived in great splendor while the laboring classes were really only bonded slaves, the money spent by the Pharaohs' on their own eternal future life seemed to be a little over the top, and the forced labor with poor wages if any was hard to understand.

The enormous stacks of stone as burial places seemed to be silly to the Orbseyns, but compared to a lot of other countries so far visited the people were quite well treated. The control of the people by priests playing on the superstitions of the uneducated, if it wasn't so pitiful would have been to the visitors rather funny. These priests seemed to have more control than the Pharaohs, but it just seemed like a lot of mumbo jumbo all mixed up to hold the people in bondage, and the method was very successful.

The source of life was the river they had named mother Nile and the annual flooding and subsequent silting of the soil was why Egypt was such a fruit bowl, but they had been defeated at war and been in bondage since the time of Alexander the Greek. He had built a great new city Alexandria, and one of his generals had founded the present Ptolemy Dynasty, and his descendants Cleopatra and her Brother had been the joint Pharaohs of Egypt.

The future European countries were still in the formative stage, the former Carthage had been the centre of trade for many countries, but since that country had been completely destroyed by the Roman Legions France, Spain and Portugal etc; had become more attached to the Roman Empire. At present they were being occasionally invaded by the German Barbarians, but they had only small populations. The German Barbarians the Orbseyns met they found to be a smelly but handsome people, who were fantastic fighters when they weren't fighting they were making babies, those were the two favorite pastimes enjoyed by both men and women.

The war and killing seemed to the tribes of Barbarians natural, but at times they did a bit of growing of food for consumption, the trouble was the weather was cold and hard, so many of the efforts to grow food were frustrated by the cold. This being the reality these Germanic Tribes was really nomads moving from place to place living off the efforts of others as they confiscated all vegetables, and animals they came across for eating; as they moved from place to place.

Their nomadic ways were exacerbated by the vigor of a people that lived in such a cold climate, which was a natural weather pattern in that western part of the world. At many times during the year they subsisted, those were the times they went looking for new homes, in new areas, but since they were nomadic they never stayed long enough to start developing, and improving by their own efforts they far preferred war and living on the efforts of others.

Spain was an area that certain tribes of Aryan Barbarians actually started to settle, but this was a country that will develop into a superior economy and will in the future have a real part to play in the development of Planet Earth. The same comments applied to, France and other adjacent areas that was still not in the process of development. The American Continent to the South of this area was where the first two of the group was let off their transport, in what would become Argentina. The next two were dropped off in what would become Central America, North America and Mexico; the last two were dropped off in what would become Canada. The group that travelled by foot down through the vastness of Canada into the top end of the future USA found native tribes, who were a beautiful friendly people happy in their own style of living, and keen to learn off the visitors.

Many happy hours were spent with the different peoples, but the populations were very small by number for what would be needed for real development. The natives were light brown in color and had a big variety of dialects all of which the visitors could understand, but they were hunter gatherers and unlikely to develop the huge resources that was in their lands.

The lands in the Mexican area down in the South had hosted high levels of civilization, but the two main cultures the Orbseyns found sickening because of the sacrifices to Gods, the people were once again deemed as subjected to the manipulation by priests and others, so that they were pleased to leave and forget them, even though they seemed to have developed an advanced level of understanding. As far as the Alien visitors were concerned planet Earth was just a barbarous world, and could not be a part of a highly advanced society such as Orbsey wanted to see developed.

India the country was obviously a subcontinent that hosted a big variety of religions, but was a really colorful one that would one day have a huge population. This was even now an advanced culture, but not in a technological sense. India has been repeatedly invaded over the years by many different peoples including repeatedly by the Chinese, Alexander the Great conquered part of India after fighting his way over the Himalayas. The country although it was huge didn't appear as if it was one that could host a colony of aliens, because of the huge internal difference in the indigenous population.

India had a lot of different religions, but the main ones were at that time Buddhist, Muslim, and Hindus. The background was far too old fashioned for the Orbseyns, they could see no attraction to try and settle in India. For centuries India had been one of the most prosperous nations on earth because of their variety of goods, and buyers from the entire known world, especially Rome and China came to trade in India.

New Zealand: The two Colonists who went to NZ found a country that was almost uninhabited, there were a few Natives but like the Aborigines of Australia they weren't much interested in their visitors. Compared to Australia the climate was colder and quite wet, the natives called themselves Morioris and were passive by nature.

The entire landscape was heavily covered in forest and bush scrub, and the biggest bird the visitors had ever seen lived in the forest. It was a giant and stood about 12 feet high at the head when standing upright, they named them Moa's. Starting at the bottom of the country and travelling by foot right to the top the scenery was beautiful, there was very little wild life if any, but the plumage and singing of the native birds were fantastic.

'The Mountain Peaks in the South as they travelled North were like visions of Icy splendor' rising out of the mists in the mornings and then clearing around 10.00 am to beautiful days. The beauty of the fjords and the waterfalls coming up the West Coast was a sight to behold, unspoiled by Earthlings of any type.

It was when they got up to the top of the North near the end of their stay that they made a wonderful discovery. The scenery had been beautiful all of the way and the birds more abundant, always bursting with song more so than in the South, but except for one major mountain there wasn't as much of the majestic scenery they had seen on the way up to the North. The bush and rivers were perhaps more beautiful than the South but in a different way, the fertility of the soil was very obvious, and there were far more of the gigantic Moa's to be seen.

It was when they got well up the Nth Island they discovered the enormous trees, (Kauri) huge straight hardwoods stretching with gigantic trunks clear of branches to fifty feet high. Only at the tops were there any branches with leaves, so that the bush appeared to be just a mass of these huge trees all reaching to the stars. The surrounding ground at the base of the trunks was all clear; obviously the giants took all of the surrounding moisture to sustain them in spite of the constant rain that fell almost daily. One of the travelers noticed that when he notched one of the trees it started to bleed a yellow resin. They tested the resin with heat and found that provided they applied the heat before the resin touched the soil, it hardened and became solid gold, this was quite interesting, and they described it in their reports later on their return, so that their discovery had great effect in the areas future. In certain parts of planet Earth gold was highly prized, and quite accidentally it was gold that from the start created an affinity between Orbseyns and Earthlings.

One night while the travelers were camping at the base of the trees; they heard a rustling and, they found that hard to understand, until they realized it was the trees talking to each other. Because Orbseyns had the ability to understand any language, they realized if they listened carefully they could hear and understand; what those mighty trees were saying. They suddenly understood they were listening to the spirits of the Kauri trees, telling each other how strangers had come who understood the blood of the trees; could if properly treated be turned to gold.

When suddenly the Orbseyns started to talk back to the tree spirits, there was for a few seconds of startled silence, before they began to rustle at a very high tempo, the Orbseyns understood immediately the great trees were laughing. As the rustling lowered they started once again to talk, "how is it that you strangers understand us when we are talking they asked, we and our ancestors have been growing here for millions of years, but no one has passed by before who understands us?"

"Well we are from another planet a long way from earth, and we have the gift of understanding all languages as well as being able to speak any language we hear, so we have no problem in understanding you and being able to talk to you." The Orbseyns replied.

The rest of the time they were at that spot, the team from Orbsey learned more about mother Earth, than the rest of the expeditions learned about their areas combined. The spirits explained they were well able to travel anywhere they pleased, and because they were thousands of years old they knew more about this planet than anyone else. The only other life on earth as old as them (except stone) were other great trees at certain parts of earth, and they met quite regularly to laugh and play whenever they felt so inclined, but normally once a year at least.

The tree spirits explained they could manifest into any beings they wished but didn't bother unless they needed to because all people and animals; had such short lives which was why they had little knowledge. But sometimes a person may pass by who had been reborn many times; then they were possibly wise and could understand the trees. Just to prove the point some of the trees manifested themselves into human beings such as they had seen, and had stored in their memories over many years.

By the end of their trip the explorers had been unable to make any friends with the few local peoples, whenever they found a village or camp site the occupants showed little interest in striking up a friendly conversation, so they didn't pursue any further attempts to get to know them.

At the very top of the Island looking out over the ocean the site was as good as any they had seen on their entire journey, but it was almost time to be picked up and returned to the Australian base. All of the travelers were back in Australia now and in general found Planet Earth although very attractive not much of a world on which to base a sophisticated colony. It was felt that this planet was very backward, and in some places still practiced human sacrifice to obscene Gods.

The recommendation at the meeting to discuss what they had seen, the traveler's opinion was that they should go home to Orbsey as quickly as possible! Those who had gone out on the exploratory expeditions, had reported what they had seen in great detail, and some of their stories were wonderful, but many were so terrible their fellows were horrified by what they heard. The only areas that were suitable to settle were in Australia, New Zealand and the many islands that were in the adjacent ocean, but nobody seemed to want to sell them land in fact they had been told to help themselves. The great desserts of Australia would have been ideal for them they had the technology to make the area fertile, but why develop land that didn't belong to them? If there had been no people at all it would have been different, but there was no denying both countries were occupied, and therefore they could only stay if they could buy, and it was obvious they couldn't buy.

CHAPTER 4/

A NEW WORLD A NEW HOME

Orlos hadn't told me of the trouble he had had with the leaders when we first arrived at the camp, he had been worried my reaction would be negative and maybe I would run away, but that would never have happened my love for him was too strong for me to have done that. He had been reprimanded for taking me from my home, the leaders had wanted him to take me back to my village, but he had steadfastly refused, until they realized they had no alternative than to take me with them.

When we had at first left Earth on what I had been told was just a little vehicle, there was no doubt about how frightened I had been. Everything was just so surreal and I could feel my knees knocking together as we walked aboard that huge thing, Orlos had held my hand firmly otherwise I would never have been able to walk the short distance needed. We were leaving my home world probably forever and my thoughts were racing, I was terrified and wanted to go back. It was only when Orlos took a hold of my shoulders and gave me his full support that sufficient strength returned to my legs enough to carry me aboard!

It was when I got my first sight of a full sized space freighter that my feelings nearly erupted, I started to cry; but for a few moments I was on the edge of hysteria, my goodness it made the machine we were in look so small.

Here was I, a little Chinese girl who had never been anywhere and now I was going into that huge frightening thing, it was unbelievable and I was scared more than I had even imagined possible. It was then my memories saved me! My old Granny telling me what was to happen in the future saved me at that moment! The terror of the moment was about to overcome me when the memory returned, only then was I able to control myself and only Orlos could feel my terror at that time.

Huge doors now opened in the side of that monolithic thing, and the now tiny craft we were in seemed to just slide noiselessly into place set for that purpose. The doors through which we had entered when boarding now opened again, and we all gradually stood and transferred to the big craft. Only now were my thoughts becoming coherent once again! Orlos and I looked at each other, and his little smile said it all I felt safe at last and we were on the way to for me a new home!

The journey was going to be nice and from the start reassuring because the staff and all of the people were so friendly. Most of the friends I had made on Earth were dispersed throughout the cabin but we soon made new friends, and they were all equally nice so there were no problems. Gradually the craft filled up as other new arrivals came aboard and took their places! Suddenly there was an announcement came over the system that we were leaving, and all passengers were urged to restrict their thoughts and direct them to the launch process. I had looked at Orlos in surprise, but he had said not for me to worry it was just that on Orbsey thought was harvested and converted to power and that what they were doing now. It was just the surge of power that would conserve energy nothing more, and it wasn't a vital ingredient towards take off!

Suddenly we were moving at great speed even with my lack of experience I could feel that, and as I watched out of one of the port windows Earth was gradually receding and becoming visually smaller by the minute. For me the journey seemed to be one long game of which they seemed to have hundreds of variety, it was great fun but all too soon over and we had arrived.

Coming down over the airoport was fascinating it was so huge, but at the same time fascinating! There was several of the big craft like the one we were in standing on the ground and dozens of small ones parked around them. Orlos explained the big craft were the International ones and the small craft bought passengers from the outlying National areas for transfer to the big ones. When we were disembarked we would be put on transport and taken to the gates, where our transfers would be made if need be?

After we had landed and been greeted by the family of Orlos I felt a little intimidated at first, but they were so nice that I soon felt very comfortable with them all, it was only that Orleb the Brother of Orlos, was over forty years older. To me that felt so strange, the thought of the old man who had been chosen for my husband at sixty was repulsive, but this man was about seventy YOA; and looked no more than a young man would look back in my home village. This man smelt nice and clean and was of a good appearance, how I wandered could there be such a big difference?

We had to take a flight from where we had landed to another state which was over 1,200 earth miles away, the flight only took two hours including the embarking and disembarking, only meant a total of around three hours for the entire journey. After we had landed we boarded a type of home air shuttle service that took us, and two other families, within fifteen minutes we were home. The home to me was bewildering, it seemed small outside, but inside was huge, it was so big that to me would be easy to get quite lost.

During the first few days there were several things, easily noticed, the first was that the days were long and the nights very short. At most stages of the day there were two Suns in the sky, and at others only one? At night and visible also during the day there were several moons rotating in the heavens, because the nights were so short the moons were in the sky night and day, so that the heavens always seemed to be lit brightly night or day.

The full day was 32 hours, but the hours seemed to be a bit longer than on earth, night was only 10 hours so the day was 22 hours. The temperatures seemed to be very much the same as it had been in my own home in Central China, but it was more constant and there were very few clouds ever in the sky. I was told that because rain was restricted to fall only where it was needed in the farming areas. Rain wasn't needed in the cities so it never rained there, except maybe a drizzle now and again!

Orlos was with me all of the time until I had settled down, and became comfortable with my new home, but the rest of the family had to work to me even that was strange. They each had an office in the house, and spent all of their working life at home, Orleb was an architect of some type, he looked very much like Orlos, but was obviously older he was a very serious type and in this sense took after both of their parents. Their father was a Professor of history and lectured to students, and their mother was a Professor of home economics, both lectured to students via; some type of home communication system. Orlos when he started again was a student of history, and would study under his father and several other lecturers, using this strange communication that to me seemed very complicated, but it all seemed so exciting. I asked Orlos what I would be able to do once I had become adjusted to my new home, and he laughed politely.

"Well you will start school via the internet and will study at home. When you have passed the exams up to University level then you will be on the same type of system as me, but you will choose what subjects you want to take. Like Mother for example she is an expert on home economics, and that is a compulsory subject for all young people, before they can take a mate and live together as a couple. There are other compulsory subjects that you will learn the basics of before you get to University, which is when the serious learning begins. You are a little young yet, but will be given special attention because you haven't grown up here?"

"Oh I love it here already it will be great to start this learning, as quickly as possible, if that's what we must do before we can live together that's fine, just let me start as soon as possible". I had already received the gift of languages, and communication by way of thoughts, but it was hard to get used to. It was still hard for me to remember there was no need to talk, we could pass and receive communication just by thinking of a person, and they would appear just as soon as they could in our minds, and on my console one we all carried everywhere. Its function was to project an image of the person one was communicating with, so that it was like being face to face". Not having to speak was a little hard to get used to, our thoughts though, could be turned off at any time we wanted privacy.

"My new life was exciting but quite frightening there just seemed so much to learn, and so little time to do it in! My love for Orlos was strong, but it seemed we would have to wait forever before we could be together! Then to top off all that learning we had to have a home of our own before we could be together, it was strictly forbidden that we could live together in the home of Orloses parents, we had to have a home of our own".

Orlos told me, "I am anxious to be together, but no exception to the rules could be allowed, mainly because my parents as two academics are very strict, and they would never consider breaking the laws in any way. Not that we want to do the wrong thing; it is just that it seemed as if it would be years before we can be together and it was a daunting prospect".

"When I had first seen moving pictures on the main wall of our home it had been a shock, I had seen them when we had first landed in Orbsey at the terminals, but hadn't thought to see them at home as well. There was all sorts of stories, and if we wanted we could watch the news all day, but really after a while it all got to be too much for me and rather boring". It was the same with anything we actually saw with our eyes during the day, it was all recorded and we could keep it on a type of tape after we had edited everything, or we could just destroy everything we had seen at the end of the day.

Orloses mother Jerrianda; and his father Orlosa decided it was time for me to start my education, so the time of just thinking about my old home was over, now it was time to learn how to be an Orbseyn. Jerrianda was quite a tall woman, but at her grand old age was starting to look a little fragile, one could see she must once have been very attractive. Orlosa was an older version of his two sons, and still a handsome man, with a strong crop of hair, but now starting to be a little bent with age. 'I thought my Orlos at that age will look like that I hope'?

My first lesson was fairly basic as could be expected, but gradually we got to more interesting subjects, but I could understand quite easily! I had learned that the planet Orbsey had been highly developed for over ten thousand years, and that the peoples of all the different countries, had originally been from all different cultures much like Earth, was or so we were taught back home?

The rain is controlled by the weather bureau, and is directed to the areas that are scheduled for rain as needed. Fresh water is controlled in the international water banks and doled out to the consumers as needed, and sewerage is collected and processed into water, and fuel for the rural farms from which the food banks are fed.

The real use of sewage wasn't told truthfully to me then, because at that stage it would have been too hard to understand what the real use was! When my understanding had progressed enough, it was explained that the sewage was kept, then dried and processed using a secret method, and became one of the main ingredients of energy, especially for the space freighters that plied the Orbseyn skies.

The food banks are there to supply the food in the amounts needed, anybody who wants more than their allocation has to pay the difference, but there is no difficulty with getting extra although very few ask for more. The food banks feed the entire population of the planet, and the variety of food was adequately diverse. One could indulge ones taste from a very big menu, but the personal choices had to be kept in one's own memory for use at any time.

Originally the different countries were made up of a variety of national races, but as the centuries went by and the countries interbred, the whole of Orbsey became as one all one color, and shape with obesity conquered. Gradually the mouth and ears of most people became redundant, so that in time these facilities became unused on most people, and gradually grew out over the years through lack of use.

The most difficult thing I had to overcome was getting to know other Orbseyns, because ours was an academic household everybody worked from home, and there were little chances to socialize with others. We went to clubs and sports clubs, but even so we didn't mix much Orlos seemed to be at a loss in the company of his fellow citizens. As far as he was concerned we had each other he had no need for anyone else, but I enjoyed the company of others as we learned how to interact socially. To me they are a very friendly people, but that may just be a personal reaction to having been so kindly treated when we first arrived.

Orlos and I had received a request to attend a seminar about our journey to the Planet Earth, I was asked to attend as an honored Earthling who had decided to come to Orbsey to live, and if possible to express my feelings about being here, and how I had been treated since my arrival. Orlos was keen to attend, but for myself; although I was happy to go with him I wasn't inclined to be giving any opinions, because it was far too early, and as yet there was little I knew about my new home. I wanted Orlos to explain I had come because I wanted to be with him, and now I was here it was a wonderful place, far better than my home on earth which seemed to be so backward, compared to what I had seen here so far.

Orlos and his family were very understanding, and suggested that I give permission for my thoughts to be read, and a simulated statement would be given that was exactly as I felt, but this couldn't be done without permission. I gave written permission, and this was what was broadcasted out. My new family explained it was a criminal offence to take thoughts without permission, and that I could if I wanted actually block my thoughts out, but that nobody could change their thoughts so as to be deceptive.

To me Orlos, the decision to return to Orbsey was a disappointment, I had hoped we would stay on Planet Earth to start a new Colony and help this world to develop, but my peers were very sure this world was too undeveloped, and our presence would be destructive. My love and pride in Li had got stronger and stronger as she faced up to our Alien presence and to her, our strange ways from the time we got aboard the recovery vessel, and we were taken back to our small settlement.

When she had told me about her dream and how she had seen a carriage with ten horses taking us to my home it was at first funny, but when I had time to think about it the seriousness of her thoughts enveloped me. I now realized that here she was so innocent that she thought we could travel through space being pulled aloft by horses. It was for me a shock should we just settle on Earth to be together or was it still fair to take her to my home in Cordiance. I pondered the problem for quite some time, but in the end felt she was strong enough to settle down in our home. I knew the immediate future was going to be very hard on Li, there would be so much to learn and adapt to. Even simple things like being able to project ourselves through space, we could travel if we wanted to from one country to the other in minutes using our travel devices, which we all had at age 18, this is what made the entire planet seem as one. The use of the fourth dimension had been widely used ever since it was discovered five hundred years previously, but sadly it was often abused by criminals who could use the system to illegally enter buildings, and to frighten the unwary. Gullible people could be frightened into thinking they were looking at spirits, when the system was used to make the user appear ghostlike.

Li was so beautiful and trusting she was quite small by our standards, but seemed to exude an inner strength that few have. Her beauty was in her facial bone structure; and clear skin unaffected by the artificial cosmetics so loved by the girls in my home state. She seemed to have an aura about her, and it wasn't only me that could see it, many of my friends commented on that when we arrived home.

All of the Orbseyns at the settlement were curious at first to meet this Earthling, but that curiosity soon abated, and we just settled in. Li stayed with a group of my friends and I stayed with another group, but by day we spent all of our time together. Our mutual trust had grown into a wonderful friendship as well as us being very much in love, but although we no longer had an established wedding ceremony on Orbsey, there were still a lot of things we had to achieve before we could live together.

The decision to return to Orbsey wasn't unexpected to me, we could all see it was quite a shock to Li, but she took it very well and never lost her ready smile, I could see though she may have shed a few tears when she was alone. Our flights back to our home in Cordiance were uneventful, and the meeting with my family was a happy one, and it was easy to see they were curious to meet Li.

It was naturally a bit tense disembarking at the Intergalactic Terminal which was only ever used for joy flights into space, by many of us who had just wanted the thrill of space travel it was really very cheap, but usually reserved for those with a clear imagination of what they wanted. The joy flights were very popular and hundreds of interstellar flights left daily, and perhaps one or two hundred International flights also left each day, usually cruisers with up to five hundred passengers. By comparasion with the size of the population there wasn't such a great number in International flights, because many people used their travel devices.

The sight of so many faces all with neither mouth nor ears must have been intimidating for Li, but she never hesitated, and retained that smile all of the time. She was a bit tense at meeting my family, but that soon passed and we were very quickly back at our home in Cordiance 0000,455, this was how we named all of the districts in the different countries by numbers. There was no change to this system no matter what country or state you came from, everyone area was numbered.

My family was full of thoughts to us and since Li had already become used to inter thought communication, there were no problems for everybody to get to know each other; by the time we had arrived home the flow of thoughts was easy and happy. As is usual in Orbsey, my family indicated their strong support for my loved one Li, she was fully accepted and always would be.

The news that the colonists including my brother were coming home wasn't a surprise, we had heard from the scientists that the new found life sustaining World was still very much undeveloped, and they believed there was a good chance this first effort would have to be aborted quite quickly. Our mother in particular was ecstatic she had never wanted Orlos to go on this, in her mind, mad mission in the first place, and when we heard he was bringing back an Earthling to be his future partner we were intrigued. As my brother we weren't close because of the age differences, Orlos used to call me Orleb the bully, but that wasn't true it was just when he was born my first career was already started.

There had never been any worry about the Intergalactic travel such journeys into Space had been available as Joy flights for hundreds of years. Incontinent travel was almost no different than getting in an Aerocar and taking a quick journey anywhere on our Planet Orbsey, or one could travel using our devices.

Mother and Father now each close to 185 YOA and looking forward to retirement the acceptable age being 210, but this was expected to be extended soon as the average age was now up to 300 and the working age expected to be increased to 260 YOA. My parents were strongly objecting to the increase in their working life, they had both worked from the age of 30 so it was a lot of years, they just felt 250 was too long and they wanted to retire ASAP.

Although when we are young the career demands don't seem at all onerous, as we get older time seems to stand still. Changing from one career to another isn't as easy as it sounds; the demands become greater as the responsibility increases, our parents already looked exhausted yet they had another 55 years of work ahead. Mother in particular seemed for at least a year go into a state of shock!

We are all expected to work for 180 years before we retire and during that time we were to have four different careers, each of 45 years duration. Now we wondered if we would have five careers! My second career was getting close to starting, and I had chosen to do Civil Administration as my next, my first had been as a Civil Draught person. It was expected that the careers one chose during one's life should be compatible, so that as little new training as possible had to be undergone when one changed over, from one career to the next. Since we are a family of academics we are all able to work at home, but that was optional it was quite permissible to find work to which we have to travel to an office daily, it was very simple to do this if that's what one preferred.

Orlos had been training for an academic life he would be expected once he had finished his education to first go into a Police Career, and he would spend the first stage of his Career in the Uniform Police, the next would be Plain Clothes Police, then as a Lawyer and Barrister, and finally to either as a judge or a Politician. It would depend on ones record where one finished up!

Depending on how just well one had performed their duties as to how high one rose on the way through in each career, just how good that final career would be. Mother and Father were both on their last careers, but if the new law was passed then they may have to spend another one before they could retire?

The method of reward for work done on Orbsey was by a system of credits, and these credits could be accumulated and used as required. Credits could be used to buy anything but every Orbseyn couple when both had started work received 100,000 credits into their account from the govt. These credits can only be used to buy a home and an aerocar which if one only wanted the average home and aerocar would take all of one's credits and need never be repaid.

All people were eligible for the payment no matter how wealthy the family, because the system was such that there could never be any large inheritance left to individuals. It was thought that large fortunes were impossible to accumulate on Orbsey, but a few later in their lives such as Orlos and his partner were very successful. To be honest though that was only because of their earnings from Earth sourced products!

Ones monthly credits (income) could be used for whatever was required for all and every service wanted including daily sustenance and all services, but all and anything that is required to live a decent life, which requires very few credits. All extras such as an extra nice home or fancy aerocar took up a lot of credits, which must be available in ones account at time of purchase, because there is no trading or borrowing of credits. Our parents cannot donate or loan to us any of their credits, nor can we borrow off any organization, credits are a Government function and there are no variations allowed.

Our society has been for many years sectionalized and effective throughout the entire Planet! The economy has for many years been tax free for all whom live on govt; sponsored credits, and we all have that right. The private economy is fully financed initially by govt; credits, the system is a little like the public economy in that the initial credits for business is supplied by application to the dept. of business, but must trade in private credits, so that all private trade is controlled by credit banks. The banks can only control the credit flow; they do not issue or lend credits, only the govt may supply new credits, the banks are a govt; branch institution.

There is no such thing as interest being charged, but private credits are transferable, extra trade credits earned by any business big or small must be shared with the workers and must be converted to govt; credits by those workers. Any business big or small must distribute excess credits to workers or management as decided by the Board of Directors, but the level of the distribution must be pro rata; to the individual's contribution to the earning of those aforesaid credits.

There are several major groupings of the work force 1/ Academics, 2/ Professions, 3/ Govt Employees, 4/ Trades, 5/ Business and the 6/ the laboring classes. These groups break down to hundreds of other classes as decided by the various workers unions. All Orbseyns are classified first at birth and then at age thirty the year they are first expected to start work. There are exceptions for special projects when time is allowed, this for example would apply to all who had been selected to be possible Colonists on planet Earth, they were given gratis time credits on their return to Orbsey.

There are no direct taxes on Orbsey but there are consumption taxes, all consumption carries a price expressed as credits and that cost includes a fee to the govt; which uses the credits for all of its costs. Private business is strongly encouraged, and the State never interferes in how a business is run, but since there are no taxes there is no need for tax returns nor any other govt control. This is because all private credits must get converted by the govt; somewhere along the way, and in this way controls are inevitable.

There are few hospitals on Orbsey, because private practice is encouraged, and all General Practitioner's can replace body parts, heart lungs etc; but not brains, these are still managed in special hospitals that only do work on the head ie eyes, nose, brain, cranium, tongue etc; but such hospitals are owned and operated by the specialists. These highly skilled specialists can become very wealthy, but they can only spend and enjoy their own wealth, they cannot pass it on to their children or family.

Money related crime on Orbsey doesn't exist because there is no way the credits can be transferred, even the origins of private credits have to be confirmed and proved before being able to convert to govt credits. There is a lot of other crime, fighting and destroying private property is common, dissenting to laws being enacted causes many problems, petty theft is really bad etc.

Sex crimes are unusual on Orbsey because any male rapist found guilty is immediately turned into a eunuch, and sexual perversion such as same gender sex, pedophilia etc is treated medically as soon as found and rectified, there is no appeal once found guilty of any sexual perversion whatsoever, the medical changes are automatic and cannot be stopped.

Orbsey has for over two millennia had all of its citizens being of one race, the inter breeding had accomplished that naturally, there had been no laws put in place to force the issue it had just gradually happened. The foods that are all ingested by way of thought, are all artificially flavored, but there were menus that supply the genuine product at higher prices supplied by private restaurants, and roadside cafes. The same applies with clothes one has a menu of clothes in their memory, and can be changed at will at any time during the day, this includes effective body cleansing, and there is no need for baths or showers.

The Orbseyn form of Govt should be considered a Socialistic Egalitarian one, in that the Central Govt funds the first home and vehicle, when a couple comes together with the intent to stay together. They must stay that way for five years if they want to split up they cannot until the term is served, and the home and vehicle must be returned, no further assistance is given to either party if they should set up a new relationship.

From the time they split up the couple are put off any form of govt assistance such as Home, Vehicle, Food, Clothing, Medical Credits etc; they must go on private credits and they rarely manage to return to the govt; system. They must still convert their private credits to govt; credits, for their consumer goods, and they can only redeem their situation by depositing 100,000 credits to their Govt account, only then they will be restored completely to the system. The intent is to keep family separation as low as possible?

There is no real military on Orbsey, but the Police Force does enforce all govt; policy over the entire Planet. Cordiance is the biggest and major Country within which the Orbsey Central Govt is stationed. There was a two level form of Govt for all countries with a population under 100 million citizens, for countries with a population of 100 million and over the system has a three level format.

The two level forms allowed for State and National Govt, with the State Govt running all of the Govt; Programs not run from the Center of Govt. With the three levels Govt; there was an added Council of the people, which deals with the State Govt; which in turn deals with the Central or Federal Govt.

Simply put all credits had to flow through the govt; system then all credits would be used by the govt; to settle all credits due from various sources. For example the methodology of feeding the Planet was developed by the food Industry in tandem with the medical Profession, meaning the systems were actually owned by those two groups. The industry produced the material and processed it to the status of food etc and then the Medical Profession had the responsibility to control the methods of consumption, all the govt; does is to pass the credits due to the industry through the banks.

This method is used for the main consumer products namely, White Goods, Clothes, Footwear, Medical Costs, all other products are direct trade, but using converted credits from prvt; to govt; credits, then all payments are passed through the govt; agency. The payments made on behalf of the consumer have an 'on cost' that includes the handling fee which was essentially a consumer tax.

The populations are all treated the same, because all young couples have the right subject to qualification to start off equal, with 100,000 consumer credits for a home and a vehicle; in this way the state creates the base for the egalitarian state. There is no reason not to sell the assets so granted by the state, but if in so doing the couple finishes up with nothing they will be passed into a govt; controlled home and wouldn't have a vehicle.

Such drop outs are expected to work and rehabilitate themselves, but they would get no help on the way and if they did manage to get back on their feet they would simply be reinstated, if not they would be put on simple govt; work for the rest of their lives. The credits they were entitled to would be used to keep them; sickness wasn't an issue because all medical conditions were under control and free except after retirement.

There were animal parks all over the Planet and each country had the responsibility to have large areas set aside for wild animals and Flora and Fauna. There is little animal culling, all protein is created by the Medical Scientists, and animals aren't kept for killing and processing for food. There was a huge variety of animals kept as pets and there were many hobby farms just for this purpose, as there are also for all Flora and Fauna, that had been kept from the old world before Orbsey became so sophisticated.

There were very strict laws to ensure that animals were well cared for, many creatures were still being bred that had survived for many millions of years. It is important here to understand the function of animals is still farmed for eggs, milk, wool, and many other uses it's just that they aren't killed, at the end of their useful life, they are retired.

Sport is a major industry, and elite athletes are treated with great respect, but they were still controlled within the spectrum of the govt; credits system, adulation from the masses is fine, but excessive credits aren't acceptable. The abuse of athletes by managers etc is strictly controlled, and they are locked into the system of credits, but the creativity hasn't in any way hindered promoters they are treated with respect as are their protégés.

Each country has retained their natural culture, the assimilation of the races has been achieved by inter marriage over several millennia! After this long period all of the original indigenous races look alike, and have the appearance of one single race, now there is a Orbseyn culture of which all are proud, but also an indigenous culture of which the independent countries are equally proud!

Business citizens are allowed to accumulate as much credits as they want, the problem came for them in their final Wills, there was no such things as Family Trusts or other devices to instruct, and create any way the credits could be distributed after death. There is a maximum that can be left to a single beneficiary, but one could name any number of them, if there is any credits left over they must go to some charity, and that must be settled within 30 days of the funeral or the entire estate would be transferred to the govt.

At a family gathering it was revealed that Orlos would get a credit of six months, for the period he had been away from Orbsey, and he would continue his education, that would now have about twelve months to complete as an engineer, he had changed his future vocation, but was able to do so because he was just starting out.

Everything was so complicated that Li was having difficulty understanding what was happening, she knew what was being done was in her best interests but had little idea what her future really was to be.

Often at night when she was alone her mind would wonder to her family back home, and she would shed a few tears thinking of them. Even her father was remembered with love! Li knew that what he had tried to do was preserve the integrity of his family, but the cost to her would have been enormous. She knew her Granny had predicted she would never go home while any of her family was still alive, and that made her very sad. But she also knew she had no regrets her love for Orlos was stronger than ever!

Li had received a tertiary grant and had been allocated to a first legal career starting with the uniform police force, her education would start immediately and she was the only one in the house who had to work away from the home her education was to be one of on patrol duty and daily seminars at the police college.

There was 30 days to appeal the positions for both Li and Orlos, if no appeal was received both would have to start within 30 days., they would be eligible for the credits grant when their education was completed and they were fully employed, and they could have their own home and aerocar. Both Orlos and Li had agreed to the grant and the terms were as usual so no letter of appeal was sent or needed and Li was now delighted because she knew what her career path was to be, and she was delighted!

Orlos now explained to Li, they would have to wait until she had finished her education, and both were actually working so the better she did with her schooling, the sooner they could be together, and in the Orbseyn belief of good society committed to each other. With the family of Orlos there was a family ritual, and had been so for several millennia, on both sides of their family tree, neither Li nor Orlos would dream of breaking that important family thread.

Still now that Li knew her future would be she was very happy, she still thought periodically of her home and family, but the specter of that ugly old man interfering with her body soon dispelled any longings for home, she knew she had been blessed and had a wonderful family now, she had escaped from hell!

CHAPTER 5/

EDUCATION AND WORK

The day to start her education had arrived, and it was time to go out on her own, Orlos took her to the police college, and told her to send him a thought message when she was ready to come home, he would pick her up then. When Li entered the college grounds and then entered the office, it was as if she was just another old student coming back from a vacation. She was escorted to the Masters office; he in turn took her to the classrooms immediately. She was introduced to her tutor and the other students, as the earthling who had come to settle in their neighborhood, and had been allocated to be one of their fellow trainees.

There was a little curiosity after all she was from a different planet, and had ears and a mouth which to them looked a little strange, but apart from that she was no different and they soon forgot her being a stranger, and just treated her as one of their own.

The lectures during the day were eight hours by length of time including a break of twenty minutes inclusive, every two hours. Then after that there was another six hours including breaks spent as a trainee on patrol, it was now that Li started to see the real Orbseyns at work and play.

The patrols where staggered with vehicles leaving every hour on the hour, the first call they got was to a break in at a Jewelers store. They were alerted and on the scene within five minutes, but the culprits were well gone; within minutes all of the information at the site had been processed, and sent to the plain clothes division. The next call was to a rape, the same procedure and again within minutes the data had been sent to the plain clothes team.

This continued for the rest of her day and then she was finished and Orlos was there to pick her up! Li was so happy she had loved every minute of her day, and couldn't stop remembering, and passing her memories to any in the family who cared to tune in to her thoughts. Orlos was delighted because Li had enjoyed herself so much, he was now certain she would settle in her new home.

He then started to share his thoughts that it was nice to be back at where he had left off, and most of his old buddies were still there, and keen to know his thoughts about Planet Earth. Later that night when Orlos had gone home; and Li was in bed she once again sank into a reverie, of remembering especially her beloved mum, and her siblings none of whom she would ever forget, even after they were long dead. Even her father was in her thoughts, she knew he had done the only thing he could do in the sad circumstances he had got into, but she was relieved she had not been forced to marry that ugly old coot?

Because Li loved her education time went quickly for her, the years seemed to fly by. First Orlos had passed all of his exams and now it was up to Li as soon as she was finished her exams they could finally be together. They were both proving to be fairly strong sexually, and the restraints were becoming hard to contain, but they had honored Orlos parents and strictly abstained. To achieve this chastity they had refrained from being alone in compromising situations, and had refrained from too much contact such as dancing etc; anything that put them too close together was not to be allowed by their own choice.

Li was doing well and her actual Orbseyn age had now been calculated and she was 26YOA and had been in the country for eight years, she was in every respect now an Orbseyn in fact as well as in her heart, she really loved her new world family, and Orlos as well as her education; it was all really wonderful the little girl from China felt at home in every way.

The education she had been getting gave her a full view of Orbseyn society; she could see the wealthy and those that would be wealthy. There was the criminals that really couldn't help themselves, and were truly victims of their own poor mental level. There were the many people who just couldn't help but get into trouble, and have to pay the penalty for their own cupidity; there were so many forms of crime that Li just couldn't believe what she was learning.

Gradually she was sitting and passing her exams she thrived on every test they gave her, she was already one year ahead of where she was expected to be, the family were all delighted with their new daughter and sister to be, they were not to know the natural acuity of her forebears.

Li had become a type of teachers pet they really loved her at the police college, and were fascinated by their earthling student, who supposedly came from a backward culture, yet found the Orbseyn education so simple. Out on the road on patrols in the prowling aerocars she was again very popular with her quick grasp of the job; frequent comments were made about her rising very quickly through the ranks, achieving high command in the police force.

All of their friends and her police associates had predicted Li would be one of the highest ranked females ever in the force, achieving that stature during her career, and retaining her personal popularity was her own perceived goal. For herself Li quickly demonstrated just how ambitious she was, her personality was fully controlled, but at the same time always looking for ways to improve herself. The physical regime in the force, Li in spite of being small proved she could take the training, and lead the way when leadership was needed; she was in every way an Orbseyn in thought and appearance in spite of still having a nose and ears, there was no longer and mention of her origins, her colleagues seemed to have forgotten her unique background.

In spite of her apparent progress Li was always very nervous about how she would succeed as the responsibility increased, what would happen when she a tiny female had to arrest a large male? Would she be able to make an arrest and at the same time force respect, she was well aware that she was considered a joke by many of the local criminals!

When she had occasion to arrest vagrants of whatever type they were always intrigued at how funny, to them she looked, many were the laughs she shared with her workmates as the crims stared at her in wonder, and to some even fear.

One afternoon Li was making an arrest a very large person who didn't like being stopped by somebody who he thought was deformed, he went to strike Li with his big fists, suddenly he had been flipped on his back, and shaking his head in horror. Li's tutor in the vehicle just sat and roared with laughter; while the bully shook his head in shock, he stood up looked at Li in disbelief, and stuck out his arms for the electronic shackles, two hours later he was still shaking his head in disbelief.

When Li sat for her license to control and drive/fly an aerocar, she passed first time tested, from then on she was allowed to be in charge of the patrol vehicle she was out with, her tutors were always glad of the rest. Li passed her final exams at the age of 28 two years quicker than was normal; she was now a fully qualified police-woman in the state of Cordiance on the planet Orbsey the first earthling to be so honored. Her Family was very proud; finally Li & Orlos were fully qualified for the starting 100,000 credits, and the right to have their own home and vehicle.

The young couple was so excited finally they would be as one in a home of their own on, the waiting was almost over and they both had their careers well underway. It was now time to be recognized by the family Orlosa and they would be on their own this was to be done in the near future when the entire family could assemble to wish them well for their life's ambitions.

The funding of small to medium sized business and the support for growth is also designed to eliminate debt from money lenders; the govt; wants to see its citizens free of all financial entanglements that can create financial slavery. So far it seems to be working, but it's a mammoth job that is still being put in place, changes are being made as problems are found. Like all things theory is great but the next stage is the reality, it was tried first for twenty years in the smallest country on the planet then slowly developed until the system had been fully implemented.

There are still problems that frequently come up, but they are all based around the sheer size of the program, the intent is right and the goal has been proved, but good administration is still being implemented. Li was learning daily and she loved it, "Why she asked Orlos is this planet so far ahead of Earth, when I think back of how life was at home it's confusing! Everything is so far behind and yet our people are just as bright as they are here, will that always be the case or will one day we be equal?"

"It's only because we have such a long time advantage, several thousand years! It will take many years for Earth to catch up, but they will eventually! The business world has been revolutionized as debt is cancelled out with govt; credits and production starts to flow unhindered by stress for business people as they grow their businesses. Another two hundred years will find the system fully in place on Orbsey, and the entire population freed from debt, by govt funding, these are none recourse govt; contributions never to be repaid unless for family break down or criminal activities. It is these and other emerging improvements that will be available for Earth to one day copy! At present they are just too far behind and that is why we had to come home, the continual wars on Earth is unacceptable to us so here we are now ready to set up our own home."

'Li sighed with pleasure her thoughts for the future was so encouraging, she whispered tell me more about my new home please!'

Orlos continued, "The banks have become administrators only for the govt; controlling the flow of credits govt and private. Govts; are barred from any commercial activities unless specifically ordered from the Central Parliament, for some natural disaster etc. Distribution has been beaten by the method of part processing on production, before the products are sent off for final process, and converted to whatever system for which each product is designed, ie food is initially processed within each country then beamed into a central grid for distribution via the thought demands. Private product is distributed by a private grid; that is strictly for products being bought within the private economy! The reliance on the Cyber system is enormous, but the power of thought has been harnessed as the main power source, and ensures that computer back up is always in place. The attacks on the system have been very persistent as criminals have tried to break into and fraudulently tried to beat the system, this has held up progress for many years but is now back under control. The stealing of the finished products was a problem for years, as the difficulties were so hard to solve, then when the system was up and operational the criminal element for years diverted the credits through fraudulent claims, this also worked for a while, but was gradually controlled. The attacks on business again by criminals to force credits to be paid out, without any rights were also another problem now beaten! It's been a long hard journey but finally the improvements are working!"

Finally Li and Orlos had the right alone together and selecting a home was pretty easy, these after all are cheap first home owner's property as was the vehicle, all mass produced well made in each country for its own citizens. They had enough credits left over to furnish their home they were now ready for life as a couple. Li and Orlos had been together for eight years nearly all that time spent on the planet Orbsey, and now it was time they were recognized to have the status of adults, and would be given the 'grant for life' as it was called.

Although there was no form of marriage on the planet, each family had their own traditions, and the family Orlosa certainly had its long traditions, the youngsters never left home without a celebration, and they were expected to be virgins when the happy to leave time arrived. If they weren't then there was no celebration they simply left, and they were dropped from the family tree, the idea being to keep the tree pure to family tradition.

The celebration was in full swing and the family bloodlines were all represented, Li was dazzled by the size of her new family and was happier than ever, when the main celebrations were over. It had been a long and laborious journey, but the time had arrived for them to really be a couple at long last!

The blood Patriarch rose and gave a great thought welcome to Li; who really would inject new blood as he succinctly thought, it would bedazzle all of the other blood lines of whatever stature, and it would be millennia before it would happen again. Then Orlosa spoke of their pride in their earthling daughter, after that they all danced the night away! Many got drunk as they filled themselves with alcoholic through thoughts of booze, and it was a great night of celebration!

The next day the young couple shifted into their home, and at last they were together. Both were Virgins and not so sure of what they were to do, they had had all of the lessons, but now it was time for the real thing. That first night was very difficult for them both, but having broken their virginity, they both decided they liked this sex game, and they found they could practice all they wanted to; neither of them would be fertile until they were 120 YOA and that was over 90 years away, there would be plenty of practice before then.

On the first night Orlos found it difficult to get ready he was scared, and when he did finally rise to the occasion he couldn't succeed because Li had just lost interest in fright. Several hours after starting to try they succeeded, but it wasn't so great at that point, the next time same night it was easier, by then they were both sore, Li internally and Orlos thought his private was a flame.

After the next night trying again to get it right it was a lot easier for both of them, but after a week they were quite the experts. Li and Orlos were really in their own private version of heaven, the years of abstinence which they didn't really understand anyhow, until they finally did get together was time well spent.

They adored each other and their honeymoon lasted for many years, they never seemed to tire of sharing each other's body, and when ninety years later their first child was born; he was the true fruit of his parents love for each other. Still that was a long way in the future for now it was just them by themselves, and they ate of the fruit liberally. For the first five years they spent all free time in bed practicing at how to make babies, both found it to be a wonderful pastime, and they had to have a spell period infrequently, which really was just as well else they would have both faded away to become walking shadows.

Orlos was now involved in the construction industry as a major construction engineer, and he was known as that fellow with the foreign mate, this made him inordinately happy; he loved it knowing that his wife was different. On the other hand Li's workmates had forgotten she was an Earthling, and truly loved her and her dedication to her work and her fellow workers, she would do anything for her colleagues take the extra shift wait back for someone running late; for her nothing was a problem. Even as she was lifted rapidly through the ranks they never demurred, and were happy for the little Earthling who was small yet so capable.

There had been many times when she had arrested big angry men, and had to pacify them before they would do what she wanted, but it was never a problem big or small they all finished up groveling on their backs, much to the amusement of Li's male colleagues, and the respect of the other females in the dept; none of whom displayed any signs of jealousy.

One of the things Li found hard to get used too was never having to cook and clean for her man, it was all done automatically by a house robot, which was more intelligent than many of the criminals Li had to deal with daily.

It was a net twelve hour day allowing for breaks, but the pace was constant, there were a hell of a lot of crims living in Cordiance, and they seemed to just keep rolling through. Because of thought control and the controls available to stop a prisoner telling lies the flow through the courts etc was very quick, there was no time wasting, from arrest to court then sentence took no more than two days. The free labor supplied by the criminal section of Orbseyn society; was a big contribution to the state budget.

One day Li came into work and found a very dismal situation in the usually cheery Police Station, two of her colleagues had been abducted, the note received was that they were to be killed, and their bodies destroyed by fire unless certain conditions were met. This was a serious threat there was no way the medical fraternity could restore ashes, to bring the men back to life, there was no doubt the threats were genuine because, if caught the culprits would be executed within days, so the situation was serious.

Because the captives were from Li's precinct they had the right to try and get their friends back, but the ransom conditions were so onerous it was doubtful if the Chief Justice would meet the terms set out so all would die, the crooks and their captives. Knowing she was so small that the criminals would never take her for a police-person Li without permission managed to find her way to where the hideout was and enter without suspicion.

To Orbseyns who didn't know her she looked deformed and a bit of a joke, but she had her laser stun gun, and her own lethal hands which the abductors weren't aware of. After getting into the hideaway quite openly she made herself at home acting the part of a deformed clown, she soon had the criminals in thoughts of laughter. The prisoners who knew her were astonished here she was playing the clown, what was she going to do; they looked at each other in wonder and watched? LI herself had to subdue her own fear she was well aware these criminals were desperate and wouldn't hesitate to attack her if they realized she was a copper, but she continued in spite of her internal quaking!

There were three crims all as nervous as could be; they knew what they had done was a capital offence, but Li's antics were breaking down the fear that was pervading the room. When she had gained their confidence and they weren't being so watchful suddenly Li went into action, within the space of a few minutes she had stunned with her laser two of the crims, and disarmed the other by flipping him on his back. It all happened so fast the prisoners were astonished; suddenly they were free and had three prisoners.

When all arrived at their station there was a gasp of surprise, this little woman had overpowered three real thugs on her own, she was an instant hero from then, her journey to the top was unstoppable.

Orlos had been retained to do the engineering design for a new building that was to be 140 stories high, and he loved the challenge. His Father was a close friend of the developer, he had put in a good word for his son, and when he got the contract father and son were both delighted, it would keep Orlos working for three years or more. Because it was a private contract Orlos would earn a lot of private credits, there was no govt credit rate control on this work.

The credits for work performance were not high working for the govt, the private sector was far more attractive, but eventually all private credits had to be converted to govt; credits so Orlos was in the position that he needed advice on how to work out the terms of his contract. All that needed to be done was to send the data to a business consultant, then meet with them by thought process. The expert suggested he should set himself up as an independent, and write the contract in his own name rather than as a govt employee. This he did and was pleasantly surprised at how well he would be remunerated, as a self employed contractor. The young couple was indeed both doing well at their chosen professions.

Li and Orlos were now on their own and rapidly setting up a circle of friends, most in different professions, but mainly academics or older friends reaching the top of their careers, who were very well respected in Cordiance Society. As was quite normal the couples would often come together, and enjoyed each other's company sometimes for many hours in the evenings, and long weekends.

The Orbseyn work week was four days at work or study, then another four days work free. Since the normal days work was fourteen hours the normal working week is fifty six hours, balanced out by the next four day weekend.

When relaxing often stories are told of their work, and one evening the following story was told, with much hilarity within the group as they listened. The story was told by a Legal worker who had reached a high level in his chosen vocation.

A young man a future lawyer by profession wanted to become a developer of Real Estate, but he wasn't interested in starting at the bottom, he wanted to use his legal knowledge to climb rapidly into being a big player in that industry. First he searched out properties of a decent size all with a net earning; of surplus in trade credits for sale, after negotiating prices he then set out option terms, each one which would come to the call at the same time by date and hour.

The option term was 90 days and time of day was 13 hours which was one hour before the change of shift. Then having got a lot of Properties under legal options he set about raising the credits, that he needed knowing that he couldn't go into debt, so he had to have investors, with enough trade credits to settle. The law in Cordiance is explicit when the time for settlement had finally arrived; it must be completed by the one clerk in the registration office, and if that clerk cannot complete the documents in time they must be rolled over, and the terms of the option started all over again. Neither the Vendor nor the Buyer may withdraw if the option holder had committed to complete by agreeing to the settlement.

This lawyer had acquired twenty options on major developments, and he had set them at a time that the stamp duties office wouldn't be able to complete more than one maybe two contracts in the time before knock off. Effectively he had got himself delayed settlements by time the 20 were settled of almost 36 months, by which time he would be well able to settle all contracts. When the time came for settlement both sides are presented to the office, but when the advisors for the vendors asked how many settlements where due our hero said why twenty is there a problem? There was an immediate outburst of rage, this they claimed is a trick and you have done this deliberately.

Not so he replied I am not a property lawyer I didn't know how long settlements take. "Quite so said the clerk he has never had a settlement before, but the law applies, what I have done by time I finish work is what will be processed this time around." Now leave me be and taking the first contract he was only able to complete that one, and half of the next so the balance of them had to be rolled over until the next time.

There was uproar and an immediate application was listed with the equity court for the next day. The next day as required the equity judge said he would need time to examine all of the implications, he would give a decision the following day. The next day he was very explicit the law was fair, the buyer was now committed to a full contract not an option, but all of the terms still stood. The lawyer had got himself twenty major properties, for which he had heaps of time to find investors who had surplus govt; credits. The whole party exploded into thoughts of admiration, what a smart move they all thought, he is best as an Entrepreneur, he needs to change his vocation.

CHAPTER 6

THE EYE IN THE SKY

The spy in the sky control of the population was one that Li had only just come to grips with; much to her amazement she found that 95% of the people were all recorded on the systems data base, the ones that weren't were not worth bothering about. Li was shocked at the amount of control that spy in the sky had, there was literally millions of cameras all reporting back to the eye in the sky, and even all of the leaders were subject to that control. It wasn't a matter of any instructions being issued it wasn't needed; 'the eye' had all of the legal controls also the practical understanding of anything, and everything that was happening.

Li quickly learned that that eye was the real ruler of Orbsey. All of the people were totally controlled, and this included the plebiscite leaders, if and when one died he wasn't replaced until the elections, and then only those with impeccable records according to the eye were eligible to contest elections.

The plebiscite members were men who had reached their last term of work, and they were eligible for the post if nominated and elected. Li had begun to understand the reality of life on Orbsey was good while young, but the aged struggled to keep up to the harsh demands. When she had first heard the age average on Orbsey she had thought how wonderful, but then she began to see how tired the parents of Orlos were, and their constant wish to be able to retire in peace. The sorrow in their eyes when the age work average was lifted by forty five years showed it was a terrible disappointment to them both.

Then short of committing suicide there was no way out, because no matter what the medical profession could keep those alive fit and well up to the end of the last work term, but the tiredness of mind couldn't be overcome.

Even after 300 YOA if one was so inclined life could go on, but there was very few that even made it to the 300, let alone living any longer, once the govt; stopped forcing the medical people to keep people going at the end of the last term, many just sat back and waited to die.

'The Eye' over viewed every aspect of life, work, relaxation, having babies, work performance everything, mind there was the good side of it all too! There was little abuse of wives and children by recalcitrant males, because they were soon bought to order by the eye, and punishment was swift and harsh, the same applied to any female abusers, and there were quite a few.

The entire planet of Orbsey was the same, many years before the Eye there had been different races from different countries, but marriage or a type union between the young of each country had greatly increased. The advent of a superior travel system became so cheap, that it wasn't long before the young thought very little of shifting to a different country, too settle down.

Then with the advent of the Eye, racial disharmony was banished forever, because anyone found guilty of creating such problems were charged with serious disturbance of the peace, and branded as trouble makers. Aerocar theft was another crime that was too dangerous even to think about; the eye seemed to be able to read the mind of thieves, stealing of any type was normally quickly brought to justice by the police, with a lot of help from the Eye. Even career criminals had a tough time getting through the system because they had to prove the source of their income, which was very hard to do with the Eye constantly keeping everybody under surveillance.

Whenever a crime of any sort was committed the police would text a message away and within a few minutes receive back the name of all possible culprits that were in the area at the times given. Nine times out of ten a catch would be made and the case before the courts the next day! Li had begun to wonder who actually ran the planet, was it the elected officials or was it that all 'Seeing Eye' in the sky that seemed to know everything.

When the parents of Orlos had finally finished their last term Li and Orlos went to visit them and were amazed at how worn out and tired they both were, it was no surprise they just wanted to pass away in peace, with no more medicine keeping them working. Sure enough within a month they had both passed away and finally looked as if they were at rest. But the sad part was they had had little or no real opportunity to enjoy their life and their family. Li found that hard!

Li began to work out her own future as a servant of the eye! At 120 YOA she would be able to have her first child, and then at 150 YOA her second would be allowed. After that she would have to work for another over 100 years, my goodness she felt tired just at the thought, and she was only 100 YOA so it must be tough doing that last stretch.

Living in Cordiance on Orbsey: Li and Orlos had both completed their first careers and both had achieved high honors, Li had graduated top out of 50,000 who had completed the course with her. Her colleagues were proud of her on her last day; the precinct had set up enormous banners proclaiming their affection, for the little Earthling who had stolen their hearts. The next step was into plain clothes within the quick reaction division. This meant they got the smaller style petty criminals. It was a division which had an average 60% success rate to find and convict criminals within three days. Any that were then unsolved were handed over to the hard crime division.

Li and Orlos had done well in accumulating quite a large surplus in Govt credits, the remuneration was all in the credit control system, she had earned nowhere near as much as Orlos. Orlos had graduated well and had now moved on to the architectural side of high rise engineering, he was self employed and had accumulated a large surplus in Govt credits.

They had now the surplus in credits to look for a better home, and could become a two vehicle couple, which they did with two better quality aerocars, the one they had, was handed back to the Govt; with all of their white goods for recycling, and their full 100,000 of govt; credits reinstated, after they had found a new home. It was simple they handed in the keys for the old one to the govt; and the home was either passed on to another new owner, or recycled through the system it was irrelevant; there was no loss to anyone.

Li and Orlos now moved into a new home that cost them 200,000 govt credits and with furniture, white goods and two new vehicles had spent over 250,000 credits, but still had a healthy surplus. Orlos now talked to Li about his ambition to create a construction company, and to license his business to become a real estate developer; building high rise homes under semi contract to the state govt. His goal was to build the complexes, and to keep them as investments owned by themselves, and other friends who had surplus credits they wanted to use up.

The usual return on this type of investment was about 8-10%, tax free of course! Li was happy with her own career so that she gave the idea little thought, but agreed immediately to Orlos doing whatever it was he wanted. Orlos had never shown himself as an astute trader, he had been successful as a subcontractor, but that didn't involve risk. It was the developer who took all of the risks, now Orlos would be taking the chances it was a completely different world, one that can bring heartache or pleasure, to the semi skilled often heartache.

Li had been promoted to the plain clothes petty crime division, and found it easy so again she flourished as she had done in the uniform police. It wasn't long before she was just as admired and respected within the new division, her rescue of her two male colleagues had never been forgotten, and she was respected by everyone. It wasn't very long before she was getting promoted, and soon found herself working in the hard crime arena, one that would really test her skills and nerve. Because now she was into working on murder, rape, violence of every type etc; it wasn't a pretty world. In spite of being so high tech Cordiance had it all in abundance, criminals who never seemed to learn were always being found. Li was to learn some vicious lessons over the coming years as indeed was Orlos; they were now part of the real world one that can be very hard and unforgiving, it was a high tech paradise and often very complicated.

Li's next promotion to the serious crime division was quick and unexpected, but the elevation was based purely on her performance in uniform; and plain clothes petty crime. She had received three promotions within 10 years and now at the age of ninety YOA she was only up to the middle of her new career and looked as if she would go to the top before she was 95.

One of the first serious crimes she had received and solved was high level fraud, and in solving this case she had proved her ability with numbers as well as her many other skills. A large development company had been accused of enticing people to invest their surplus govt; or private credits in a scheme to promote the purchase of production rights, for a new health product. The company had claimed the rights for the product, and an agreement to sell through the private thought food delivery system. Shortly after the credits had been received claims of fraud were made against the promoter of the scheme.

The case was put onto Li's work list and she was quick to respond. The promoter produced reports, and claimed options; all seemed reasonable, the business should have been able to do what was claimed. Li after careful research could see a fault in the claims made, but it wasn't easy to prove. Very carefully she indicated she thought the proposals were possibly ok, but in fact she was getting a police employed forensic accountant to check the projections. It was quickly seen that the claims were in error, but it would be hard to prove, so Li had to set up a trap for the very glib promoter. She set up a very subtle trap and within two days the wily fellow was caught, and on his way to a future working for the govt.

Her next case was a serious murder which seemed to suggest a serial killer, who in spite of the high tech police weapons had been able to avoid capture, but when caught he/she would be executed promptly. There had been a rampage of killing in the state of Cordiance, and had been narrowed down to Li's precinct area.

There had been over thirty women killed and raped over a period of five years, and it was thought to be someone with a police background;

they appeared to have a sound knowledge of the detection methods used, and avoided all of the traps. Li spent days and many hours following all of the threads she could find, until finally she thought she had a trace, but she needed some bait and there was only herself she could, and would commit to the danger.

Having set the trap and walking into the bait position she had to wait to see if the rat would bite, finally after three days there was a tentative nibble, but it was really very tentative. The rat smelled the bait and liked it, but wasn't yet ready to bite, plenty of smelling but no bite. Using the analogy of cheese she placed out a stronger cheese, still the rat smelt but no bite, and every day became more dangerous for Li, her nerves were starting to fray. But she still persisted and again strengthened the cheese, finally a bite, but what a bite.

Li had been taken for a whore, when suddenly she was invited to a very interesting party. After setting up a backup she went and was invited by a very suave looking character to have a little comfort, again she accepted even though she had been laughed at because of her nose, and ears the risks were now very high.

Suddenly she was attacked with the perpetrator being first after sex, which would be followed by her death, of this her attacker boasted. He also now knew he had the famous Earthling, and she was a high ranking police officer, it seemed to him she was a loose funny looking woman; this seemed to urge him on to greater dreams of what he intended to do before he killed her. He had restricted his thoughts to Li, but foolishly forgot she could redirect his thoughts through her own, and that she could signal the danger and the time to attack. The serial rapist/killer moved to molest her, he hadn't known of her notoriety in defense suddenly like so many others he was cringing on the floor in fright, while she had him secured by laser handcuffs, he was asleep after having been convicted within five days.

Li's success rate soared, but unknown to her Orlos was on his way to serious trouble. He had moved ahead and won a development on the usual terms of funding part govt; and part private, sadly he was a good engineer, but a less than accomplished developer. It was soon obvious he had under quoted for the development and the govt; under no circumstances would raise the price they would pay for the finished product.

As with all developers he had set his targets markets etc with the govt; as a back stop for sales if needed, he had done all of that work very well and accurately, but he had committed the ultimate folly. He had badly under costed the development and now his projected losses were very heavy, in fact he would finish up bankrupt unless he could find a way out of his predicament.

Li had been so immersed in her own work she didn't notice how her mate was sinking into negativity, hers was nothing but success; and she thought Orlos was the same. Sadly the day wasn't far off when he would be the target of attention from one of her colleagues. Foolishly Orlos had turned to downgrading the quality of the material he was using on his development, it wasn't a criminal action unless he didn't specify on his specifications what he had done, that's where he had gone astray he didn't follow the right proto cols, and got caught.

The development was over 80% finished, when the use of downgraded products was found, and a real uproar developed. It was an involved case during which the police had needed to bring in forensic accountants, leading to serious problems being found and charges were laid.

Li had no prior knowledge when one of her colleagues had to tell her that her mate would probably be charged for fraud, and he would be in serious trouble with the courts. The charges wouldn't have been referred to Li anyhow it wasn't serious enough to reach her level, it was a civil not criminal case, but she was devastated, how could her beloved Orlos have got into such trouble? Then when she started to think she realized all of the signs were there, but she had been so wrapped up in herself she hadn't reacted, and was now truly ashamed of herself, her Chinese heritage was still with her.

She was so deeply in love with Orlos that she had queried nothing he had been doing, nor tried in any way to help him, but there was nothing she could now do just let the law take its course. Within three days Orlos had been found guilty and been ordered to pay the state an enormous amount of compensation credits his development had been downgraded to govt only stock, and sold off cheap.

The shame for the family was severe but that wasn't held against Orlos, his job now was to fight his way back, and repay the state the credits he owed. Li had been affected very little she was tough, and took their fall from grace stoically, but Orlos wasn't so easy to adjust, he had disgraced his family the more they stood by him the worse he felt, he gradually sank into a miasma of self pity.

Li was so very worried what was she to do? She went home to her In Laws for advice, but they too were unable to advise what to do, it seemed they would have to insist he take medical treatment, to heal his problems such as depression. They hated to bring up the subject with Orlos, all they did know was he could be cured with treatment, but it would be at the hospital that specialized with problems of the brain, and that would be hard to convince him to do, in spite of the difficulties it must be done, as quickly as possible.

Like Li his mother was frantic, "We will do anything we can to help, but we know our son he can be so stubborn and sensitive, the disgrace to us in his mind isn't that bad he is too young to worry so much?" His father simply said, "My son is strong he will be ok just be patient you two, and wait for a while."

Li knew she must start to try and encourage her mate to lift himself up, she felt if he could be convinced they could get out of their mess quite quickly, he would become enthusiastic again and they could work off the debt together. There was now a debt of two million credits to be repaid, the big problem was he wouldn't talk about what had happened just bottled it up inside.

At last Li summoned the courage to speak to him, "I know you are in pain and that has caused you to sink into depression, but if you can't recover you will have to take treatment, I love you so much it is causing me pain as well, before long I will be in the same state as you are now?"

The reaction from Orlos was immediate, "I will go in today my darling even more than losing our credits, the thought of hurting you is far worse, I am so sorry." That's all it took and soon Orlos was on the way to recovery having been treated, and his problem corrected quickly.

On a night she would never forget one of Li's dreams had proved to be prophetic, she saw an image of Orlos and another man standing in front of a hill, that glowed as if it was gold, and when she got a good look she discovered it was gold. They were smiling and congratulating each other in such a manner that Li could only assume the gold was theirs.

A large group of men were standing around watching Orlos and his friend, but quite suddenly the group of men was joined by women and children, who were all shouting their pleasure at finding the men. The men all seemed to be Warriors of some type and there was even a few Chinese among them, but the most were quite obviously Romans who were still in their battledress. Li was surprised at the volume of the activity that was going on around the men, but what surprised her more was that there was a huge spaceship that the men, women and children had started to board as she watched.

Suddenly several workmen came into view and started to dig up some of the gold and put it into sacks which they loaded into the hold of the spacecraft. Then a man who was dressed in fancy clothes came with some of his own workers, and bagged up what was left, when there was none left on the ground they carried the bags away to where Li couldn't see, but they didn't load the bags on the spacecraft.

After the two men had finished watching the gold and people had been properly loaded they shook hands enthusiastically, and finally went aboard themselves, she could hear a cheer as they entered the cabin. Li was left behind and could only ponder about what she had seen, but suddenly she was home in Cordiance and the ship was being unloaded.

First out was the men and after a considerable pause out came the women and children; finally the gold was unloaded and then loaded onto a small cruiser which then with the two men aboard was whisked away, to a destination quite some twenty minutes flight time away.

The gold was unloaded at some sort of warehouse where several men came to see it, to apparently value the gold that was there. The two men when it was over had smiles of obvious delight on their faces, and they could hardly contain their pleasure.

They then went to where the new arrivals were, with a man from a govt; dept was counting all of the men, women and children as if they were being sold by the number. It was all so strange to Li she had no idea what it could mean, but then she suddenly awoke, and it was just a dream which she thought no more of for some time later; when the prophetic nature of her dream became a reality.

Returning home one day Li was surprised to find Orlos waiting for her with a visitor, a friend from his work she didn't know. Orlos was very excited and on introducing the visitor it was clear why, this person owned the business he was working for, he was an experienced developer.

Orlos then asked if Li remembered the report from the team that had gone to New Zealand.

"Why yes I remember that well why do you ask?"Li responded.

"Do you remember one of the important discoveries they made near the end of their journey and the sample they bought back?" Orlos asked with rising excitement obvious in his thoughts.

"Well yes they discovered how to get pure gold from the sap of the huge trees they found, yes I remember that's why they didn't want to come back, they wanted to stay and collect gold," replied Li with a smile. "but what has that got to do with us now that's way back on Earth not much we can do about it from here is there?" Li asked.

"I have kept a copy of those reports and I know all about how they processed that gold, Coreum here is a developer and he is interested in putting a consortium together to visit planet Earth, and get a load of gold and bring it back home. We would also like to try and find some earthlings who would like to emigrate here to Cordiance, and set up a tiny colony here." Li didn't interrupt so he continued, "The idea is to get our govt; to subsidize the flight cost of the biggest freighter we have, and bring back the gold and about 1,000 Earthlings. You would need to get leave to come with us so as to demonstrate to your fellow beings they will be safe with us, and that you are indeed the first interplanetary expat, one who has been here for over fifty years will you do it?" He asked eagerly.

"Well until I know what it s all about I don't know, but if it's going to help us and it's all legal of course you could count on me?" She said with a warm smile.

"We are to share half of any profits from the trip and Coreum will be coming with us, this would more than pay of my debt to the govt; we would be free again. But more importantly it would be great to go back again, we could even visit your home so what do you think?" asked Orlos both men looked very excited waiting for her answer.

"As I have just said if it all comes together under full scrutiny yes thanks."

Li remembered her dream and was excited herself but she didn't allow her feeling to show instead she asked, "Why don't you get the trip and everything arranged and approved first, if the numbers and the govt; guarantees look right I think it will be fine. First get it set up then we will know its real and not just a dream?"

Both of the males let out a sigh of excitement and relief, they had thought Li might not want to make such a trip, but her love for Orlos was so strong she would try almost anything to get him out of trouble.

As usual on Orbsey everything moved very quickly, within a week Coreum had the cost and terms, for the trip to use the biggest Space Ship in the fleet, plus one small Cruiser for the International travel on Planet Earth. The state had also agreed to subsidize the trip and pay for each immigrant they bought to settle on Orbsey, this was a great chance for their state and they would very much like to set up an Intergalactic Colony the first on record.

As for the harvesting of gold that wasn't so important on Orbsey, there was a good value on the product, but it was suggested the promoters might like to sell the gold to the Egyptians; they seemed almost obsessed with that product. The problem was how the Egyptians were going to pay for the gold, they didn't have anything that was wanted on Orbsey, and the Space Ship was expected to be full of immigrants, how the problem could be solved was a puzzle.

Li had checked out the materials used in Orbsey for clothes and had discovered they had no silk, she suggested they bring back a load of silk and spices, and that the immigrants should include experts who knew how to work with silk. If possible they should try to bring back with them the silkworms, thus setting up a new industry on Orbsey; they would have the experts to really make it work. Li's Chinese pragmatism was coming out even after all of the years away. Sadly she realized that all of her sibling and her parents would have by now died of old age, because she was now in Earths terms over ninety YOA.

Finally Coreum had all of the numbers in and they confirmed the project would be a success. The project with govt; help was viable, and would make a surplus of several millions in govt; credits because the state had agreed to underwrite the project. If the gold couldn't be used for trade on Earth then they were to bring it all back home, it would be credited at the value of gold on Orbsey. The value of the proposed colony of earthlings was considered to be very high, so that even if they only bought back 100 earthlings the govt; would be very satisfied.

After all of the information had been collated and filed; Li took it to the police forensic accounting lab; to have all of the details checked! It was returned with a very good result re cost and feasibility, it was only then she sat down with Orlos and Coreum for a final meeting, to set out the terms of a contract to be drawn up between the two parties. Li and Orlos were to own one share and Coreum would own the other share.

'Within 32 hours after the meeting the final contracts had been signed, the expedition to Planet Earth was a reality'. Now there was a surge of excitement, Li was busy arranging an extended furlough of six months. Orlos was finishing up his job and handing back what he had been doing, and Coreum was putting his business in order for the period he would be away.

'The Space Freighter had been loaded and a cruiser was sitting nicely in the hold with two aerocars as well', the cruiser would not be bought back to Orbsey, but put in permanent orbit around earth which could last for fifty years, if it wasn't reclaimed in that time it would simply disintegrate, and become space junk. The freighter had been fitted with living accommodation for 1200 coming back, with the facilities to put them all into an unconscious state; so there could be no problem with frightened and rebellious earthlings.

There would be no harm done at any stage to the hoped for new Earth colony on Orbsey', but the safety of the mission had to be ensured, and if that meant the new travelers had to be put to sleep it would be done, with every precaution for their comfort. 'The number of earthlings they wanted to bring back to Orbsey was, 150 Chinese, 150, English, 150 Germans, 150 Indians, 150 Sth Americans, 150 Africans 150 Egyptians, 150 American Indians, 50 Australians, a total of 1250 plus any children' who were part of any family groups, the more the better.

The Space Freighter' was ready to launch now at any time, but Li wanted a last round of checks before takeoff, and they found one problem. Since a lot of the power to move from one Galaxy to the other was thought powered, how were they going to get such a big freighter through with only ten persons on board. Then coming back the Earthlings could hardly be expected to provide thought power so how again were they to move from one Galaxy to the other. This wasn't really a problem, but it would change the cost dynamic for the Govt, that extra cost had to be approved, and it was necessary to install another piece of equipment to facilitate the use of stored thought power. It was an embarrassment to the scientists that such a fundamental mistake had been made, but to Li just another example of how thorough she was in everything she did.

Finally they were all set up and ready to leave there was to be no more delay and the partners were becoming more excited as takeoff time approached. The launch to planet Earth was smooth, and easy not much different than a normal international flight, it was like rising on a cushion of air, but when reaching above the gravitational pull of Orbsey is when the real flight begins. Suddenly without apparent disturbance the Spacecraft was through the fourth dimension and into the 'Planet Earths Galaxy' and the real flight was underway, but there was no sense of the enormous speed generated.

They were very quickly moving back in time, but none including the Pilots were aware of anything, many light years backward had been traversed over the entire trip to planet earth it was the year 100 AD when they arrived, they had left in approximately 70BC; but the actual distance from Planet to Planet was a thousand Light Years.

All on board now settled down for the week's journey to Planet Earth, there was plenty to keep all types amused, but for Li and Orlos it was a time for memories shared so lovingly, they clung to each other the whole way. As they relaxed aboard an empty huge Space Craft, it was like going back in time, but now they were mated so they had a second honeymoon, both wished it would never end.

Quite suddenly the Captain announced, well folks we are here, it will soon be time to launch the cruiser, myself and most of the crew will stay aboard to check everything is fine for the trip home. The Cruiser has two travel jets aboard with the same controls as an aerocar on Orbsey; these are at the disposal of your team leaders. We will have one here, but that is only for use if you need help, and then you must call for it to be sent down. The Cruiser will return to us, the mother ship automatically just press the homing button that's all you need to do.

"When you have cargo to be sent back let us know and we will send down the cruiser, it will pick up, and return your passengers for the trip home. We have two medical specialists on board who will if necessary anesthetize, the earthlings until you return, then you will look at them and may in consultation with me revive any you think can travel with us, the rest will be left to sleep until we get home. If you have too many immigrants for the cruiser to carry and take with us, we can just beam them straight up and sedate them on the way".

"That's good then we are prepared for any eventuality and know that we can rely on you," said Coreum with a smile.

"That's right and as you know this is a private trip so when you leave us you are on your own, but we are here to help if necessary. Once you are all back on board you will again be in the crew and my safety umbrella, until then good luck and we on board hope the goals of your trip is fully successful". 'The cruiser was ready to arrive at destination Central Australia, the disembarkation hold was opened, and they glided free safely within a few minutes were landed on Terra Australis'.

The first day was spent just orienting to the earth's slightly weaker gravitational pull, but the next day it was time to start work. The team of four going to New Zealand had the coordinates, and would take one of the aerocars, the others would travel on the other aerocar, but would only stay there long enough to see the team settled, and then they would fly to Egypt.

'All of the travelers had been treated so they had mouths and ears; they all looked just like Earthlings. The trip to New Zealand took 45 minutes and they had found the gigantic trees in minutes. They landed and as expected there was no signs of life the areas were completely deserted, just as Australia had been when they landed.'

They all spent a day there following through the instructions that had been left by the previous Orbseyn group, and were quickly all set up to heat the mineral gold just as quickly as they could farm the trees. It was exciting to notch the trees at several points around the trunks and watch the flow of the gold colored resin, exactly as the reports they had, said it would. Collecting the resin and then heating them into ingot shaped containers, it was obvious that one tonne of gold could be collected easily in no more than three days, so the target was increased to four tons of gold within three weeks. Meantime the other craft with the leaders aboard was off to Egypt.

The trip to Egypt took them almost three hours; the speed could be felt these vehicles weren't meant for this type of work, but the performance was still formidable. Outside of Egypt the vessel was hidden they took on the appearance of the local people and entered the capital Alexandria quietly; they wanted to see the Pharaoh, and abduct twenty of his citizens.

The visit to the Pharaoh wasn't easy to arrange they had to change into being aristocrats, but once they had done that it was easy. The offer to sell three tonnes of gold was enthusiastically accepted provided the source could be proved, but then the problem was how they were to be paid, not only for the gold, but the secret of where the gold was to be found and processed. What could an ancient culture provide Orbseyns with, there could only be trade goods, but what goods did they have that Orbsey could use on their world.

The start could be the supply of 150 people from the areas as listed; these must know they were going to a new culture as new settlers. A team of experts were needed to grow mulberry trees and silk worms for a new industry on Orbsey. This was a different type of silk and it wasn't available on Orbsey, but a sample of the cloth had been found and inspected by Coreum and Orlos both agreed such beautiful clothe, would be very popular in their country.

Families with children were preferred for the new colony, and since the Govt; would reimburse them on a headage basis, it seemed they would be best to take more colonists for the immigrants wanted by the govt; the silk for private industry was the only unsold product.

The information on how to find and process the gold would be handed over when the new immigrants were made available, Trans shipped to Australia at Egyptian cost. What was being given to the Egyptians was not of great value to the Orbseyns, but to the Earthlings had great trading and other values. It was left to Li to value what they were getting, in exchange for what they were trading, and after reflection she said, "If we take back one tonne of gold and 1250 immigrants for an Earthling colony in Cordiance it will be a very valuable, profitable cargo that's what we need to do and thus stop trying to find other products when it is almost impossible".

They now knew the main product Earth has is immigrants so the more they could take the better, a check with the mother ship confirmed 1200 plus children, but all would have to be kept semi conscious, there would be too many to be left conscious, because they may run riot in fright.

The problem for the Egyptian Pharaoh was to get the immigrants to Australia it would take months, on a fleet of Carthaginian boats going into an area that was unknown to them. The team had offered to take the Pharaoh to have a look at the gold producing trees, but to do so they had to reveal a little about themselves.

At the end when everything was ready the Cruiser would be called in to take Pharaoh and his court to New Zealand, part of the deal was that the Orbseyns would never again harvest gold, but they may come back for more immigrants. It had been agreed the immigrants would be beamed up to the cargo ship and sedated on the way up; this made it far easier for the Egyptians to reach the delivery points.

'Finally the agreement was approved', there was to be twelve hundred adults plus child immigrants, and the silk etc in return for three tonne of gold and the secret of how to find the gold trees. There was no offer to provide transport of the gold, the only information sold was where to find the gold, and how to harvest it properly.

CHAPTER 7/

NEW IMMIGRANTS

The Pharaohs advisors had sent out runners to collect the people selected for the immigration to Orbsey, and arrangements were ready to have them beamed up to the Mother Ship, but it would take too much of the stored energy so the cruiser would have to be sent. But how would the people be transferred even to the cruiser it was a real problem, these people may panic when they got sight of the strange vehicle, and then there would be a problem to get them aboard. The cruiser could carry up to 250 people at a time, there was no alternative, they would have to be put to sleep as soon as they were embarked which in itself was a big job.

When reaching the Mother Ship they would have to be carried on board and put into their lay back seats for takeoff, but that was going to be far too difficult. Finally it was decided they would have to be sedated just enough to sooth their fears, and then once they were aboard the Mother Ship they would be kept awake just enough so they could be lectured by Li.

Because she was herself an Earthling it was expected to calm them down, and it was hoped the message would keep them all quiet until arrival at the airport in Cordiance. The authorities would be asked to clear the terminal of all Orbseyns before the ship was disembarked so the new immigrants wouldn't be frightened. It had been agreed that any immigrants that couldn't settle in Orbsey would be sent back after five years and released near their old home, first having their memory of Orbsey and their travels completely removed.

Finally everything was in place the new immigrants were being assembled as close as possible to the ratios asked for, except the Australians it was decided to leave them out, their culture was just so ancient the shock would be too much, they would never be able to settle on Orbsey. It was time to order down the Cruiser to transport Pharaoh, and his assistants to New Zealand to witness the gold being harvested. Orlos and Coreum had decided this was a highly commercial opportunity, and if the Earthlings settled well on Orbsey they would apply to the govt; to return with a fleet big enough to take at least 22,000 new settlers back. In modern day jargon they got greedy and now wanted to make huge sums of credits, such was the Entrepreneurial spirit as strong as ever in spite of the anti capitalistic state from which these men had emerged. They were real gamblers!!!

If the settlers they were taking now failed to settle they would have to be bought back at govt; cost! The men decided to get two of their staff to stay on Earth, and prepare at least 22,000 Earthlings for the next trip! It was hoped with that number they would then have a viable colony on Orbsey, and they could be trained to one day in the future; send some of their young back to help develop their own mother Earth.

The main goal would be to train Earth to exist without wars, and get rid of all weapons of death, as had been done on Orbsey. One day they hoped Earth and Orbsey may be planets working together, both with advanced technology, this was possible only if peace prevailed. If it was found to be impossible to control crime and killing on earth, the only thing that could be done was to cut it back as much as possible, to be as compatible with Orbsey as possible, but all killing must be controlled.

The cruiser was now hovering high over Egypt ready to come in to receive the 'Pharaoh', and his group of about forty people; all was set to leave the next morning. The group including 'Pharaoh and his wife' had been well versed on what was to happen, and they were to meet the Cruiser alone with as few observers as possible.

The group in New Zealand knew of the group's arrival and was ready to load four tonne of gold onto the ship as soon as they arrived. The embarking and disembarking was very easy, the Egyptians were very nervous at first, but as soon as they were underway they settled down and enjoyed the ride. The high speed of the Cruiser compared to an aerocar, meant they were ready to land in NZ one hour after liftoff in Egypt.

After they had disembarked at the site of the trees and had seen how the gold was harvested, all of the Egyptians clapped their hands in glee at the sight of the 'three tonne of gold they were to receive for the immigrants they were to supply', but they had no idea the people were going to another planet.

On their arrival back in Egypt Pharaoh was asked how two men would be treated if they were left in Egypt until the return of the fleet for more Immigrants possibly 22,000 of them in several years time. He was most amenable to the idea, and promised the men would be kept as special envoys with access to the Pharaoh, whenever they felt they needed his or the help of one of his ministers. That would apply as long as they didn't abuse that privilege, which in the end they did?

The new immigrants had been assembled before Pharaoh and he told them should have no fear, and that he himself had already taken a trip on the strange machine, and seen wonderful things in a far off land. The people cheered their ruler, but some from far off were still anxious, then when Li stepped forward and told them she had lived with the strangers for many years, all became quiet and said they were all ready to leave in the strange boat that floated through the air.

The Cruiser had taken the first tranche of the immigrants on board, and then had left for the Space ship to unload them, and the one tonne of gold going to Orbsey. Before they took off they were all given a powerful sedative that would keep them quiet for several days, by which time they would have landed in Orbsey.

While the last load was being embarked onto the Mother ship there was a final meeting between Orlos, Coreum, Li, Pharaoh and his courtiers, the Orbseyns promised they wanted 22,000 more settlers, and any that were unhappy would be bought back. The two men who were staying behind were introduced, and the Egyptians were told they were staying to find the people to take back on the next trip. If when the space ships got back no way had been found for the Egyptians to harvest the gold in New Zealand, then they would get another three tonne harvested for them by the Orbseyns.

The Cruiser was now ready for the team, several trips had been completed to load the immigrants, and it was time to leave? The passengers were all loaded and sedated; it was time for the Leaders from Orbsey to go on board. One aerocar was being left for the two men who were staying, but it was hidden so that it wouldn't be wrecked by intruders.

Li hadn't been so sure it was a good idea to leave the aerocar, but it had been promised so it was too late to change this arrangement. Li had said the aerocars would give the two persons left behind too much power, and they may abuse that power over the Egyptians. Orlos and Coreum before they left warned the two, that they would be subject to the laws of Orbsey on the fleets return, so they should defer to the laws of Orbsey at all times not of Egypt.

The goodbyes had been said to 'Pharaoh and his Court', then their two comrades who were staying; after which the cruiser lifted off they were on their way back home. On their way back to the freighter as a gift to Li the cruiser drifted over her old home, and she had a few moments to look back and remember. There had been little change, and Li could see where she had played when she was a little girl, she shed a few tears until Orlos reached over and kissed her, then she was ready to go home to Orbsey. 'There had been little excitement on the flight back to Orbsey, the transfer from one Galaxy to the other was just as quick as usual and the flight to Orbsey uneventful'.

All of the Earthlings had been lightly sedated as the heavy affects had worn off, they had been told only they were traveling to a new home far away from Egypt. They were being fed in the usual Earthling way and were quite content; they were now coming in for landing, like floating down to the hanger on a cushion of air. Li could now see inside the terminal and it was deserted, they were now able to receive thoughts from the ground, and they knew the Earthlings were to be isolated until they could be got used to their new environment.

Special Staff had been appointed, and given mouths and ears so as not to frighten the newcomers, while they were being transported to new quarters from which they would be debriefed for as long as needed. Finally it was complete the immigrants had been unloaded, and we're all doing well, they were being left for the sedation to fully wear off.

Li, Orlos and Coreum would have to help with the newcomers, just by appearing they would be reassured, it was especially important for Li to be there because she was an immigrant, and could reassure her compatriots they were safe and headed for a better life. 'Li had to stay at the immigration office for thirty days' by which time most of the newcomers were settled down, most had even got used to the strange look of their new owners.

There had been trouble until Li had told them they had been bought off the 'Egyptian Pharaoh for gold', but if they couldn't settle down in five years they would be returned to Planet Earth. This worked wonders they knew what slavery meant they had come from servitude, not always slavery but all had lived under harsh conditions.

The Egyptians were the hardest to settle their religion dictated they had to die within the borders of Egypt to earn eternal life. Li's comment that on this planet they could live to at least 300 YOA; and then be reincarnated gave them pause to think that maybe this wasn't such a bad idea after all.

The total load had been twelve hundred adults plus children, but there were more children than adults; as far as the promoters were concerned it had been a huge success, the total of new immigrants bought back was over 3,800 including babies in arms. The gold also was valuable, but not as valuable as it seemed to be on Earth, all up it had been a wonderful and very prosperous trip. Li and Orlos were out of trouble with all of the govt; credits now paid, and a huge surplus of almost 5 million commercial credits from the sale of the gold, and the bonus from the govt; for each of the new persons, and their children who were bought back.

Li was back at work as soon as her furlough was up, and Orlos had the money now to be a developer. He joined up with Coreum as a full and equal partner, in building high rise apartments, and scheming about their next trip to Earth. It was most important to them both that the new immigrants settled down well and liked their new home, so they kept their Earthling appearance, and frequently visited the new development that had been especially built for the new arrivals. The new homes were much more than they would have had at home on Earth, and they had land so they could grow their own vegetables etc, but 'the meats were processed protein and given to them to be cooked.

The new arrivals were more curious than frightened, they had been reassured by Pharaoh; and Li, they were going to be safe so it had calmed the men down; the women had been settled from the start. The children were no problem at all the average age was only six YOA so they thought it was all an adventure? The babies, all they were interested in was the milk from mummies' breast; for the rest they knew nothing. On arrival then being held in a type of detention the men began to get restless, but they knew they had to wait until their new masters were ready to expose them, to this new world.

'The day they first saw the real Orbseyns they were terrified for a little while', but Li, Orlos and Coreum were with them so they were reassured. The next day it was all forgotten their new masters were a different race, but obviously couldn't eat them if they had no mouths, but then they also had no ears so how did they hear each other. This had been explained so they were fine with that also, very quickly. The govt; Representatives were delighted with how well their new people had settled down, and accepted their new home, they had heard of slavery in their own history, but that was at least 5,000 years ago, now all were free and equal, unless of course a few messed up for themselves which happened now and again.

The govt; decided that the newcomers could work out among themselves when and how they wanted to be fed, and have their thoughts arranged like the Orbseyns there would be no pressure. They had also agreed that if and when this group had settled down, another expedition would be sent with a full fleet to bring several thousand immigrants back to join their compatriots, but this would only be if the present group was a complete success. It was also decided that if after five years they wanted to go home to Earth, then they would be sent with no hesitation and no questions asked.

All of this had been told to the Earthlings but already it seemed that 90% of them loved their new homes, the other 10% would never be happy anywhere, and they were being ridiculed as idiots by the majority who could see a great future for themselves. Not least of the advantages was the idea of living for so long! The length of life they couldn't easily understand three hundred years goodness that was a prize indeed, and amazing that would really be something to try to get.

Even Li warning them they may be sick of life well before the allotted time span, but they could be kept alive even longer if wanted or if they had a serious accident, didn't stop them from thinking it was all great, but time would teach them.

Li had also warned them that the law was very severe on Orbsey and criminals were usually caught very quickly, she stressed that capital crimes were judged harshly and execution was quick if found guilty. The reaction to that was well on Earth the law is immediate, and criminals are executed immediately without being really able to seek fair justice, so that wasn't new to most of them, especially the men had seen beheadings before, they were very servile when it came to that part of the new society.

When they were first shown their new homes they were very happy, and the cleanliness to the women was wonderful, the men were only creatures of habit anyhow and would soon settle down. The children had been especially catered to, because they were the real persons that would decide if the family was happy or not, so a special effort was being made to ensure their happiness.

Special schools were built for the children, and teachers were found among the group to teach them as a few had been taught on Earth, but then special Orbseyn teachers were arranged to teach about Orbsey. Then there was another program which was compulsory for the adults, this was strictly controlled by teachers who would give lessons about the history of Orbsey.

Within twelve months most of the earthlings had converted to the Orbseyn way of life and were settling in, all were on course to be naturalized, of them all there was only two who were holding out, and declaring they wanted to go home. In another twelve months all had been converted except the same two who still held out, and said they wanted to go home, the problem was they were married men with children and they wanted to take their families with them, but their wives and children didn't want to leave with them.

In total there was twelve who may have to be repatriated. All of the others even the trouble makers families had settled in, but after three years these two men still held out, they seemed to glory in the attention they were getting; and after four years were still insisting they wanted to go home. Li was more than happy at all times to send them home, but the problem was their families who were refusing to leave with them, they had to go unless their men would stay, herein was Li's problem.

Li was bought in, the authorities had hoped she may have some way to convince the rebels they were wrong, she was given a free hand to speak to the two recalcitrant's in the group. After persevering for over two months, Li walked into their compound one day and said, "I have convinced the govt; to send the two families home within one week so please prepare yourselves to leave; there is no going back the govt; is sick of the intransigence of these two men so as they wish it so it shall be, you are all including the families going home," then she turned and walked out without any further discussion, but behind she left an uproar.

The two men had been basking in their notoriety as the only ones who had held out, but now it was time to go, they were terrified! Their wives and children were refusing to go with them, so they were going home alone! Li had called their bluff now they were the ones in trouble, they had no way to know it was a bluff, they didn't know there was no way the govt; would send a ship just for them, but they would go on the next space craft.

The next day they were chasing around for Li, who had refused to come at first, but when they sent a message they had changed their minds she finally came with a very severe look on her face, "well what do you two want are you ready to go I can arrange a Cruiser for you now if you are ready?" She said with no malice in her thoughts.

"No we want to stay now because we were wrong can you speak to the govt; men and plead for us please, we are so sorry and will never play up again," they whined.

"Is this really you or your families I will only arrange the change if you all sign now you are going to stay of your own accord, there is no way then you can change your mind, so sign and we will have the return cancelled, but only this once, any more of your nonsense and you will be treated as a criminal, our promise that you could go home has always been clear, but its only your wives who have stopped your wishes being respected, they don't want to go home never have," Li said finally with a smile she had won again, but for the families not herself it didn't affect her whether they went or stayed.

About one week after settling the dispute with the two Earthlings she arrived home one night to find Orlos and Coreum waving an official govt; letter, they had been chosen to lead a fleet of freighters back to Earth; to bring back fifty thousand new Immigrants, the last lot had settled in so well it had been decided to set up a full sized earth community. They would be leaving in twelve months time, and would be backed by a full fleet with all of the necessary aerocars and cruisers to service the entire program, just as soon as the numbers on Earth were ready to leave. In the beginning they would be going in just one spaceship with a cruiser in the hold!

CHAPTER 8/

NEW CHALLENGES

On her return to work after the first trip to Earth Li had quickly settled down at her job and was soon back to her old self, because she had no need to worry anymore about Orlos she was once again able to concentrate. Her work load and success was soon back to the previous level, but her superiors had been told she was to be part of an expedition to collect fifty thousand Earthlings back to Orbsey which may take up to twelve months to complete, that was a lot of new people to find and a lot of work to be done on planet Earth. There was no problem she was granted twelve months furlough on full pay; because she was still working for a govt; dept. of Cordiance.

Orlos and Coreum were very busy they wanted to complete all of the private work before they left for earth; they were very excited the credits for each person they bought back would be quite large, and once again they were allowed to bring back one tonne of gold. They had got a better price than they expected for the last load of gold, so this time there would be a huge profit.

The development they were currently working on was 140 stories and there were 1,000 condominiums in total, all had been costed out properly and would just be finished in time; if they added extra contractors to the teams that were already working on them. Li had already solved two major cases of fraud and the conspirators were, now working for the govt.

The condominiums were quite nice, but as with all govts; the product wasn't as good as the private homes built with owners funds. They were like 'first home buyers' homes on Earth in the 21st century; the point was there was no debt to acquire those homes and first car, a great start for any young couple. As with the young in all cultures, given a good start they will prosper, on Earth they often start off with debt and out of control.

Li's next case was a major homicide one of the severity unheard of for many years on Orbsey, and had forced the police authorities into urgent investigations; even the eye in the sky was unable to give them any helpful information. Six of the planets top politicians had already been murdered, and the killer had sent a note to police headquarters that twenty four more were scheduled to die over the next twelve months.

It was a very unique case in that the method of killing was with a bow and arrow; it was obviously a specially designed weapon that must have been a miniature handmade version. The killings had all been of Leaders in the Orbseyn Plebiscite and at the time seemed to be a most bizarre and unlikely method, but it was effective.

The arrows that had killed all six of the men had pierced the heart and death had been instantaneous, but must have been quick and painless. By the miracle of Orbseyn surgery all of the victims had recovered and grown new hearts, but they had to be on an artificial heart for nine months. Even though the men had recovered it was in Orbseyn law homicide because the five victims had actually been dead, but bought back to life by the doctors who had received the bodies, and instructed to revive all of the victims.

The type of weapon used seemed to indicate the killer was an Earthling because they were the only ones skilled with the bow and arrows. There were plenty of trainees who were being taught the use of that old fashioned weapon, but it was thought there was none with the skill required to do what the marksman had done. It was because the Earthlings were under suspicion the case was given to Li to try and solve, and she liked the idea of the challenge. Li was well aware of the proper function of a bow and arrow; it was a weapon very popular and used in China when she had been just a girl, before she met Orlos and the Orbseyn team he had been with.

The arrows were of a type Li had never seen before and were obviously of a technical design way beyond anything the Earthlings could make, and it was because of this Li was sure the culprits weren't Earthlings, but Orbseyns with a grudge trying to blame others. The arrows were only ten cm long and very finely finished; there was a device in a capsule on the tip that was sensitive to odor. The tip carried a small sample of the victim's hair or something similar, and the arrow would follow the odor, which was targeted to pierce the victim's heart. The arrows were a fine example of a scientific invention of which the Earthlings would have no clue how to devise, they were all fighting men, killers yes, inventors no, and Li could only laugh at the idea.

With the total resources of the division at her disposal Li seemed to be getting nowhere with her efforts, she was becoming more anxious each day with her lack of tangible results. Then another three prominent politicians were killed, and had to receive medical help to recover, each one was off work for at least nine months, but then only able to work on none stress duties for another twelve months.

Then almost immediately afterwards another three were attacked the same way and would be off work for over eighteen months, this it seemed to Li was her first real clue. Who in the govt; would benefit from the absence of such senior ministers, and who would have access to such inventive knowledge to be able to murder at random? Even to hire assassins to do the job would be dangerous most persons with such knowledge would be already under scrutiny by the authorities?

Every politician with influence in the Parliament was already being scrutinized, but Li increased the range of investigation to any inventive knowledge of the scrutinees that could be found. There were still very few real results, Li's frustration was increasing daily, but her nerves were good and she stayed focused on her investigation. After a thorough search of the background of all senior politicians, who may benefit from the increasing number of absentees; Li could find no reason to be suspicious of even one of them; all were categorized as above reproach and this line of investigation had to be cancelled.

Li was in a quandary; what should she do now, then another three were killed and had to be off work for a time. This really upset the entire system even Li's most fervent admirers in the dept; were asking questions of the brilliant earthling, what is happening was the oft repeated question, but Li had no answers she had no idea where to look anymore.

Then out of nowhere a recurring thought came into her mind, what if one of the Earthlings or a group of them were behind the attacks, and she hadn't checked them out, it seemed impossible but there was a culprit somewhere and they had to be found. She instructed her team to switch their efforts to investigating the Earthlings, but more especially any connections they may have with highly inventive Orbseyns. The investigation was now switched with an emphathis on any group of Earthlings that were associated with any criminal elements, but again there were no results.

Li held another think tank of her senior officers, but again there were no answers, could there be someone trying to discredit Li and show her lack of ability in a real crisis, but whom and why? Li gave orders for every conviction of substance she had achieved to be analyzed, they were again to try and find someone of inventive genius, but even with Li closely following all leads from the start of her investigation they could find nothing. Obviously the criminals were well versed in the procedures that would be used to search for them, and had covered all eventualities. Li was now spending all of her time on this one serious case; all of her other jobs had been passed over to another officer, and she was free just to concentrate on catching a very clever crook or bunch of crooks.

On her own Li started to investigate all of her promotions and check out any officer who had been passed over to make way for her, finally she seemed to have found a clue; not very strong one yet, but a clue that could have some substance. How was she to mature her thoughts in secret she didn't want to warn her quarry in any way, if she was wrong she would be discredited more than she had been so far?

Then there was another six victims added to the already long list of convalescents, and Li's pressure went up higher than ever. What her senior officers were asking are you doing, and when can we see some results? Li still had nothing she was prepared to divulge, she told them they had to wait. It was a mark of the high esteem Li enjoyed that her superiors agreed and stepped back, but they in their turn were under pressure from the politicians, they were worrying about which of them would be next to be attacked?

Li had noticed that the attacks were always pursued whenever there was a group of politicians together generally at some public or celebratory function, and the attacks were all in groups of three. Why she asked herself was that so? She could easily understand why the attacks would be during a function, but why in groups of three there had to be a reason? The victims were always well known to each other, and were standing when attacked; they were always fairly close together. There had to be a reason, but what was it? Li deduced there was no bow the arrows were fired using some different instrument, and it fired three arrows at once. It had to be a spring loaded device with an exceptionally powerful force to propel the missiles, and it had to be small so it could be used without arousing interest from bystanders.

Li calculated the mechanism had to be a barrel like instrument, and would be large enough to hold three arrows that would leave the barrel almost simultaneously but not quite; there would be a one second gap between each arrow. From the information she had Li was able to draw up a picture of what the gun would look like, and she could also calculate the power required; so she felt her depiction of the weapon was accurate. As an incidental the weapon wouldn't be illegal on Orbsey as it didn't use explosive power, Li thought it was purely compressed air and wasn't illegal.

The colleague whom Li had started to have suspicions about had been senior to her, and for six months had been her boss. It had been a surprise when Li had been promoted, suddenly she was senior and her old boss was now under her charge, he had clearly resented the fact still did, but he didn't allow it to show only he and Li understood the animosity that was just below the surface.

In her hard search for clues to the perpetrators of the crimes against politicians, the animosity in her case was all she had, and was too small with which to mount a credible accusation, but Li was sure she was on the right path, as always when an opportunity came her way Li usually won with her dogged persistence. Li knew her quarry was an arms expert; and had access to all of the expertise required to design such a weapon.

Her quarry was well aware of all police procedures, better still he was aware of Li's efforts to find a formula, he would also be aware she would be following an agenda of her own, and he would be watching her very closely if indeed he was the culprit. Suspicion is one thing Li was well aware she was a long way from proving anything, and her quarry wouldn't be making her task any easier, he probably knew she was aware of him and he was enjoying the chase. If he was prudent he would stop the attacks immediately, and he would probably never be caught or charged, it could have been the perfect crime, but his ego was too big only a month later another three victims were successfully attacked.

Now Li was sure she was right about the culprit, and she reported the facts to her superiors, but she stressed none of the charges would prevail in court her evidence was too circumstantial, they had to wait and take their own pressures as best they could while she gathered concrete evidence.

Li had to work out the methodology used for each attack; the gun had to be fired from a location, and yet nobody had ever reported a strange instrument of any kind being aimed at the victims. Hidden locations were hard to work out because the attacks where all at different locations, and there was no way to duplicate the same opportunity at each venue.

The gun had to be small enough to be hidden under a coat or some type of uniform, and it had to be fired easily without attracting attention, the only answer could be that it was strong enough to be fired from quite a distance away from the targets. The sensitivity in the nose cone had to be such; that the targets were as good as dead from the moment the weapon was fired.

It seemed to Li she now understood the fundamentals of the attack weapon, but apart from personal jealousy against her, there must surely be another motive; what could that possibly be and what if any was the final agenda? There were no political meetings of any consequence for at least another two months, so Li set about discreetly investigating her suspicions and all of the information she could about her quarry, but it wasn't easy, he had covered his tracks very well the harder she looked the less she found.

She had to face the fact that much of her information may be wrong, she may indeed be on a wild chase with no credible ending, but her instincts were clear she knew she had the guilty party what she had to do was actually catch him, with the weapon loaded and ready to fire. Then one day at a think tank meeting at which all senior officers in Li's division were obligated to attend, her target officer was in attendance a question was posed for which he ventured an answer, and seemed to give Li a clue as to how her quarry thought, and what he would do in certain circumstances. He had said in answer to a question, "under those circumstances no sensible criminal would do the job himself, because he knew he was being watched, he would use a surrogate while he gave the orders from a hidden position".

The man was well aware Li was at the meeting so she was left to wander if he had made a slip or had deliberately baited her, if it was only bait she knew he would now wait for her to make a move, but she wasn't sure what her move was going to be? Having thought the challenge over carefully, Li now leaked out what pertained to be sensitive information, first she gave out a description of the gun and its capabilities, also that such a weapon wasn't illegal.

Then she gave out a description of her quarry that was entirely fictitious; she wanted her quarry to be laughing at her fumbling attempts to find out the truth, during the entire period she went about her work, as if she didn't have a problem in the world. Then finally she leaked out the guilty party was a police officer in a powerful position, but she was only waiting for his next move, then she would have him or her, but she had emphathized the word him.

Now it was a real cat and mouse game, the mouse Li was apparently on the run, and the cat, her quarry was playing with the mouse so that the poor mouse seemed to be in a flurry of nerves, but in reality didn't show any nerves only fright so the cat became too sure of itself, and was beginning to make mistakes.

The next political public meeting was due in a week's time, but there was some ideas put forward to cancel until the assassin had been caught. The idea was canvassed but gained little support, most politicians saw the cancellation as giving way or being held hostage by a criminal, so the meeting was to be continued, but special help was to be given to Li and her force on the day of the gathering.

Li was busy preparing for the big day, she was sure her quarry would strike again using a surrogate, and she was sure it would be outside, and not close proximity to the gathering place. The eye in the sky had been warned of the situation, and Li was certain that no one would be able to fire any missile without being seen, she was sure this time she would catch her quarry, or at least whoever was designated to fire the arrows on that day.

One can only imagine Li's horror when once again a successful attack was carried out, and another three victims were recovered from the dead, and condemned to the period of forced inactivity.

To compound Li's woes she received a note from the guilty party informing her there would only be another two attacks, and then they were going to retire, but if she wanted to catch them badly enough they would advise her when and how the next attack would be carried out, then they signed off with a rather silly joke about Earthlings who lived above their natural station in life, from a true Orbseyn patriot.

The taunt was translated into a challenge by Li, but in fact it was a mistake because it indicated a reason for the attacks, she was if possible even more determined to catch her foe, and she worked night and day to find the answers she needed. The 'seeing eye' had failed, her own calculations hadn't come to any fruition, and she was being harassed now daily from her superiors all mindful of their own insecurities from superiors above them.

Then one day Li began to ponder over the meaning of a surrogate, what message that word really sent her. Someone other than her suspect was the one who fired the missiles, but that didn't have to be a person it could be a robot for example or it could be pre set and left to be fired by a radio signal, this was a common ploy, but which was it and how was it concealed?

Li began to list out the facts of which she was quite certain were correct. She knew the main culprit, but she didn't know if they used a surrogate. The weapon had to be fired from a height so as to have a clear view of the targets, and once fired had to self destruct in this way leaving no evidence it had ever existed. The weapon was built for each attack out of a prepared mould, and this was why there had to be three victims during each attack.

The motive was partially jealousy but there had to be more than that the crimes were way to serious to be motivated by simple jealousy, then she remembered the slight on Earthlings, that had to be the main motivating force.

Looking at what she had Li concluded that the weapon was dropped from a height and fired by radio wave, and the nose cone was highly sensitive to each particular politician, so how did they get the material that was the base of that sensitivity, this was an entirely new direction that Li had missed up until now.

What did all of the politicians have in common? Of course it was free makeup and hair dressing before any political meeting, and this was common to them all, everyone loved getting made up at no cost to themselves, it was a must for them all. Now Li had a handpicked team investigate the makeup and barbers, who prepared the politicians before their meetings, and quite soon positive results were coming in that showed a definite connection between the barber and Li's quarry. One of the barbers was getting paid to keep samples of politician's hair for the rogue police officer, but that was all he was doing.

Li was getting closer, but not quickly enough because the next day she got a warning two hours before the attack, and soon another three politicians had been slain and were being treated the same as all of the rest, in total there had now been twenty seven victims, only three more would be attacked before the campaign was ended.

The last evidence Li had to find was how the weapon was fired and from where, but she knew it had to be from quite some height, because there had to be a clear path to the victims, otherwise the wrong targets would be killed. Finally the launch pad for the arrows was found, it was at the base of a traffic control watch tower, and could be put in place several weeks before the attack then launched at will. Li now had all of the evidence she needed, but she couldn't prove her case against the person she felt to be the sole guilty party, who was of course her rogue police colleague.

The hairdresser insisted he had only saved some hair from certain politicians, and had no idea what the hair was wanted for, he further claimed not to know who was paying him he merely left the hair where he was instructed and received payments with govt credits. This at last was Li's big chance she hoped, but it wasn't to be that easy there were many twists still to be found before she could arrest her quarry.

The credits were from a private account in payment for a debt; but the payer didn't know the payee he just paid as he was instructed to do, so for Li it was another dead end just one of many during this very trying time in her so far illustrious career. Li now went to her immediate superior and set out her case, she was worried there would be another attack before she could close her case and press charges. Her revelations about what she knew were greeted with a lot of enthusiasm, but agreed she didn't have enough to prove who the guilty party was.

Her boss authorized Li to report to her division the results she had achieved because it was necessary to stop the attacks, even though the evidence wasn't yet strong enough to enforce an arrest warrant. What Li had would go a long way to damp down the heat from higher up, and she could continue her investigation with less pressure from above. She was warned her position in the near future could become dangerous, if her ideas about who was the guilty party proved in the end to be wrong.

On the day that Li reported to a gathering of her colleagues her rogue adversary was present, and sat with a sneer on his face as she outlined the case she had uncovered so far. At the end of the meeting all except that one, came up to congratulate her for the progress she had made, but her supposed adversary left the room still with the sneer on his face. The next day the barber who had kept the hair samples was reported missing, he was found a two days later dead, the time elapsed was too long for him to be medically treated, and bought back to life, Li's only possible witness was dead for real.

Several weeks went by and one day much to Li's horror, she received a letter informing her that another three politicians were going to be attacked the next day, but the letter also stated, "You will be glad to know this will be the last attack in this series it completes the number we warned you of in the first instance, so this will be goodbye, and we wish you well in your efforts to find us. So far you are well off the mark, but that's for you to find out goodbye." Li had always loved a challenge but this was ridiculous or so she thought, the next day when another three politicians were assassinated in the same way, she was dumb founded.

How can this be possible she wandered all of her work now looked as it had been for nothing, and she would have to start all over again? But she was certain she had been, and was on the right track this she was sure was an attempt to sidetrack her, and lead her away from the true culprit, even when she was again confronted by her boss she insisted she was right, and she would prove her case within one month, or resign from the case.

The same day Li sent one of her detectives out to pick up the person who had paid the barber, she wanted to herself assess just how reliable the person was, and if the truth was being told. She had made it clear she didn't want anyone to know what she was doing and the detective assigned to the task was one who for several years had been loyal to Li at all times good and bad, she would trust him to the maximum, and he had never failed her. When the person was bought in it was obvious from the start he was very nervous, and the more Li queried him the more nervous he became.

Finally she asked, "Is there some reason for you to be nervous after all you aren't being accused of anything, there will be no problem if you answer honestly, and you have my guarantee about that."

The reply was instant, "And did you give that guarantee to the barber who is now dead it seems your guarantees are worth nothing?"

Li's answer was equally quick, "I gave no guarantees to anybody, but when I do give a guarantee it will be honored if not my whole career is at stake and that's no joking matter, we both know that. Nobody but my most trusted colleague even knows you are here, and only we two know what we are talking about; the information will never get out while you are at any risk, and if I think you are at risk you will be protected until the case is closed. That is my guarantee and I have the authority to back that guarantee up with the full support of this dept; now what can you tell me if anything?"

"I know a member of this division paid me to contact the barber and pick up some envelopes for him, then the barber was to be paid out of my govt; credit account and certain reimbursements would be made in my favor. I delivered over one hundred envelopes over a period of twelve months, but for this I was generously paid. The only reason for me to speak now is because the barber is dead, and it's time for me to fear for my own life, but before I will swear that in court I have to be guaranteed immunity for any crime that

I may have committed not deliberately, but indirectly without knowing what was really going on. There is no way I would ever have been involved had I known at the start what I know now. So if you can protect me then I will tell you everything I know," he said.

"Ok you are protected from now if you tell me the truth and if that truth is worthwhile, but your fears may be groundless, and then my guarantee won't be needed, tell me and let me judge how exposed to danger you really are," Li said.

"Both the barber and myself found it strange what our contact wanted, a lock of hair from all politicians, what for we asked ourselves? But we never guessed the reason until several politicians had been attacked and had to be off work for so long, and then we realized they were all those who were strong supporters of setting up colonies from other planets if and when it could be done. But most significantly they were all against special conditions for planet Earth; this was anathema to us because we were both supporters of colonists from Earth; even if they were to be stolen. Both of us felt the more that came the better it would be for our planet eventually because they are so like us anyhow, but unwisely the barber told our contact what he felt, whereas I never did. Now give me a sheet of paper, and I will write the name of our contact down and seal it in an envelope, if you think my story is worth your guarantee you may open and read it. If not give me the envelope back and that will be the finish of the matter and we will discuss the matter no more, now what do you say do we have a deal or not?" he asked.

There wasn't a moment's hesitation from Li she agreed to the arrangement immediately, and with a nod from her informant she opened the envelope. There were three names written down, two politicians and the rogue police man. Li was so surprised she couldn't help herself, but let out a gasp of surprise, it was only now she realized just how big this case really was. The first thing Li did was to honor her safety guarantee to her informant; this was done by her trusted aide.

Then she arranged a meeting with her boss to discuss the new events that had now turned up, and the truth for which she now had a material witness whom she had placed in a safe house in a different country, but where he could be questioned at any time. She had done a search on the two politicians named and found they were both foremost in speaking out against Earthlings in particular, they named Earthlings as plain murderers who had no place on the planet Orbsey.

Li's boss was as shocked as she had been, "Are you sure of this was; his first question?" After that he settled down and started to listen in earnest to what Li had to say, both of them knew that to accuse politicians at that level could be very dangerous, and neither of them could afford to make a mistake.

They both decided Li should try and find corroborating evidence, while her boss dug deeply into the backgrounds of the two politicians, he would at the same time do a complete new check on their rogue colleague, to find everything he could about him perhaps something had been missed.

The search for more confirmation about the allegations against the trio was now underway with no secrecy; it was now common knowledge that something very big was afoot within Li's investigation, and there was a lot of interest within her division from sincere colleagues.

First Li went looking for an outside collaborator, but could find nothing. Then she started to look for how the radio signal was sent to initiate the attack, but still nothing could be traced there was no trace on the radio signals because as Li began to realize there had been none, so how was it all done. The stress was becoming very strong there was a lot of pressure from above to prove up or shut up, and if she had to shut up she would have to apologize to all of the parties she had targeted.

Finally Li got the break she needed, she noticed that the traffic watch tower sent out a low frequency message at the same time every day aimed at a specific police audience. When she compared the times of the messages there seemed to be one at almost the same time as each arrow attack, could that be the signal that was timed to fire the secret weapon? She started to make discreet enquiries, and found that just before each attack her rogue colleague had rung in to confirm a time was being kept for a certain broadcast signal.

There was often a different officer in charge and every call was kept in a log book, the police didn't use thought communication because that system was too open to abuse for police work. This was a major clue for Li because there were at least ten different in charge personal, who would testify to the accuracy of the reports and the identity of their caller, but she still had to prove the signal was the fire order to the weapon that was sitting at the base of the station. This was the last clue needed to prove her case, but Li was to find out it was the hardest yet, and it took her another month to find the answer.

Li's assistant approached the top radio intelligence experts in Cordiance for advice, but none could be specific without the weapon for examination, but those had been destroyed. The alternative was to find the mould from which the weapon had been made; it would be a difficult task because it would likely have been destroyed but they had to try it seemed the only hope to finalize the case. Then Li remembered the meeting during which her rogue colleague had mentioned a surrogate, what had he been implying?

At first Li had thought he was referring to the signals from the traffic control tower, now she wasn't so sure there had to be more in that comment, which she believed had been made to tease her. What was the surrogate he was referring to and where was it kept; was it a valuable piece of weaponry that would cost a lot to make and wouldn't be destroyed unless there was a danger it would be found.

Li decided to try and set a trap the object being to flush out the mould, its whereabouts was only known to one person; if she could catch him in possession of it his guilt would be easy to prove, or so she hoped. But her quarry couldn't be underestimated they were very intelligent men and would be closing ranks now for their mutual defense; just in case the police did press ahead with charges.

Leaks began to flow out of Li's division, it was rumored she now had a case and charges were being processed, but it would be another week until formalities were complete and formal charges laid against the three parties. The three men were now under full surveillance by the police and by every link back to the eye in the sky; they couldn't even go to the toilet without being watched in some way.

Then another leak went out, Li was just about ready to pick up the mould that was used to create the weapons, and when that was done she would have a case that would be 100% certain to convict and order the death penalty. The three suspects were now under great pressure, they needed to meet and plan strategy, but how could they do that without being seen they all knew the depth of surveillance Li had available to her, so how could they meet without her knowing?

Li was watching them like a spider waiting to catch flies in its web, and her assistant was just as vigilant the trap was set which fly would be the one to take the bait and fire the trap. The least likely was the rogue policeman he was looking as confident as ever, but that was because he knew police procedure, but sadly for the trio they couldn't meet together to ease the tension off the politicians; they needed reassurance badly.

Finally one of the politicians cracked, and was seen to go to an unknown (to the police) address; he went in and came out with a parcel under his left arm and a stun gun in his right hand. With very little trouble he was apprehended and the missing mould had been found, Li's case was complete only the formalities remained to be finalized, the court case would begin within at most a week.

The charges had now been issued and the three accused had been put into their temporary restricted activity shackles, a type of incarceration reserved for serious cases that could lead to death penalties. The defense team had filed its documents and the prosecution had done likewise! The prosecution charged criminal assault and murder of thirty politicians whom in the course of performing their duties, were at odds with the beliefs of the three accused!

The prosecution asked for the death penalty to be commuted to a two hundred year sleep facility, such penalty in Cordiance law being equal to the death sentence. The intent had been to deprive the country of planet Orbsey the right to bring Earthlings to Cordiance even though the act had been approved by the Presidium. It was further noted the Earthlings had in 99% of all cases been abducted, and were given no choice before being bought to Orbsey.

The defense case was the three accused are servants of the country Cordiance, and were acting for the betterment of the citizens of that country if their judgment's were indeed wrong it was personal error not an attempt to kill. All of the defendants knew the victims would only be temporarily incapacitated and would suffer only an enforced time off work.

The court found the defendants guilty, but they were sentenced to only one hundred years of sleep imprisonment, the penalties under the circumstances were too lenient in the opinion of Li's comrades in the police force.

Chapter 9/

A new Planet in a different Galaxy

The scientists announced another Planet had been found that looked lot like earth, but unmanned probes were being sent out, and if they could they would land to find out more and give a better more accurate report. This Planet was a much greater distance away from Orbsey than Earth was, and sounded much more developed than Earth. The radio signals being picked up were definitely sent by beings of a more advanced caliber than maybe even Orbsey, so the probes would be very careful, but the scientist's knew the technology was far more advanced than they had found on planet earth.

Suddenly the news broke about the new find, it had taken four months for the round trip by a new advanced type of probe; they had landed for a quick reconnoiter but hadn't stayed long. This new planet was very advanced not up to Orbsey standard but quite close, and they were a very warlike one.

The scientists were perturbed at the thought of a warlike planet within easy reach, they would have to send a manned probe to see if the weapons could be neutralized, but also they may have to construct a shield right over Orbsey to protect their world if need be.

Another two probes were sent out one to land and try to find the weapons first, and then to destroy them if they could! The other would stand by and be able to report back if the first probe was attacked in any way! Finally both probes were back and reported they had failed in their mission, so the cover over Orbsey had to be decided and if necessary erected, but it wasn't an emergency just to be on the alert and send for more information. It was certain the tyranny of distance hadn't yet been beaten on the new planet as it had been on Orbsey two millennia ago, so it would take travelers from the new planet hundreds of years to reach Orbsey.

It wasn't such a big deal to cover Orbsey, but there was some thought given to the fact that the coming fleet being sent on the mission to earth should be held back for at least another twelve months. The leaders could only agree fully, that there was no use bringing back a load of Immigrants only to find they had been locked out by the shield, and had to float in space possibly to be destroyed by an aggressive neighbor. All plans were put on hold until further notice, but even if they went in twelve months time they would still be four years earlier than promised.

There was a lot of controversy now in the govt; most didn't like the idea of a shield around the entire planet, it would stop the flights out into the stratosphere and ruin a lot of ticket sales that kept the huge Orbseyn fleet viable. The scientists were instructed to find out if there was some way the weapons of war could be nullified, another two probes were sent out with plans to try and bring back an example of the type of weapons in common use, in the new Planet named by their own peoples Xalafeu.

Within six months the Probes were back with a load of weapons they had managed to steal from one of the bases on Xalafeu, and the scientists were immediately looking for ways to nullify the deadly potential of the strange weapons. It didn't take very long before they had worked out a way to nullify the weapons, but the question now became how many more of these warlike planets are there out there.

Orbsey shunned war but what needs to be done to protect themselves in the future. So far they had found planet Earth, and felt it would be at least two thousand years for them to develop any real weapons of war, they were still driving around with horse and carts. Xalafeu was a very different world it had weapons well able to destroy their own planet, and so presumably wouldn't hesitate to destroy another world.

All Orbsey was interested in was peace, they had no desire to destroy or even fight other worlds they had been civilized for too long, the idea of wars between the planets, was really anathema to the leaders and the citizens alike. Wars as they were waged on earth were not really a problem, they could only kill a few thousand, but Xalafeu were different they could destroy planets even ones as big and as advanced as Orbsey. Decisions no matter how unpalatable had to be made, it was decided that a screen had to be developed that could be erected from its base, to cover the Planet Orbsey within three days.

The space freighter going to planet Earth would be leaving with Li, Orlos and Coreum aboard, with extra 10 staff men of their own, and the usual crew of four were aboard, they would signal how many warriors they had ready to bring back before the fleet left their base in Orbsey. There was one Cruiser and three aerocars in the docking bay, but there may be a need to leave an extra aerocar behind, so the men left on Earth could travel to various countries, and find the families of those they were taking to Orbsey.

The lift off and flight to Earth was quite uneventful and when they arrived on the ground in Egypt their two men were waiting for them, happy to see persons from home, but sadly for them their happiness was short-lived.

An immediate meeting had been arranged with Pharaoh and his entourage, who were all anxious to see the travelers; they hadn't been able to find a way to get the gold from New Zealand. The Southern Oceans were just too turbulent for the Carthaginian boats to navigate safely, and the Egyptian treasury needed gold urgently.

The Gold was ready but way to heavy for the aerocars to carry, the cruiser would have to be sent down to carry the gold from New Zealand to Egypt, Pharaoh was keen to do anything the strangers needed to get that gold, his army hadn't been paid for two months. The Orbseyn mission expressed the need for hardened warriors! Pharaoh suggested they take 20,000 Romans, and he would be pleased to see them go, but the exercise wasn't just to please Pharaoh they wanted a blend of warriors including some Egyptians.

To keep Pharaoh happy the cruiser was ordered down and the gold that had been harvested for him had been transferred; one tonne was kept to be taken back to Orbsey. The need for caution was important the men that were going to be abducted, were prime fighting men, who would object strongly if they were not treated properly.

It had been suggested by Li that a trial should be done with only one freighter probably one thousand to twelve hundred men at most, then she suggested all of the problems with men of this type could be known before a fleet load were taken. It would also establish just how the men would react, when they were again conscious but still sedated.

Li was turning out to be by far the best thinker of the team, and since female leaders were quite common on Orbsey her leadership was quite easily accepted by her fellow traders, for they were after all traders in the sense that they were stealing men and taking them to another life, in return for a reward. It was true that Orbsey offered a far better and longer life than they could ever conceive of on Earth, but that didn't change the truth they were stealing human beings to Trans plant into another world. Li had decided to take a trip by aerocar to New Zealand to check what the men had been doing and was surprised at the amount of gold that had obviously been taken, "What she asked have you two been doing, it looks to me as if over eight tonne of gold has been processed where is the rest?"

Unfortunately for the two men even on earth they could read each other's thoughts so there was no alternative, "we have processed the extra and sold it in India they confessed, but it's not stealing this gold belongs to anyone who can get it," they protested.

"Is that so well as far as I am concerned the gold belongs to us because we provided the facilities to get it, were it not so you would still be at home on Orbsey," Li smiled. Now she continued, "what other mischief have you two been up to tell me quick before I get angry, and remember my position in the police force, because you seem to be getting into a lot of trouble here. It is lucky for you we are on Earth because was that not so you would both be in court tomorrow."

The two were natives of the Cordiance State and were not intimidated by Li, at the start, but instead were inclined to be cheeky. "Well we were left here on Earth and not given any rules, the Orbseyn laws don't apply here they sneered."

"You were explicitly told you still came under the jurisdiction of Orbsey law," was that not so asked Li.

The two men refused to answer although their thoughts confirmed they were.

Li now said "Let me explain! If we lock you into laser chains and take you back that way you will think you have been hard done by, but I think that's just what we will do, now what do you think of that?" Li said with a pleasant smile.

Orlos and Coreum looked on in wonder, they hadn't thought of something like this happening, but they didn't dare to dispute with Li what she was doing. The two men were laser cuffed and beamed up to the Space Freighter within minutes; they were now two very downcast looking men.

On the return to Egypt when asked where the two who had stayed on earth were, Pharaoh was told they were in jail for stealing gold, but he expressed no surprise except to say they could have sold all of the gold to us, who did they sell it to?

"Our laws are not the same as yours it doesn't matter who they sold it to it only matters that they are thieves and must pay the penalty, the next ones we leave won't be so silly and do that again."

But protested Pharaoh, "our agreement was we could take all of the gold we wanted, so really they were stealing off me not you?"

"No the truth is you can take all of the gold you want, but you must transport it here on your own boats, it's only when we carry it for you do we get paid." Smiled Li "and that's what we have done transported to you three tonne of gold now we want payment. Even if you don't mind persons stealing off you we do, those men will be dealt with under our laws. Under our agreement we want the warriors we ordered off you now, and when we get back we want 22,000 more, but we will bring you another eight tonne of gold does that keep you happy?" Pharaoh was beaming with delight he had already forgotten the other two persons, he was thinking about eight tonne of gold, he already knew this was only a trial so he had to have the number of warriors, and to him that was the problem.

But when Li explained they were just going to take them and put them to sleep until they got home he was jubilant, "Why we have a camp with 100,000 Romans they won't even miss what you take, the sooner you take them the better. Are you sure you don't want to take the lot he asked it would be a mercy for us!"

"No we will take 10,000 of them and 6,000 Egyptians hows that and 6,000 Mongols," replied Li.

"Well I guess that's what it will have to be, but these accursed Romans are so hated here I would like you to take all of them, but I guess you can take some of my own troops as well, but they aren't as good as the Romans at fighting," he said with a last desperate try to persuade.

Li just smiled and said this is what will happen, "one of our big ships will hover above and we will pick out the men we want, they will be beamed up to our ship but will be sedated on the way, then when they are aboard they will be put to sleep for the journey home, it's really very simple and you will have earned your gold.

The loading operation was started the following day, much to the confusion among the ranks. Some leaders were taken with those from among the ranks, to ensure continued control when they were rehabilitated later in Orbsey. The whole operation was completed easily and quickly; within two days the warriors were settled and sound asleep in the Space Freighters, and on their way to their destination Planet Orbsey.

There was little or no fuss on arrival at the space terminal, the warriors were semi awakened and allowed to walk off the ship, but kept heavily sedated at all times. It was over a month until the new arrivals were left to become fully conscious, but even so laser guns were held by their attendants at all times.

Li had been in constant control of their settling in program, and even though to be controlled by a female was anathema especially to the Romans they had finally realized there was no alternative, they were on an Alien Planet and the old rules of home no longer applied. As time went by they became used to Li being around and obviously in control of them, but then they began the program that had been developed for new persons who were being settled on this strange place.

When told that Li was almost ninety YOA and the average age on Orbsey was 250-300 years they were silenced from complaints for the present. When they were asked about wives and families of the 22,000 men in the total draft, 20,000 had families, and when all added up the total came to another 50,000 future immigrants to be bought to Orbsey depending on how many decided to settle and stay they were happy, and only wanted to know when this was all going to happen?

It had been decided to again leave two men on Planet Earth to search for and advise the families what had happened, but also to ensure the families were looked after financially by the Orbseyn treasury. The ease with which these violent men were settling in amazed the authorities; and they put the success down to Li primarily and her two compatriots secondly. An assessment had been made and finally it was decided to send a fleet of forty Space Freighters to collect another forty thousand new warriors to join their compatriots already in full training.

The men had been told exactly why they had been bought to Planet Orbsey, and that their mission was to train the natives to be the focus of old style war in this world. It was also explained that in the modern age whole planets could be destroyed, but that the aim of the authorities in Orbsey was to lower the level of war to what it was on earth which in a planet such as Orbsey; was considered very low tech.

The two men who had been arrested in NZ came before Li in her position now of being high up in the legal chain, and were sentenced to 10 years in the military with a nominal monthly credits allowance. The money they had earned from selling gold to India was transferred to the controllers of the trip the three partners.

It was only a few days later that the order arrived elevating Li to a position never before held by any person on Orbsey, she became the supreme commander of the fleet, in the search for interplanetary immigrants. Hence forth she was to be in charge of all immigrants from any planet including planet Xalafeu, since it had been decided the best way to get to know that planet was to abduct some of their citizens and get the information they wanted that way.

The fleet was going to planet Earth again, and by time the full program was completed it was estimated there would be about 50,000 (plus families) Earthlings living in Planet Orbsey and hopefully settling down. There was fifty Space freighters each equipped with a cruiser and an aerocar in their holding bays, and all especially equipped to deal with any troublesome warriors, but no problems were expected the trial load had been very successful, they were ready for their mission when Li and her team was ready to call on them.

Their arrival back in Egypt was greeted with great enthusiasm by Pharaoh, no doubt boosted by the thought of the eight tonnes of gold his treasury was to receive, but a bit tempered by the number of men his people had to find. First the gold had to be processed in New Zealand, and then freighted to Egypt. Orlos and Coreum where now acting alone as agents. Li no longer had a position within their activities except to check that Orlos was doing nothing illegal.

She was now a high govt; official and couldn't afford to be worried about any commercial sidelines. It wasn't certain they would have any involvement with the next job she had, bringing men from Xalafeu, but that was in the future and not on her mind just now.

They took their full team to New Zealand and within two weeks had processed twelve tonnes of gold, eight for Pharaoh and four for Orlos and Coreum, they had both been surprised that there was such a good market for gold on Orbsey, and they had become very rich men. However the govt; had cancelled all commissions for fees on each new immigrant bought back, they didn't need to pay that cost now they had Li as a govt official.

Pharaoh had got all of the men, needed and the transfers were just as easy as before with no hassles what so ever. After arranging to leave two men behind and promising to be back within twelve months, Li had assembled all of the crews on her command ship, ensured all was well and the fleet left immediately for Orbsey. The timing was the same as the previous three flights and soon they were home again in Orbsey, but this time with a big load of mainly Romans.

These warriors were just as easy to deal with as the trial run, as soon as they heard their families could be bought to them, and they would have at least a two hundred and fifty year life span nearly all were very happy. When the calculations were done for all of the families the final count was another eighty thousand of wives and children to come as soon as possible, but only after Li had done a trip of exploration to Xalafeu.

CHAPTER 10

XALAFEU AND OTHER PLANETS

Three months after the last trip to earth a VIP cruiser, was ready to take Li to Xalafeu, this really was a dangerous mission, and one that would set the three planets on a peaceful path, as it had been on Orbsey for several millennia; or one that could degenerate into war. As soon as Li returned there was to be a space craft go to Xalafeu to bring back 1200 of their persons for processing, Li now held the position of being in charge of all of those new immigrants to Orbsey. Because this planet was far more developed than Earth it wasn't expected their people would want to stay, unless like Earth there were special reasons like the increased length of life, and far better conditions than on their home planet.

This was a far more hazardous trip than the ones to Earth, and Li was very aware of the dangers. Her partners Orlos and Coreum had decided to go with her, they were very wealthy men now, and had millions of govt; credits in surplus held by the Orbsey treasury. They weren't interested in the profits unless they could find another bonanza like Kauri Gold, for that's what they had named the trees that had made them so wealthy in New Zealand.

Xalafeu was in a different galaxy than both Orbsey and Earth so using their fourth dimension facility the space ships had to go through three galaxies, and on arrival at the closest point to Xalafeu they still had several months travel. It wasn't the overall distance that took the time, it was the point at which the Orbseyn freighters entered the relevant galaxy, the closer they could emerge to their target planet the better and quicker the trip.

Finally the space freighter was loaded, it was a far longer trip to Xalafeu, and would take from up to six months by time they passed through three different galaxies, and then to their final destination. By time they had arrived at Xalafeu it had been a long boring trip, but Li would go on far longer voyages during her career as the commander for aliens, being bought either peacefully or forcefully to Orbsey, and she would many times face life threatening situations, with the equanimity for which she was becoming famous.

During her long career Li was to bring or manage settlers from another eight distant planets to her home base on Orbsey, hers was a new career but a dangerous one. The constant travel was very hard on the bodies stress system, and at the end of each tour of duty she was allowed a long rest at home.

Li when had landed and changed herself to the shape and understood the communication that were used by the Xalafeuns, she was ready to start work. The first thing was they seemed to have an antenna protruding from their foreheads, their eyes situated higher in the head were quite large and they had a mouth and ears, the first sign they weren't as far advanced as Orbsey.

Their bodies were very thin and looked almost malnourished, which later proved to be a fact. The govt; of this planet was only interested in war and were spending all of its resources to that end. The dream was that some day they would conquer space and the tyranny of distance, and they were prepared to use force on other worlds to make them submit to their will, these things the Orbseyns had been doing, but lacked the drive to wage war on others.

The main reason for embarking on a program bringing the people of foreign worlds to Orbsey was to learn all about them, and to be able to ensure their world was safe not living in a fool's paradise. Li went carefully into the city but was uneasy all of the time, the people seemed to argue a lot and had no love for their govt; and she soon found that the greatest need was food, for hunger weakened them all.

There was prime land in abundance, but everything produced went to the govt; for redistribution at the set prices that's where the profits were made. There were animals to slaughter for food, and fishing fleets bringing in their catch, but all food had to be sold through govt; controlled markets.

Li spent time searching out the armaments factories, and found them as being far behind Orbsey, but pushing ahead. They had atomic reactors and the ability to deliver bombs over a maximum 7-8,000 miles no more, so it all seemed to be pretty safe for Orbsey so far, but Li was well aware of what her job was. Having spent enough time searching out information and being ready to do a full report for the Orbsey govt, she decided to have the space ship sent ASAP. They would beam up one thousand persons, and then wait for the safety of home to interrogate them.

It was a long trip home during which Li prepared a full report for the govt, but Orlos and Coreum were totally bored and were relieved to get home.

They had found no gold or other mineral they could take back to Orbsey so it for them was time wasted, but at least that was their own decision not one made by Li for Orlos.

They had said that Xalafeu was not anywhere near as beautiful as either Earth or Orbsey. The Xalafeuns when they were stolen were sedated, because it was a long trip and it was a lot safer that way. But as soon as they were taken off the space craft sedation had been reduced at the hostel that had been specially created for Li, and her immigrants they became aggressive, so Li ordered them fully sedated again immediately.

It took another two months for these persons to be controllable without being sedated, but after they came right they were model immigrants, and settled in quickly, with them the abundance of food was the main catalyst, all of them could never remember not being hungry. The abundance of food was something they found hard to believe, in Xalafeu only the wealthy could eat like they were being fed on Orbsey.

The problem was they had families to get and that would be another eighteen hundred people, plus it was still problematic how many Xalafeuns the govt; wanted to bring in total. That decision would be left to them; but at first the reaction seemed they wanted as many Xalafeuns as they had Earthlings.

Li's report was well received in the Parliament, and the Orbseyns were so relieved to find there was no immediate threat, but the intent was to make sure there would never be a major threat, now they were alerted to a future possibility. The debriefing of the new arrivals was quite slow they seemed far more suspicious than even the Roman warriors had been, but once they had settled down became very friendly.

Their world they confirmed was a very hard one compared to what they now found to be the case on Orbsey. The leaders on their world were fanatical in the belief that one day theirs would be a superior culture, and all must be prepared to make sacrifices for the good of that future. Their world only honored the strong; the weak were considered to be a liability, which is why there are so many malnourished in Xalafeu.

Their scientists had recently discovered nuclear power, and now they were trying to find ways to harness the power of the atom, but so far the success had been limited. There were over one hundred different countries on that world, but all were controlled by a central govt; found necessary because of the constant war and bickering over the centuries gone by.

Like the other Planets Xalafeu was mostly water, but with less fresh water, so the drinking water shortage was a constant threat; and ways to control the problem were underway. Desalination was being tried; it seemed as if the answer had been found to the problem. All agreed that there seemed to be a better standard of living on Orbsey, but they couldn't settle until they knew their families were going to be bought to live with them. It seemed that would be a bigger task than reuniting the Earthlings they obviously had bigger families, so much so that to bring them back together there would be over 2,500 new immigrants. Unlike Earth the risks were far higher, because there was no Pharaoh on Xalafeu to help them in return for lots of gold; Li was still searching for what they could bribe the leaders with.

The Planet Corrdeloo The scientists had announced another planet, this time a little closer to home a big one almost as big as Orbsey, but not as densely populated. Li decided she was going to take a trip to the new Planet, and reconnoiter before deciding what they were going to do; this planet was in a different Galaxy than the others. But she only had to go through one galaxy to get there; her position was now such that she could order up whatever Space Craft whenever she needed to help do her job.

The new planet was huge Li thought it was just as big, if not a little bigger than Orbsey? It was quickly recognized, as obviously if anything, a little backward compared to Orbsey, but well ahead of Earth. There were many great cities built, and high rises covered the great city centers, but nuclear development was still in its infancy. It was easy for Li to identify the nuclear powered huge navel and merchant ships, that were big enough to deal with the violent waters; they needed the mammoth size that kept them safe?

Li and her crew did a trip around the new Planet taking photographs, and film of the entire planet. There were ice caps at North and South poles, and a huge area of tremendously raging, seas with very few areas that could be seen to be relatively smooth, most and possibly all were just as wild as, or wilder than the southern seas of planet Earth.

The land area was also very large and densely covered with bush and trees, but there were big areas that were being cultivated using fairly ancient style equipment. Having gathered a lot of information from the air, Li had landed and with one other crew member had gone off to check the appearance of the people, but changed their own appearance to make themselves able to mix in easily.

A device had now been provided to Li that meant she and her companions could move from continent to continent and from country to country without having to have an aircraft. It was a simple device which enabled them to go to wherever they needed without any fuss, and not having to call for help from their craft floating above stationery, waiting to ensure help was available if they needed any.

The persons living on this Planet seemed to be a happy well fed lot, they quite resembled Earthlings and Orbseyns in facial characteristics they had mouths and ears, plus the tentacles on their foreheads like the Xalafeuns, but were completely hairless, this was a characteristic they had to themselves, because on the other planets the natives were quite hairy; similar to planet Earth. Their torsos were long, large and muscular, but the legs were very short, the overall effect was that they were about the same height as the people on planet Earth, with a similar friendly appearance.

There were at least twelve medium sized continents with very few island type small countries, but that could just be an oversight created because of the quick assessment that had been done by Li and her assistants. It was later found there were a few islands, but the hostile seas made them unsatisfactory to be heavily populated, these weren't in general a sea going people, but that was natural considering the constant high winds creating violent storms.

Li returned home knowing there was no immediate danger from any of the Planets so far found, but aware of her govts; desire to set up local colonies from all new planets found; so they could be studied and a peaceful future assured for all of the planets people's, not just Orbseyns.

Li decided some colonists from the latest planet found, should be bought to Orbsey for research, and then no more, apart from populating the colonist numbers to the same level as the ones that they already had, which was already a wonderful success.

After that no more planetary work was to be done for at least five years to allow the research on the colonies they had to be completed. Li was in full agreement with everything they were doing, and she was pleased this Planet was as close to Orbsey as Earth was, so the trips weren't so arduous it was only a matter of time, and they would have been incorporated another local colony.

First she and her team went out and just bought back a full load of people, she loaded up her Craft sedated them as they were being loaded, then had them put into an unconscious state, and came straight home. They unloaded them still as unconscious persons, then Li left it to her dept; to do the rest she had a holiday to wait for the reports which she knew would come in quite quickly.

The reports about the Coordeloons were very positive, they would fit in very well with the Orbseyns, just as well as the Earthlings did, but it was essential to bring in the families, and properly populate their colony for them to settle down. They had not caused any trouble, and seemed quite content apart from missing their partners a natural reaction; they seemed to like the Earthlings, and the Xalafeuns which was helping them through their loneliness. Their planet was a peaceful one which was a lot more developed than planet Earth, but they were a democracy of a type that was in later years to be attempted by the Greeks on planet earth.

Coordeloo is a highly animal powered society which was beginning to change and become mechanized, the inventors had successfully pioneered powered flight, but hadn't yet developed an abundant source for the fuels needed. There were no horses or other animals such as dominated on Earth, but there were other animals that had the same strength, and courage of horses and could run equally as fast. Li had seen on her trip around the planet animals that looked a little like a type of camel, but they didn't seem to have been domesticated and just ran wild in the hot areas of the various continents.

This was a planet way behind Orbsey but ahead of planet Earth much to Li's disappointment, earth was a long way behind all of the planets so far found, and she had hoped to find one more lacking in development than her own home planet, but so far it was not to be. Li and her guards left with a team of the natives to pick up the families as promised, and they took again four natives of the area from whence they had taken the first lot, plus they carried extra staff to go searching for the families, they had to find. This time the collection of the families was very quick, and within three days they were on their way home fully loaded with their passengers lightly sedated just in case, but they were back on the ground at home within four weeks.

The noise and cheering from the impatiently waiting family members was intense, and the excitement when they came together made Li's job ever so fulfilling. But as ever it was back to work, now the teams would go back on a single freighter, and find enough who wanted to immigrate, but this time she sent an extra team because, she wanted this area of her work to be finalized quickly just for now. The thought of a five year break away from constant space travel, and strange countries was exciting to her; the work had worn her down she needed the break.

The report that the full number of immigrants was ready came all too quickly, and once again Li and her guards were back in a space freighter going to the latest planet, but Orlos could see his mate was exhausted, and he worried about her, she had been a mountain of strength, but that strength was fast running out.

Space flights were long and boring with sometimes months of doing nothing and life became very difficult! There were thousands of movies and hundreds of games to play but day after day just looking out at the vastness of space made ones isolation seem more and more relevant daily. The lack of a day and night just added to the feeling of insignificance, sleeping and eating was only necessary when the need was felt. Large objects hurtling past during the never ending days became no longer of interest, and questions about how those objects were avoided were no longer asked.

When the fleet arrived over Coordeloons Li barely left their stateroom,

Orlos took her place and settled the fleet into loading stations as was needed and reported daily their progress back to Li. They were on their way back with forty fully loaded Space Craft now, and when they arrived, Li was immediately beamed down and taken home to rest!

Orlos and Coreum did the entire job including having the terminal cleared again, this part of the work was now becoming automatic it was repetitive and easily done? The cleared terminal was to allow all of the spacecraft that couldn't land immediately to beam down their big loads. There was pandemonium in the terminal as old friends met so far from home, with the ones who had been in Orbsey longer, telling the newcomers what a wonderful new home they had been lucky enough to find.

Back to Earth and Egypt: It was now time to return to planet Earth to bring the families of the warriors, who were starting to languish, this from not knowing how their loved ones were getting on without them. Li had been in touch with the two persons on Earth, and they were nearly ready with 90% of the families found they asked for another month to find the rest. In the meantime Li spent time with her fellow Earthlings all of whom were curious about how an Earthling could have risen to such a high position in govt; service.

They had many questions and were so keen to get into the training program that Li was setting up, that Li had to ask for an assistant to help her, because the work load was so big. The govt; didn't want to prejudice her time spent on other planets, and their scientists were almost ready to announce other finds so the immigration from Earth, had to be finalized as quickly as possible. It was expected that by the time she was next back from Earth there would be another planet to visit and bring back settlers. Word now came through that all of the families had been found, and all of them were ready to be reunited with their husbands and fathers.

Orlos and Coreum were both going on this final trip, gold had to be processed for Pharaoh, and they wanted a final load for themselves. There would be no future windfalls on any of the other Planets because the Govt; had realized just how commercially valuable some of what they may find could be.

The trip to Earth was really anticlimactic, and while the immigrants were being assembled the men were off to get the last load of Kauri Gold for themselves and Pharaoh. Pharaoh had as usual been delighted to see them and was anticipating his new load of gold, but he was saddened that his Alien friends would not be back, he had hoped they would clear the earth of all Romans, he even said he wouldn't expect any gold.

On her return to Egypt the men were back and Pharaoh was looking very happy once again, but he wasn't happy at the thought his friends wouldn't be back, for a long time except with smaller craft on scouting missions only. The setting up of an Earth colony on Orbsey would be complete, and they would now let it grow naturally. The next day the gathered families were all beamed up on the Space Freighters and loaded, but only semi sedated these people was happy to be going back to their men folk it was a happy time for everybody.

Only Pharaoh was sad at the prospect of no more gold. Even Li reminding him he knew where the gold was, and how to refine it from the trees didn't reassure him, no he said we won't get there the seas are too strong for the boats of our friends, and anyhow if we did tell them they would only steal it all for themselves. And so it was they left Mother Earth not to return for several years and then only on a research mission.

The return and landing at the terminal was an exciting time for everyone, the new comers had been told all about their new home before they had arrived, but even so natives from Orbsey were kept away, to allow them first to be reunited with their men. The men were all in the terminal waiting and cheering so loudly, that their families could hear the noise as they were disembarking, that had made the occasion even more exciting. Finally the big moment had arrived and Li led all of her charges out into the huge palladium; that was used on these very important occasions.

There were squeals of children calling dad, and mothers sobbing at being back with their men, for Li the best trip of them all. For Orlos and Coreum too it was a very good trip, they had bought back four tonnes of gold for themselves a fortune indeed, but not really needed.

There was now a time to settle in the first immigrants from Xalafeu, but first it was time for a two month furlough. It was a holiday well earned and for the first week Li did nothing, she and her husband had a second honeymoon with their love life as strong as it was at the start. Though they had been forced to spend a lot of time apart; there was that very strong bond that had endured the years, and the time spent away on govt; work.

The intensity of their love had been strong at the start, but had grown over the years so that now it was really over different time periods they had to spend some loving time for each other. Their physical love had always been strong, and now had developed into warm soft encounters within which both were entirely satisfied. Their love making had always been regular and passionate; their increasing ages had certainly reduced the frequency but not the feeling.

They had two wonderful months idling at home, and doing nothing beyond making love and occasionally making the marital bed, but mostly that was just pulling their bed together, after a busy night. It would be only twenty odd years now and they would be allowed to have their first child, and thirty years after that the second child would be allowed, but there would be no more, not even for valuable citizens like Li and Orlos.

The Xalafeuns were as usual looking for more concessions than they had, such as being well fed and housed. Greatly extended life expectancy, were simply accepted as their right because they were superior beings, far in advance of the Earthlings and at least on a par with the Orbseyns. Unfortunately for them the general opinion of the Orbseyns was that the Earthlings although not as advanced in their technology were superior to all, but the Orbseyns, and taken in the time of advancement, doing as well the Orbseyns were at the early stage in their history.

As a result the Xalafeuns were unpopular even in their small group, and it was being debated as to whether they should be sent home. They could be treated so there was no memory of what they had experienced on Orbsey; all that needed to be done was to drop them off and then forget them. Li decided to face them and give them the choice, they could be returned home as soon as possible or they could be increased in number, and also bring their families to join them. There was an immediate heated debate among them; at present there were only twelve hundred of them, their families hadn't yet even been searched for.

After a week they came back with a list of demands that Li unilaterally refused, and informed them they should pack their goods they would be back home in no more than two weeks. This response from Li elicited shouts of anger at which point Li walked out of the meeting with the final instructions to pack or she would have them forcefully sedated, and loaded on board a Space Craft, and rendered unconscious; when they regained consciousness they would be back in a paddock in their own country on Xalafeu.

The police were sent to serve official notice and the recalcitrant men were told very bluntly they were no longer welcome on Orbsey, but now the mood was changed. They asked for a meeting with Li, this she agreed to but had a full unit of police on hand to ensure her own safety. Li started the meeting by saying the Xalafeuns were now persona none gratis on Orbsey because of their arrogant attitude, and that she really didn't care if they stayed or left. What she did say was that like it or not Orbseyns were a more superior culture than any of the worlds she had visited so far, and that they left at their own loss not hers she just didn't care.

Suddenly these arrogant persons were groveling and apologizing to Li for their own foolishness they wanted to stay with no strings requested, and they did want to see a full and successful colony such as the Earth colony was. Li never agreed at that point she said she would have to reconsider their request, orders had been given for a forced evacuation, and she would have to try and get that order reversed if she could, but she gave no promises. As Li left the meeting the persons from Xalafeu seemed a very dejected group! Li immediately called a meeting of her senior staff and the thoughts of them all were correlated, for or against the request to stay! It was only by a slim margin the Xalafeuns request to stay was accepted, but they were to be warned that any future misconduct they would be sent home without any hearing.

The Xalafeuns were given the message, then requested to nominate four men to be taken home, and given the job to bring the families together in 5-6 small groups, and then to be collected by the Orbseyn freighters. It had been decided they were to collect new colonists to come to Orbsey for settlement into a Xalafeuns colon! There would be two Orbseyns with each Xalafeun to ensure the job was done properly, and when all was in place a fleet of Space Freighters would be sent to pick them all up. They were also told the trip was a long one millions of light years away, and could only be done because of Orbseyn superior technology.

Finally if any of the men who would be going on the trip tried to play up, their memory's would be cancelled of all details about their visit to Orbsey, and they would be dumped somewhere on Xalafeu. Li was going to ensure all the new colonists were gathered up properly, but she didn't expect to work with the groups, rather she was going to spend time in the capital cities by herself just to learn as much as she could about these people. She needed to know as part of her work!

When she told Orlos what was happening he asked if he could come with her! He was he explained tired of being by himself, and wanted to spend the time from now on traveling with his mate; and retiring from his partnership as a developer. His partner Coreum wasn't surprised; he had no need to work any longer, and was also interested in getting employed within Li's Dept; even for a menial job, hopefully also traveling from planet to planet with Li's entourage. Both men were given positions immediately as guards escorting Li while she was on duty, this of course necessitated them traveling on Li's space flights, to all of the other worlds.

It was time to go to find the families of the Persons from Xalafeu, the four who had been nominated by their peers to find their families, and to help find more settlers were ready to leave. The space freighter with a cruiser and an extra aerocar aboard with the usual crew of four was ready and keen to leave.

There was an extra eight guards on board to accompany the four from Xalafeu in their search first for the families, and next for the new persons to be abducted. It was probable the new colonists would only be randomly selected as before, and the families collected later, that hadn't been decided until Li made a decision about how many Space Ships would be in the fleet.

On arrival over Xalafeu the search party was dispatched immediately, and then Li, Orlos and Coreum left to see if they could find an official, such as they had in the Pharaoh on earth. That had made things a lot easier, yet really had cost nothing because the gold was collected from New Zealand; and all it took was a little time and work. Li was doubtful they would be so lucky ever again, but she was still going to try who knows maybe there were gold producing trees in Xalafeu, they would never know if they didn't check.

They didn't need an aerocar but they took one anyhow, just for the memory, but in the end they were quite glad they had it! They had as well the new method of being able to beam their bodies from place to place, just by thinking about where they wanted to be, and holding hands before they left going from one place to another. They could make long as well as short trips and didn't have to keep concealing the aerocar which made life a lot easier. It was only if they wanted to take something or someone with them back to their space craft that the aerocar could be handy.

They were soon in the capital city of the biggest and most populous state, but like the citizens everything seemed to be rather spartan, for a world that had seemed to be quite well developed in a technological sense. They soon found looks were misleading, and the advances as pictured by the scientist's back in Orbsey were correct this was a very well developed technological economy.

The capability to produce nuclear energy and use it for war or production was well advanced, but way behind what had been achieved on Orbsey. The people were starved of consumer goods, because all of the planets wealth had been directed to the nuclear development program! The subjugation of all of the countries in this world system was complete, and none could act freely without full permission from the Central Govt. If they didn't obey most were quickly executed, there were no jails in this world you either obeyed or you died, there were no exceptions, except possibly at the very top. The executions were real not sleep centers, once executed there was no revival possible.

Li's group travelled extensively quickly, and found an array of different countries all totally in subjugation to the one at the top, none dared to make decisions of any type on their own, and this created an enormous beauracracy all ruled by fear. There was no way anywhere they traveled that they could find any independence of thought, the ruling emotion was fear. The entire population of the entire planet was fearful! Li soon decided the search for any assistance couldn't be found by outsiders like them, better to let the locals do the job, just take the number they wanted there was no doubt now there would be plenty of the population who would be keen to leave, and never come back.

They would get enough just from extended families of those who were already in Orbsey, for the first time in their lives, they were free of fear, yet they had still tried to extract better conditions, these persons would be good immigrants for Orbsey. There was no use searching any further, Li had done her job thoroughly and now she was prepared to take a load and go home, then come back with a major fleet to gather a full colony for the new Xalafeu homes on Orbsey, it would be a job well done!

On arrival back at the Space Craft it was still about another week before they heard from the search teams on the ground, they had the families of the present colonists ready to go, and by time the full fleet returned they would have the full contingent of 45,000 ready to pick up. The ones waiting were to be bought up immediately.

Before she left Li warned they must only use thought communication as radio may be picked up, and if found they could be executed as spies immediately, no question asked and no quarter given. In this way there could be no communication by radio from Orbsey, they should work to a program of the fleet being in place in six months, because Li wouldn't be using radio to give out any information which could put her own staff at risk.

The Xalafeuns when they had all been beamed up from the Planet below were very quiet and subdued. They weren't surprised or intimidated by the Orbseyns; they had been well exposed to their countries ambitions to be a leader among planets by bringing others into bondage, so another planet arriving first didn't surprise them. They all appeared to be very relieved to be leaving and finding their male folk again, it had been desperately hard without them and they had been interrogated for months, with fear of death if the males didn't return soon.

The arrival in Orbsey terminal once again loaded with families was Li's triumph, and was a pleasure to see these tough males crying over their families was a deep emotion to Li and her guards, but it had been a long trip they would have a month off before they left again. The trip back to Xalafeu was uneventful if long, but Li understood that without their unique thought propulsion they would never be able to travel so extensively like they did, so she was grateful for the speed in which they were back.

As soon as they were within thought communication distance she was in touch with the ground crew, and very relieved they were all ready to load and leave, in their words this Godless world of death. It took a further three months to settle the colony down, but that was up to her staff, Li had completed her part and glad she was off for a short rest at home.

CHAPTER 11/

LI PROMOTED

A Plebiscite decision confirmed that there would be no more planets from which colonies were to be developed for at least five years, to allow the ones they already had to settle down, and their home planets to be properly researched the same as planet Earth had been. During that time all of the Orbseyn foreign colonies; would be bought up to the size of the Earthling one. A new govt; division had been created, and was responsible for working with the colonists, and settling them down.

Meantime the scientists were to continue searching for new Planets that were peopled with beings similar to those already found. Each planet found the only work done would be an observation by Li or her staff. Li's work had been incorporated into the new division, and she had been with her agreement, given the top job of Managing Commander, responsible only to the Plebiscite of Orbsey.

Li was empowered to staff her new division, and ensure the usual schooling agenda was put in place, they all realized the future governance of space colonies was vital, and must be fully catered too by people trained for the job over their entire life. This was the usual approach in Orbsey, when a new govt; need was found outside the norm; it had to be catered for at the present, and schooled for the future by those who had the hands on knowledge to pass on.

Li certainly had the hands on knowledge, but so far she had had no problems since she had eloped from her little village in Central China, she had never been shaped in the stress of real problems. Orlos had been her mentor and only lover from a very early age in Orbseyn time, she would have to prove herself in the stress of trouble in the future, but that was over twenty years away.

At this stage of her life she seemed as if she just couldn't make a mistake, but she was still young with another 120 years of working life. She had been promoted rapidly because she had been the only one who really understood how to deal with the colonists, and her career in the police training academy had been outstanding. But she hadn't done the years of training usually expected of those in high office. Orbsey, and although she had been brilliant she was still very young, and this was a disadvantage in the eyes of some of the leaders.

But now her strength had run out the batteries needed to be charged up the Doctors insisted she take six months leave of absence, and allow her staff to do the work. Three planets now had functioning colonies, and she could pass the work over to Orlos and Coreum for those six months. The report that came back from the Doctor's was that Li had heart, lungs and kidney problems she would have to be set up to have her body initiate the replacement of those sick organs, she would be laid up for twelve months or there abouts.

Medical procedures had to be initiated and the replacement organs must be started up to grow as quickly as possible; because her old organs were well on the way to complete shutdown. This was because she was of Earthling origin, and her vital organs had simply grown old! The new ones now being grown would see her through easily for the two hundred years she still had to live. Even in her body she was preparing the way for the doctors to know what they could expect from persons, who had been brought in from distant planets, but it was a painful process as her own organs shut down and new ones were grown. Even on Orbsey the pain of kidney problems had never been beaten except by replacement, but even that was very painful.

By the time Orlos got home from unloading and settling down the new arrivals Li was in extreme pain, and the growth hormones had been injected into her body so that the new organs could start to grow. Her old organs had expired from old age and would soon be removed; then she would go on artificial help until the new organs could take over. Li didn't need to go into hospital because there was none anyhow, but a day nurse would look after her and if necessary a night nurse would also be supplied.

Within six months Li's new organs were working, but were assisted for the time being artificially, the advice the doctors gave Orlos was that within another three months she would be fit and strong, and well able to work in 10-12 months. They had now learned what had to be done to strengthen the bodies of the new Colonist, so their organs would last for the full period without failure. It was well within medical knowledge to deal with the problems early, and ensure that on the whole there would be few problems with aging organs, in the future for Earthlings.

Better than the Doctor's had predicted Li was back at work in another eight months as fit and as energetic as ever, much to the relief of her family and mate. It had seemed to them for a while, the Earthling wasn't strong enough to live the life term of three hundred years as was average for Orbseyns, but once again she had beaten the odds and won. Not only that, but she had set the example of how all of the newcomers needed to be treated; because none of the planets so far found had an average life span of more than 160 years.

By time Li had got back to work the three Alien Colonies had settled down, and had each been separated to different parts of the state, each with different functions. The Earthling were there for the training of the Orbseyns in basic military tactics, The Xalafeuns were settled into industrial developmental work, and the Coordeloons were settled into agricultural work, all meant to help in the further advancement of Orbseyn understanding of their neighbor planets.

Another colony from planet Earth is ready! While the preparations were being made for the trip to TeKahanui to pick up the start of another new colony, and as she was instructed to do by the govt. Apparently Earthlings were proving valuable as immigrants and that's why the govt wanted to get more. Li decided to take a freighter to planet Earth, and pick up the new settlers as set out in the new instructions that had been given her by the Plebiscite.

She knew they could go, and just take without permission what was needed; then go back for the families, but she decided to go with one freighter, and then order the full number of craft needed to bring back the full number for a colony in one trip. They were also taking with them fifty mixed men and women, from the colony on Orbsey so they could go out and arrange the new settlers, and their families.

The trip to Earth wasn't so bad because it was a fairly short one, but trips in the future like going to Xalafeu, and a six month return time would soon create transporter problems new space freighters were needed ASAP. The length of time going to different planets varied greatly depending on the various craft, the space freighters were slow and cumbersome like modern day big trucks on Earth, the VIP cruisers were very fast, like racing cars and there were all the in between vehicles. Li mostly used VIP or freighters, but sometimes couldn't get them and had to settle for what she could get?

There were two planets of equidistant still to be explored by Li and her team, so the new craft were desperately needed. The scientists had been instructed to go no further out than the distance they had already gone, because beyond that the time, and stress on the fleet was going to be just too much. Further they had been instructed that only another two from the ones they had already discovered; would be considered for the setting up of new colonies. The trio had been asked to try and negotiate with the planets they had arranged colony's with for leadership discussions, such as was being set up with TeKahanui.

The trip to Earth would collect more gold which this time would belong to the state, Orlos and Coreum didn't care about that anymore, they had both accumulated huge numbers of govt; credits which they couldn't use up anyhow. The privilege of being ambassadors for their planet was now more important than gold, and the two males were very happy with their positions, most of which they knew was because of Li.

They left Orbsey two days after Li had decided it was time to go, they had the team of Earthlings aboard. The agenda was that they would first beam down the Earthlings to wherever they wanted, and wait for them to signal one week before they were ready. At this point Li would order forty space freighters to come to Earth as ASAP.

All of the Earthlings now had the Orbseyn gift of languages and thought communication, and as well they all had the devices to be able to move freely whenever, and wherever they needed to go. It was almost a month until the new colonists were ready, by which time Orlos and Coreum were back with their load of gold and lots of happy talk of their visit with the tree spirits. It took only a few hours after the fleet had arrived for all of the newcomers to be beamed up, and just to be certain all of them were lightly sedated for safety sake.

Their arrival in Orbsey this time was just business as usual, they were met at the terminal by a lot of Earthlings who obviously had relations coming, and once again there were wonderful scenes of family reunion, which brought tears to Li's eyes. It was decided by the trio to take another trip to earth before Li went into her two year period off work; they were going to take six earthlings with them to see if some form of representation could be bought from Earth to Orbsey.

Li now wanted to visit the Kauri reserves, but when she did was in for a surprise. She found one of the young female tree spirits only 500 years of age had gone off to China and the taken on the image of Li; this was fine for a while, until she had fallen in love with a young man, and so there was a tragedy in the making. The young man had also fallen in love and wanted to marry her, but that of course was impossible! He wouldn't accept that, and he wouldn't believe she was really a tree, all he could see was the women he loved, and he insisted they be married. Sadly the spirit had to admit she loved him too, but that didn't change the truth she was a tree spirit and could never be a real human!

The couple was really upset, even though she was 500 YOA in kauri tree terms, but in human terms she was far younger than her lover. It was all a real disaster she could never be a permanent human, she could only stay in her adopted shape for twelve months at a time, then she had to come back and look after her body the huge tree that she really was. Then she couldn't manifest as Li again for another twelve months, she could keep doing this living a double life, but her human lover had to be without her every other twelve months.

He was insanely jealous and didn't believe she was really the spirit of a tree he believed she was going off with another lover, and was causing a lot of problems for her. At this time she was in China with her lover, but the twelve months were nearly up and she would have to return any day soon. In China the tree spirit who had kept the image of Li was with her lover, and they were trying to part as she tried to explain once again that she was an alien.

"But my daring I have now told you so many times I am an alien, and have to return every twelve months to my tribe far away, why can't you understand and accept that? I have no choice I have to go and you just have to believe that I will be back in another twelve months, look let me show you I will change for you now and you will see its true what I have been telling you," so saying she manifested and became once again just a spirit.

But Yuan had seen this many times before even though she now became Li's image once again, he just ignored that and still kept insisting she stay, "I love you so much and I cannot live for twelve months without you, if you leave me again I shall kill myself, and I won't be here when you come back, I don't believe you, there is someone else and you only come, to drive me crazy with my desire for you."

"I keep trying to show you I am a spirit, but you won't listen so there is nothing I can do, it's either that or my huge tree body will perish and the blame will be on both of us, why can't you accept that?" she cried.

"Oh my darling I love you, I love you, I love you, and I cannot live without you, life is terrible without you I cannot bear it again it's just too much, leave your lover please and stay with me, I beg you stay with me, what does he mean that I don't can't you see how I feel?"

Yuan was prostrated in his grief and she was so sad, but there really nothing she could do! If she didn't go in a week she would be taken away anyhow, by the other tree spirits, but worse they would be very angry with her, because her tree body would suffer gravely if she didn't appear of her own accord. There was absolutely nothing she could do she was really a kauri tree spirit, and that would never change probably for at least another 2,000 years.

Being a little more firm she now said, "Yuan I have always told you the truth I am an alien from another world, I have to spend twelve months out of every twenty four in my own country why cannot you accept that? I have always told you the truth. I love you deeply my love it's not my choice to go it's my tribes, but there is none other than you, and it will always be that I can only be with you for the time I am telling you".

"There is no point anymore twelve months away is too much it's so lonely without you, just go and let me try to solve my own problems," he said but was just fishing for sympathy.

"I love you I really do and I would never be unfaithful to you in any way, but you have to know that when I go it's me as well as you that hurts, and that will always be so. I am just as hopeless as you if only you could come with me and stay with me while I have to live as a spirit, but it is far away and I cannot take you, then you will see that all would be well with us if only you could get there, but you cannot. You must always believe that I love you dearly and if I could I would give up my other life just to show you just how much I love you?"

"Why can't you just stay with me and forget that being a spirit, they can do without you, but I cannot, if you go I am going to kill myself because I cannot wait for a year, it's just torture here wondering how and where you are oh my darling I love you so much my life isn't worth living without you?" Yuan cried again.

"If I don't go the tree for which I am a spirit will suffer greatly, its body reaches to the stars higher than you can imagine, but after twelve months it starts to suffer. Perhaps next year when I can get away we should try to find our way to my country then you could be with me all of the time, what do you think of that my darling? We should have done that this year but we were too busy thinking of ourselves so now we have to wait. But the trip will be dangerous, do you want to try? It is a long trip to the ends of this world and the seas are dangerous but with me guiding you we can make it, what do you think shall we try?" she asked.

"Yes I will gladly try but first I have to get through this twelve months that will be harder than any long trip, oh I love you , I love you, I cannot live for another twelve months without you it's impossible I shall just kill myself to get out of this misery. I know you must go and that you are really a spirit and have no choice, but that still means I shall be alone for twelve months, no its better if I finish this misery my love, but just remember I will always love you wherever I am."

The next morning when she awoke she found she couldn't wake Yuan up he had swallowed some type of poison and seemed to be dead! As she was trying to wake him she got a slight groan and knew he was still alive but only just. Using all of the spirit skills she knew she was able to bring him back to life, but he was horrified, "why didn't you let me go he cried I don't want to live, I will wait until you are gone and just do the same thing again, oh my god I just love you so much I will not wait another 12 months I will do it again just as soon as you are gone?"

The spirit was at her wits end what shall I do now she wandered there was no use arguing, so she left and did the journey to were the trees were so she could draw up a map, then she returned to Yuan? "If while I am away you have a map to where I am do you think you could find me?" She asked "because if you can we can be together forever."

Finally looking at the map Yuan brightened up, "I will follow you to the ends of the earth if I know we are going to be together forever. I love you so much I would do anything and if I die trying to find you it will have been worth it, just having that dream makes it worth everything my love for you is so strong."

And so it was settled she went back to her Kauri tree and Yuan started to plan his trip to 'New Zealand which would take more than 12 months anyhow'.

When the spirit arrived back in New Zealand she was surprised to find Li there and her team from Orbsey they had just finished milking the trees for gold. The spirit confessed her problems to Li and said her lover was trying to find his way to the Kauri plantation which would take him over twelve months anyhow, but eventually he could live in the forest and know she was always near.

Li agreed it was a good solution because she couldn't change into a human since had run out her quota, she offered to pick Yuan up but the spirit declined he would only be fretting for me every day, better he should spend the next twelve months trying to find his way. Li had agreed, but promised she would track Yuan from Orbsey, and if he got into trouble would have one of the Orbseyn colonists chase him and keep him safe.

The spirit was really happy with that because she knew it was all her fault she shouldn't have let the situation gets out of hand. 'She was after all a spirit that would live for over 2 -3,000 years the situation had become ludicrous', but it was too late now she really loved this common human being who at best would only live another fifty years.

The next day the cruiser was loaded and they were ready to leave, there had been no possibility of finding leaders with enough power to speak for the entire Earth, just before they left Li had an idea. 'Going to the forest of Kauri trees and their spirits, she asked if they were able to travel to Orbsey and keep a human form, they agreed they could and would be happy to go there, if only to see how their seedlings were getting on in their new planet'. Li said no more but said, "We may be back in a couple of months to take about fifty of your spirits back to our world for about a month," she stressed they would only be away for about five weeks at most with that the group, then left for home.

True to her word Li kept a trace on Yuan and monitored his progress which didn't seem to be going very far, but he was trying very hard. Li had decided to carry on with their plans to have their first baby, and if there was to be another trip to Earth, then Orlos and Coreum would lead it without her, for her it was time to be a mother, and nothing was going to change her mind now. She had decided there was no reason she shouldn't keep a track on Yuan in his efforts to find his way to his hopeless love, she knew it was hopeless, but she wanted him to arrive and not to lose his life in his efforts.

'Yuan had walked firstly down thru China and slowly found his way to India', and was trying to find his way down through the subcontinent. He had had serious problems trekking down through China, but he was having far more trouble in India, first he had been attacked by Muslims, then by Hindus, but still he managed to make good time. 'Then he got down to the Indian Ocean, and after that would have to deal with wild South Pacific', it was a daunting prospect, but it never dimmed his memory of his love. All he could ever dream of was his lovely spirit day and night; he kept himself going by saying to himself, 'oh my daring I am coming I will find you either that or I will die in the effort. Oh my darling I love you so much, I am coming to you my darling' day and night her image was in front of his eyes, he dreamed of her every night and woke up whispering her name. And so it went on he had now been travelling for six months, but had only reached the Indian Ocean, now he wandered how I shall get over this ocean, and then the rest of the way'?

Finally he had worked and managed to save enough money to buy himself a boat, even though he had never been in a boat in his life. He watched the boats coming and going until he figured he knew what he was doing, and after thinking for two days of his much loved spirit girl he launched himself into the sea journey, in his flimsy craft.

Since he was still alive after two days he considered he was doing well and Li thought so as well; as she watched him sailing along the coast, but he will never get to New Zealand she thought. Taking pity on his poor efforts Li then contacted one of the leaders of their colony in Egypt, and directed him on how to find Yuan and propel him secretly to the shores of New Zealand. But she asked he be taken to the bottom of the North Island so he would have to walk right to the top; and would arrive just about when the twelve months was over.

'This was done and Yuan thought he was being propelled by the gods', and then when he was shipwrecked on the shores of New Zealand he was certain the gods had saved him. He had arrived in New Zealand down at what was one day to become Wellington, in June, the weather was cold and he had over one thousand kms left to walk, but he was in heaven he had made it to the land in which his loved one lived. He had been traveling now for ten months soon it would be time and his love would be with him, and they would never part again. Never would she have to leave him to go back to her tree, because he was going to live at the base of that tree and be with her evermore.

He began his long walk northward ever northward dreaming, and thinking every day about his lover, knowing he would soon be with her. But he didn't make it on time his love came out of her body, the Kauri tree, and she went looking for him. 'She went back to China he wasn't there, then she followed his tracks all the way to New Zealand', but she couldn't find him.

One day Li up in Orbsey looked down, and realized what had happened she didn't worry because she thought Yuan is safe they will find each other soon, but she was wrong. Yuan was close but he still had to go through the mighty Mungamuka Gorge he was only 100 kms away, and his love was close behind him when he got lost in that gorge, he wandered for days until he collapsed in exhaustion still thinking of his love.

'Still as he lay in the underbrush he was thinking of his beautiful tree spirit', and he kept whispering oh my love my love am I to die now I am so close to you? I have wandered far and the gods have brought me here. Am I to die here my love? If that be the case I will die happy knowing you are so close, and remember my love when you find me my last thoughts were of you? She found him only two days later he was really dead this time there was nothing she could do, but bury him where he had died'.

She buried him after two days of being with him then she went back to her body, the Kauri tree only 200 kms further north, for many years she thought of her human love, every year she went to visit where he had died, and stayed with him for a while. She always remembered him and said, 'oh my love you will live with me in my memory for thousands of years you will never be forgotten, while I still live I love you so if only you could have waited, but my love you would only have lived for fifty years, but you will be with me here for thousands of years'.

Meanwhile on Orbsey Li and Orlos were celebrating the birth of their first baby a son 'they named him Kauri, in honor of their friends in New Zealand'

Great Kauri trees of NZ for Orbsey: Li had read the reports about the spirit of the Kauri trees in New Zealand and was intrigued, so much so that she was considering going back to earth in a small cruiser, to see if they could get some of the seedlings for transplanting on Orbsey. Her investigations about how the silk farming was going encouraged her thoughts greatly, that industry had taken hold and was flourishing. 'They had bought silk back on their last voyage, and the ladies of fashion wanted more in fact all they could get, but it would be another two years until the industry was in production', and a hundred years before they had enough to satisfy the market. The production of pure golden rings and other adornments had also caught on in the shops so a full load of gold would quickly be sold out, now at far higher prices.

An inter galactic cruiser could bring back about six tonne of gold, and silk as much as they could get, which wouldn't be that much weight even if they managed to buy the full seasons crop. The markets for all consumer products were now very strong on Orbsey, and credit values high if they were not controlled by the state govt; which both of these products weren't. Li had passed her thoughts on to Orlos and Coreum, and suggested a private voyage could be profitable if they cared to do the investigation she would support a private trip, but they would have to hire a cruiser, and pay all credits that would be due to the govt. In a private trip to NZ; products of any type could be bought back and sold on the open market, but they had no way to get paid for immigrants, that was a govt; function now.

Within a few days Orlos and Coreum were back both very excited at the prospect of a trip to Earth, the cost of the trip had been confirmed, and they had managed to pre-sell the entire cargo so it was a very viable proposition. They would take a team of ten including the flight crew of four plus themselves, and three extra men to help with harvesting the gold while they went to buy the silk.

The hiring of the fully equipped cruiser was arranged, they had been lucky enough to get the best in the fleet, which would be able to do the trip and carry back the gold easily. Li was going because she wanted the seedlings of the Kauri trees, and she wanted to meet up with and talk to the tree spirits. Unlike the big spacecraft the cruiser could be landed on its cushion of air wherever they wanted so they had gone straight to New Zealand, and landed within walking distance of the trees. The crew had left a guard on the cruiser and come with the party to see these giant trees; they were all greatly impressed by the forest giants.

'Li, Orlos and Coreum had left soon after to go to China, and other Asian nations buying silk and silk worms all they could get', but the worms were too difficult for the smaller cruiser to transport as well as the gold so they managed to buy only the silk material, but got quite a large quantity much to the men's delight. So now it was back to the trees and collecting seedlings for the govt; which was what Li wanted, but she also wanted to spend time with the tree spirits.

Because she had read the reports Li knew what she was listening for, she asked if they remembered her "Yes we do remember and we are delighted to see you, for how long are you staying this time? How much gold are you going to collect off us?" they asked. 'All of the Orbseyns had gathered around and all could communicate with the tree spirits', for the spirits could read thoughts just as fluently as the Orbseyns could.

"We are staying for about one week, but we want to know more about you great trees. We want to take some of your seedlings back to our planet, for we know they will grow there just as well as you are doing here. I want to know how to look after the little ones so that they can grow to be huge like you are, but we want you to give us advice so that we nourish them properly and plant them in the right area?" Li said.

"Why that's wonderful we are so happy that some of our young will grow up in a new environment we have been here for so long, the thought that they will have a new home is a dream come true for us. Do you know we are the oldest living of any species on earth except rocks, and we have no doubt our species on your planet will be just the same, the longest living by a long way?

'Some of us here are over three thousand years old, but we the oldest are getting weary now and our hearts are starting to wear out, you can tell which of us are getting weak by tapping on our trunks, and it will sound hollow that's because our hearts are wearing out inside. "One day a heavy wind will come and I will fall over said one, but my spirit will move to one of the new trees, and the cycle will start again, so it has been for many millions of years".

"Well why don't some of you manifest as beings looking like us as you did last time, and we can enjoy some time together it will be so nice, do you have some girl spirits this time they can manifest to look like me," said Li with a laugh.

'All of a sudden there were over a hundred tree spirits standing around half looking like a variety of males, and the other half all identical to Li'. "Well here we are they all laughed half of us are male the other half females, the world thinks we have a boring life just standing here immobile, but it's not true, what is seen are our bodies our spirits can only be seen when we want to be seen as we are to you now," they all smiled in unison just to show they were happy to have bodies even if foreign ones just for a little while.

That evening and late into the night they all had a wonderful time, the Orbseyns had musical instruments to which the spirits loved to dance, and showed they had a great sense of fun. The Orbseyns always loved to party so they had all had a wonderful time for many hours, but gradually the eldest of the tree spirits grew tired and one by one vanished, until they were all gone and the party was over.

The next day when she could hear the tree spirits once again Li started a conversation with them by herself while the others were off collecting gold. "How long will it take our seedlings to reach maturity or at least full size?" she asked.

"Provided the conditions are right they will be mature in 100-150 years, but the soil must be right and there needs to be plenty of rain as we have here," was the reply. "We keep growing for up to fifteen hundred years until we are really fully grown."

"Will they travel all right in our space ship, do we have to do anything special to allow them to travel easily?" she asked.

"You need to take plants that have matured, and have their young spirits, without that they will wither and die quite quickly, we live for at least 3,000 years so there is nothing if we don't have a spirit to relieve our boredom of standing in one place," they replied. "But it's best if we choose seedlings for you we know the ones within which their spirits have grown well."

"There are thousands of your species here how big a colony must we have to start with?" Li asked.

"We need at least five hundred healthy seedlings to be together spaced the way we are here, as you see there is no room for other life around us as we eat up the entire nutrient in the soil, none is left for others. Because your people have the gift of languages your trees will flourish, and in time you will have a wonderful colony of trees, but you must not over milk the resin for gold. You cannot take what you do here for a long time, here there is a huge colony of very old trees we bleed anyhow, so from us you are taking nothing," was the reply.

"I notice there are huge quantities of solid nuggets on the ground here, why cannot they be turned to gold, is there a process we could follow because really you are gold producing trees?" Li asked.

"No we aren't not really what you are harvesting from us is just our normal life cycle, we bleed constantly this resin you call gold, its only that your tribe has accidentally found how to convert it to gold, we didn't know that ourselves until your first group did it. Normally the resin just bleeds out of us and flows to the ground then makes lumps, everywhere which gradually gets buried with time, the same as we ourselves get buried after we die it's all just a matter of time."

LI finally asked, "Are you all happy here as you are now, or would you like to have a different lifestyle?"

"To be honest you have shown us a new lifestyle, we can go anywhere and take on the characteristics of the people surrounding us and join in the fun if they are having fun, no we are indebted to your people you have shown us a new way of life. If they try to hurt us all we need to do is change back into our spirit and move on, we are looking forward to trying everything. One day we can be Romans, another day Egyptians, thanks to you and your kind we have a great time," and they all cheered for Li.

'Li was incredulous what she wandered had they set loose on planet earth, a host of spirits from thousands of these giant kauri trees; all the original natives of New Zealand. Over the rest of her life Li never forgot that night celebrating with the tree spirits as they did that night, but little did she know the future chain of events she was to set loose on the planet earth, not to distant in the future. Nor could she know that in less than two thousand years the wonderful trees in NZ would be destroyed by man.

In the future her seedlings would become millions of protected giants that were marveled at and loved by the citizens of Cordiance! Many would be watching the wonderful progress of the Kauri seedlings, soon to be growing strongly on Orbsey. Li allowed the secret of how to make gold die, neither she nor her mate wanted the trees to be used as gold making giants, they loved the NZ Kauri for their majesty not their gold.

The trip back to Orbsey had been routine nothing special happened, but they had a very valuable load the men were triumphant that their first private cargo, from a foreign planet had been so fruitful. They quite forgot it had been Li's idea in the first place, but she didn't care she had what she wanted five hundred seedlings complete with their baby spirits for replanting as she wanted. A huge area of land ideal for the growing of these massive trees was set aside and the tree seedlings were planted.

Li had been granted enough land so that in the future there was room for over fifteen million of these magnificent trees to be growing in that one big plantation. The Kauri's on this planet forever more, to be known as Li's trees never was there such a wonderful memorial to one person, a true pioneer for her planet earth.

'The two males found their silks sold out in no time with many persons of stature with credits clamoring for more, and the gold bought them both a huge number of credits sitting in the treasury, but sadly for them by earning so much they had to find ways to spend their credits but how'?

Li had settled down and was busy dealing with requests from her migrants who thought of her as their mother; even the Xalafeuns wanted to know if they could see Li the Earthling. The colonies were all doing well especially the Earthlings and the Corrdeloons; the tendency of the Xalafeuns to distrust everyone was destructive, and tended to isolate them even from the Orbseyns.

Li quickly found these peoples were best left to their own devices unless they started to cause trouble, then she would interfere and warn them, they could always be sent home. 'That threat always shut them up for a while until they started to forget, and get obnoxious again', finally Li called a meeting with them and gave one final warning; she had warned them the govt; had decided that they weren't worth the trouble they caused. If there was to much more trouble they were to be sent home without any chance to plead a case! She warned them if they didn't stop causing trouble they would be all sedated and sent home, and they would have no memory of where they had been or anything about Orbsey, every memory would be cleared out and forgotten. They all knew that on their planet that could mean death for all of the men, so from that time they had started to behave sensibly, but their previous behavior was never forgotten by Li and she filed her full reports to be on record for her successors.

The Earthlings were doing very well with their military training program for the Orbseyns, but they were just a trifle too physical, and were having to lighten the training schedule. The antique weapons being used were a source of much hilarity even to the Romans, but the program was achieving what the govt; wanted a toughening up of a big group of their citizens, so they would be ready if ever needed.

There was now over one million Orbseyns in training, but the aim was to have closer to ten million so there was a long way to go, and possibly a lot more Earthlings needed unless Orbseyns could be used as trainers, but at this stage this option seemed unfavorable. The Earthlings had called for another two hundred and fifty thousand trainers from somewhere not necessarily Earth, but of a similar hardy type that would help reach the govt; target.

With families this would mean at least another six hundred thousand immigrants not a real problem, but only the Plebiscite could decide to take that many so quickly, even if it was only a small number by Orbsey standards.

The following instruction came down to Li! 'She was to double the earthlings by just taking what they wanted from the battle grounds of Earth, and she was to settle full families into the Earthling colony. She was to follow up with just searching the other worlds the scientists had found to see if there were warrior types they could take and bring to Orbsey, when the scientists were ready to process more immigrants on Orbsey. If she could not find what was needed then the Corrdeloons were to be transferred to working with the Earthlings. Time to complete the program was given at five years.

Li looked at the rough diagrams of the three new planets that had been found, and decided to take a month's break to think about the planets, and study the profiles she had received from the scientists and the unmanned probes.

A new govt. dept; of Colonists affairs had been created; but so far the only members were Earthlings and Orbseyns. In spite of the immense gap in understanding, the two groups seemed highly compatible; maybe a sign of the millennia ahead during which Earth's technology might develop very fast.

The groups were made up of little fellas up to ten YOA then from 10-20 and 20-30 at 30 they all went out to their first 45 years training jobs. Orbseyns were encouraged to bring their young people and in this way help with the integration, it was explained the dept. would help both ways the Colonists to get to know Orbseyns and the Orbseyns to get to know them. Very quickly clubs sprang up all over the country wherever the Earthling Colonists were living, and quickly became a great success.

Every facility for the young was provided by the dept, and of course being young they started to get to know each other quickly. Obviously it was the mothers who spent most time at the clubs; the fathers were working very hard, and only came when they had work breaks.

Very quickly the little ones were playing and getting along beautifully, the older group was taking more time, but it was working well slowly. The oldest group where more inclined to want to hang around and flirt with each other, the mothers tried to break it up but they didn't get very far. The Orbseyns and the Earthlings found their respective opposites very attractive, and it was obvious that in the years ahead there would be a lot of mixing. This wasn't frowned on by the authorities or parents, so the future for social integration looked positive!

Naturally because the level of social understanding was so much higher on Orbsey, special classes had to be held for the Earthling parents, so they could have a better understanding of the culture they were now part of. It was always stressed that they could go back to Earth at any time, and they would be treated properly, the only thing was they would have no memory of Orbsey. What they had learned would be in their subconscious, and may occasionally pop up much to their own surprise. A new education program was being set up for the graduation of pioneers of the future.

The first period would be the study of the planets, and travelling with the space craft just as spectators, but bringing back comprehensive reports of all the planets they visited. The second period would be managing the affairs of Orbsey when it came to trading with the new planets in the distant future; these would be the future diplomats of the planetary system. The number of the young in the close to thirty age group were applying to join this new program were quite a surprise, several hundred including Earthlings had applied. The third work term was to be at the level of a diplomat eligible for transfer to any one of the planets, for variable periods, and the final term was as ambassadors at various levels according to previous performance.

The rule then came out that all who wanted to join this program would have to become naturalized Orbseyns, and in the case of colonists that would include their entire family. The idea was to enrich Orbseyn society gradually obviously there was a big gap in the educative quality of the Earthlings compared to the locals, but that would be rectified quite quickly as the education system kicked in to the advantage of the young Earthlings. Very quickly the Earth colonists were now applying to be naturalized, the parents in the hope it would be great for their children and grandchildren.

None were turned down they were a very healthy bunch of people; Li and her team were very happy to see their program turning out to be such a success. As was expected a lot of romantic intercourse soon developed, 90% of it was across the planetary divide, one young couple both thirty YOA in particular made it plain they wanted to enter into the Orbseyn style of marriage immediately.

An Orbseyn girl Desha by name was adamant she wanted to be married, and wanted the Govt; payment to buy their first home. This was refused on the grounds that her husband to be, Anthony the son of Roman parents, wouldn't be eligible for two years. Desha and her parents where extremely hostile to the govt; decision.

Anthony and his parents as Colonists decided they were best to keep out of the argument, they just agreed to the union between the two youngsters! Desha's parents where quite prominent in their community, and she was determined to create the maximum fuss about the refusal. The govt; maintained Anthony had been in Orbsey for ten years but naturalized for only three. Since the law said they must both have been citizens for five years before qualifying for the money, they had to wait for another two years to qualify. Desha asked when the law had been written into the constitution, and it was admitted it was only going through parliament now, and would be law within six months.

Then the real fuss started because ten more young couples stepped forward wanting the same as Desha was asking for. All of the proposed unions had been formed by members of the clubs that had been set up, as a joke they became known as marriage clubs as more and more, interested in permanent unions became obvious.

The normal age to even contemplate marriage on Orbsey is thirty YOA when the first serious career job is started and schooling is finished. Until this age the young normally live at home with their parents, until it's time to set up their own home, but if no union is being considered then the young stay at home with their parents.

The young cannot cavort around and try to keep secrets from the parents, because the truth is at this time hard to hide, all the usual signs apply whether for Earthlings or Orbseyns, daydreaming, from the peaks of joy to the depths of despair, being obtuse without meaning to be, and all the new communications of a highly developed society constantly being used, by that one member of the family.

A sure sign that there is an interest between youngsters is when they suddenly start blocking out their thoughts, they will normally do this to several of the opposite sex in their own group, this is so the interest to a particular party isn't so noticeable. If the interest is mutual then it quickly becomes obvious to the two involved that there is a growing attraction, and they start to get closer. At this stage the only one privy to each other's thoughts are the two involved, if it has developed this far, a full scale romance is quickly in full bloom. In this world of romance the Earthling parents are of no use to their children all they can do is sit and watch, but the Orbseyn parents are well aware of what is going on, and are fully involved.

The mating up with Earthlings is attractive, because although they are backward they are obviously extremely virile, and will strengthen any family's gene pool. The Orbseyns are so far ahead of the Earthlings, they know the effect of the interbreeding, they know the only reason the two peoples are different is the enormous period of development that has advantaged the Orbseyns. The Earthlings on the other hand no nothing, all they know is the lustful mating that is the norm on earth where they think of little else.

When Desha first saw Anthony at one of the clubs of integration she knew she wanted him for her own, she didn't want him to know that so she blocked her thoughts to all, but her parents. Then she kept watching him to see if he understood her world at all or if they would be misfits, she was delighted to find he was quite knowledgeable in the Orbseyn ways, and well integrated. Next she integrated herself to a group he was in, and pretended she hadn't noticed him, she kept her thoughts locked up, but Anthony didn't understand all these feminine wiles and his thoughts were quite open. 'Anthony was thinking, gee she looks nice, but she wouldn't look at a colonist like me, she is one of these charity types who want to help us integrate, I wish she would go away she is distracting me badly'?

Desha was delighted she went to two more meetings, but locked up her thoughts, she just kept reading Anthony's thoughts which were very unfair, but she was a woman after all. 'Anthony was thinking wish that woman would go away she is distracting me way too much, and I can't think properly'.

So finally Desha let her own thoughts free, but Anthony wasn't trying to read them, so now what was she to do? In the good old fashioned way she made a pass at Anthony, and at the same time she was thinking gosh he is nice wander what his name is?

Suddenly Anthony caught on and was reading her thoughts, it was on at last girl meets boy, and they like each other. From then on they were inseparable they couldn't see or feel enough of each other, for the next three years they were never out of each other's sight. Both lots parents could see there was true love in the air and were happy, now Anthony's six siblings became a nuisance, the only big families on Orbsey was Colonists, but in their turn they would be restricted to only two children once mated.

At all times night and day the young couple would be in touch with each other, as soon as they woke up their thoughts would link, then what they were at work they were linked with each other by thoughts, this was fine so long as it didn't interfere with their jobs, if they did they were forced to switch off their thoughts immediately, and stay off until the end of the day.

They were constantly seeking privacy and going to small intimate wine, and dine restaurants which seemed funny to Anthony since Desha only had to think of the menu to have what she wanted, but there was always an intimate corner for dancing to the modern band. Then they both turned thirty YOA; and decided they were getting together, they both had good jobs and Desha couldn't see any reason why they couldn't get the Govt. grant. For a while it was a lone journey as only Anthony and Desha kept chasing the Govt; for the credits on their own account, until unexpectedly there were others wanting to do the same thing. All of the Earthlings were in the same position as Anthony, having completed their education and now in their first careers, some from big families some from small, but all naturalized for over three years.

There was an immediate reaction on the intermedia networks that led to an uproar Orbsey wide, 'why they were asking each other, are these people being discriminated against We stole them from their homes now because their children want to intermarry with ours they aren't good enough, why?'

On and on it went the argument developed, huge numbers of the people couldn't be stopped, and the govt; was being pilloried daily for its insane insensitivity. Polls were held and most showed on average 70%; in favor of the young couples being allowed to get the credits, so they could go through the Orbseyn style togetherness immediately.

The Earthling parents were really surprised at how quickly their young were becoming integrated into their new home, but the parents themselves felt lost it was just all too much for them. One minute the fathers were in the military on Earth where life was so cheap, now they were living a lifestyle that seemed like it was all a world of fanciful dreams. Each morning father awoke to find himself lying in a bed beside his wife, and his wife would awake and for a few moments wander who this bloke was in her bed. From sleeping in tents almost always in full battledress to sleeping in a proper bed it was unbelievable, and before now seeing his wife maybe for a week each year; thy now actually lived together. All of the Earthlings loved their new home, but couldn't help but wonder how long this new life would last, all felt it was only temporary and the Orbseyns would send them home eventually.

The debates stormed on and on, why bring these people here if we don't want to look after their children same as our own, if they aren't good colonists send them home, but don't create second class citizens of their young. Finally one of the Earthlings who had been of a high rank in a Roman Legion spoke up in exasperation. "I can understand that we the parents aren't great settlers, it's just too much for us to grasp and we feel lost, but our young are integrating as we could never hope to do, and we are grateful for the better life choices they have been given here on Orbsey. It would be better to be full citizens of Earth than second rate citizens of Orbsey, so our family suggests you send us home and provided we don't get executed for desertion let us go back to our old life?" He stressed he was speaking for his own family only, but he was aware that many colonists felt the same way, either treat us as equals or send us home.

This really set up an uproar, why is this happening people were asking? Is it true we stole these people against their will from their planet Earth, sedated them and bought them here, do we really now want to treat them as second class citizens? What are we going to do with them now, and how do we get them back home safely? The uproar was really amazing, the people were well versed in the system of social communication it was the main media, and the govt; was being challenged for its lack of concern for these people, who they had bought so far from their home planet!

Finally after twelve months of controversy the govt; had adjudicated and agreed to release the funds, to the young couples of mixed heritage just as Desha had asked for. This was a belated victory for Desha and Anthony, who under the conditions now prevailing had only six months to wait anyhow, but they celebrated with hundreds of other young couples all of whom now qualified for the govt money, and all who were of the Earthling Orbseyn mix; now felt they were real citizens of Orbsey which was what they wanted.

Now that the young of the Earth colonists were finding their way, it had become obvious the parents were unsettled, because the Earth settlers had been stolen, and then persuaded they were safe and had a new home for ever. They now had to be encouraged and somehow made to really feel safe, and made to understand they did belong, and would never be let down. The problems were many, but 60% of them couldn't feel as if they belonged, everything was just so confusing.

The transition from an ancient culture to a highly developed one was for most of the parents traumatic. At home they didn't even have radio, now they had instant access to all the wonders of an ultra modern technological age, and most were still nervous of what they were being shown. Their youngsters who were up to twenty YOA; when they arrived had adopted very quickly, now in their early thirties, they were totally assimilated and many were marrying Orbseyns of the opposite gender.

The younger ones were totally at home and comfortable, as far as they were concerned this was their home, and Earth was just a distant memory. But mum and dad were totally overcome, it was just too much for them to conceive of, back home their fastest locomotion was a fast horse, now they had cars which only the bravest would drive, and only their children seemed willing to even try and learn about, it was a difficult situation for everybody. This in spite of the cars being self driven, all that had to be done was sit in the vehicle, enter on the control board where they wanted to go, then sit back the car did the rest, but for those who had only ever ridden a horse even this was frightening.

When they had first been abducted, and sedated for the journey their emotions were just too unsure of what was happening, then when they were put to sleep it was easy that's all they knew, until they were awoke on arrival at the Intergalactic Terminal. It was such a fright to wake and find beings working on them, and asking them to get up and walk off the huge thing that seemed to have bought them to this new place.

Apparently they were now prisoners of some type of being, and even though these beings were far lighter in build, they seemed to be controlling their prisoners easily, but they were also very friendly. The instincts of the men were naturally aggressive, how could they escape from this bondage, but when they first got sight at the real Orbseyns they were horrified. No mouths no ears how could they hear, but at least they had no mouths with which to eat them.

Then when they were finally in their especially built compounds until homes were available, they had a group of visitors, the leader a woman who looked Chinese, and she had some men with her that look like ordinary Earthlings, it was quite encouraging. During their period of being sedated they had seen these people, but now the images weren't blurred by the drugs, and they could see and understand quite clearly, so they had listened closely to what they were being told. First they weren't prisoners or slaves they were free and in a free society, and they could go home if after staying for a while if they didn't like their new life.

The visitors taking turns, then went on to explain where they were and what their condition was, all stressed they could go home if they didn't like this new world they were now in, and they would be landed were they had been taken from in the first place. The visitors agreed they had been stolen, but in recompense they would get a new home and vehicle, as well as all the furniture needed, and if after five years they still wanted to go home then that wish would be granted without question. The only problem could be if the parents wanted to go home to Earth, but the children wanted to stay for example, this would create unwanted friction for everybody.

The visitors stayed for three days until there were no more questions being asked, then after explaining how to make contact with them they left, with a very friendly attitude being expressed to one and all, by the colonists present. But here after some twenty odd years there was the need to reassure the colonists they were indeed, and wouldn't be in fact couldn't be forcefully sent back to Earth, because they were now naturalized Orbseyns, which didn't seem to be understood by most of the parents who came in for counseling.

The clubs were now providing a full counseling service to answer, any and all personal questions that were being asked, and they were staffed by older more understanding staff. All of the Colonists were now adept at communicating with thoughts, so the meetings were normally quite quick and easy, the ease of understanding was very simple, and there was no time wasted trying to find out what the other party meant. The main problem was with the men, "Why are we teaching these modern people the old arts of war as we know them, what use will ever it be now"?

"Well the truth is our men have become too soft and we need to toughen them up, and we also want to introduce a way of forcing these men who owe money to the state to work off their debt, and become worthy citizens. Our aim is to set up a system that will continue on even after the Earthlings have graduated to other jobs, we hope you leave a base behind for the future, when the system will be run by Orbseyns. Did you not know that all of your inductees are heavily indebted to the state; this is how we are hoping to improve this class of men and turn them into worthy citizens of our planet?" Li had told them.

'This was enlightening to the men, and they felt much more able to contribute to their new society which of course made them happy, and by extension their wives a lot happier as well'. Gradually over the years with a lot of understanding and encouragement the Earthlings were making a place for themselves in Orbseyn society; it was hard work but as deeper understanding of what their new lives meant grew, gradually all of the Earthlings were settling in and becoming as one with their Orbseyn friends.

We need only remember how backward Earth was in comparison with Orbsey to realize why we parents would have such a difficult transition, we went from a horse and chariot lifestyle, to being able to travel at supersonic speed any time we felt so inclined.

CHAPTER 12/

THE ORBSEYN DEBT TO EARTH

There had been quite some discussion within the govt; of Orbsey because it was known a large credit account in favor of planet Earth had been run up, and the difficulty was how to pay the bill. There had been the young Kauri trees that had been bought and a new plantation started; the silk worms and mulberry plantation, which had created a new fashion on Orbsey for the wealthy; these were mainly from the pacific-rim countries.

Recently there had been spices from the Indus Valley in India, and of course gold unrefined from New Zealand. Now suddenly the spirits of the Kauri trees were asking for some type of payment, not cash but ways that could be used to benefit earth and help them; advance as a planet with a future. So far Earth had been in every way except virility, far behind all of the other planets, which made them easier to be used; and little given in return. The tree spirits were only speaking out because they realized there was nobody else from Earth who could do so except Li, and they were asking for her help.

When Li explained there were already discussions in the Orbsey parliament about the problem, and how to help earth without doing any environmental or any other type of damage, the trees were happy, but when she asked for suggestions they had no quick answers either.

The main suggestion was education of the young, but how were they to do that without causing a fuss among the leadership of each area. The idea was not to take the young who were too far ahead, but to keep the education at an acceptable level, because any attempt to get too close to the young of any group of people would be rejected.

Certain groups of people understood education, like the Jewish sects had educated their children for many years; the Egyptians were quite good as were the Mexicans or Mayans. The Chinese were considered too brutal, as were the Romans and the Greeks, who were the leaders in educating their children.

A lot of conjecture followed about just taking school age children to Orbsey educating them for two years, and then sending them home. This sounded quite a good idea but they would lose all of the memories when they were sent home anyhow, and what about those who didn't want to go home, the whole idea sounded good, but had too many ifs and buts.

Memories of their education would be in the unconscious state, and pieces would keep emerging that would make these children different, in the end the whole idea was abandoned until some way could be found to help Planet Earth. The major way was education but how? That was the big question and even the oldest tree spirit had no answer to the problem, Li had several meetings with them and they couldn't find an answer.

Finally it was decided to approach the Romans, the Egyptians and the Chinese to ask if they could set up one major school in each area, they guaranteed the teaching wouldn't be subversive to the leadership of each area in any way. It was stressed they were Australians, with advanced teaching techniques that they wanted to share with the world. When asked where Australia was they told all who wanted to know it was a huge continent far away, but that the teachers had the means to travel back and forth. When they asked how much they were to get for allowing the land and building to be built, Li simply said we are here to help your children, and in so doing help you why should we pay you gold you should pay us for the knowledge we will bring your young.

In the end it was agreed that if the schools worked within two years, the Australians would pay one tonne of gold for each school; and that would allow them to run the schools for twenty years without interference. But if they didn't work within two years the project would be disbanded, and the Australians would leave without paying anything. Finally it was all agreed between the parties although on earth back in 140 AD the idea of contracts was unknown, only a shake of the hand was made by Li and her fellow negotiators to seal the deal. Not such a great idea for the Orbseyns but quite normal for the Earthlings.

Li had come to Earth on her private VIP aerocar specially fitted for her and Kauri, but he had stayed at home to study, he had ambitions that one day he would have his mother's job which he thought was real easy. One day he would find out the truth when his mother was worn out, and his father wasn't far behind Li's job was one of the toughest on Orbsey, the only one who couldn't see that was her son.

Li went home to Cordiance and met with the govt; she explained there was a way to pay the earthlings but she needed a colony of fifty Orbseyns plus their families. Li went on to explain everything that had been set up on Earth, and also said she had called the colonists Australian, so there would be no trouble with aliens. She stressed the twenty years of teaching would mean that the debt to earth would be fully repaid, further she confirmed she had had forensic accountants check the figures, and she had signed confirmation from them that all her forward projections were correct.

She also stressed she was still trying to find a way to grow the Indian spices somewhere on Orbsey so far the future for that industry wasn't good, but her dept; would keep trying. She noted the Indian spices were very popular on Orbsey, again only amongst the wealthy.

It would not take long to set up the temporary tiny colony for Earth, this had become a favorite subject among the local Orbseyns, especially when they were told there were four periods of five years each, they could sign up for whatever term they wanted from five to twenty years. Before sending the colony to Australia Li sent Coreum and Orlos to see how the construction of the schools was going. They reported back things were progressing quite well, and there would be five schools ready within one month.

It was now time to move the teaching staff and their families into place, there had to be administrators, recruiting agents, a team to set up the homes for the colony on earth, gardeners to bring the dessert around their new home into full production. All of these details had to be attended to by Orlos and Coreum while Li watched closely from Orbsey, the many pieces falling into the jigsaw puzzle until in her view all was ready.

Finally all of the pieces were in place to the standard Li had set so it was time to go, and the loading of a giant space cruiser was ready. The starting team consisted of 1,000 teachers, 500 other trades and a 250 set up team. Li and her assistants believed this number would need to be doubled within twelve months. That would be the entire commitment to pay the debt to planet earth; over twenty years, it was the only way Li could see to clear the debt.

Everything was going very well now, the teachers were all approved by the Orbsey dept; of education, and a type of delayed program had been developed for the ancient culture of planet Earth. It meant the teachers all had to dumb down to what to them was a very low level of an education program. In many ways this was far harder than teaching at home in Orbsey, and it took a lot of serious discussions for some of the teachers chosen to really get the idea, of what they were trying to do.

The idea was trying to introduce the concept of school for the children of the poor, not a particularly popular concept at all on Earth in those days.

Education was only for the sons of the wealthy who had no entitlement to an inheritance or some members of the churches who were again manly scions of the wealthy with no inheritance chances.

The schools had been operational very successfully for two years and the fee of one tonne of gold for each school had been paid. Unfortunately the idea of educating the sons of the poor was difficult for the aristocracy to accept, from the start the schools were for girls and boys, but this had created uproar and had to be changed now it was boys only.

The rulers in the different areas were soon asking why the wealthy weren't included in the rolls, and soon they began insisting they were to be included. This demand was quickly refused on the grounds that the schools were owned by the Australians, and they had paid pure gold to run the schools the way they wanted to; for the next eighteen years which was what they intended to do.

The Roman reply was they would do as they were ordered to by the Senate or they would be moved out, and the schools burnt to the ground. The Australians replied that they would seek redress from the Senate, because of the Emperor breaking his word, and if they had to they would try and defend their own property.

Li had met with the tree spirits and explained the new problem that had come up, and they had told her they would field for defense over two hundred and fifty thousand troops to defend the school properties. 'And how she had asked are you going to do that, what happens if they are all killed in the fight'? This created a great deal of laughter among the trees, and 'how they asked are they going to kill us we are spirits, we cannot be killed, but we can kill we would really only be there as a bluff, but if someone calls the bluff it will all be a big laugh'.

And so it was all set up the Romans sent out a small legion to destroy a school, but when they arrived there was quite a large army of troops waiting for them, showing not one iota of aggression, but looking ready to defend the school if need be. Looking rather shocked the leader of the Romans sent back for more troops, but instead was told to withdraw until further notice.

One of the Emperors warrior sons then came to the school and asked, "What are you people doing do you intend to refuse entry to the Emperor"?

"Yes if he is going to destroy the school, after all we paid him a tonne of gold to be here now he wants to evict us is that Roman justice if it is then we don't want to be part of it, because that's not justice especially after he gave his word. A week later the envoy was back with a message that the Emperor had realized his mistake and his word would be honored, there would be no more attacks on the school".

There were no problems with the Egyptians or the Chinese they never wavered from the agreement even though their aristocrats and the Egyptian priests caused trouble.

There was the school in an area controlled by Germanic Barbarians and this school was the most successful of the lot, the parents were keen to see their sons educated, and they had no aristocrats.

Finally there were the Mongols they turned out to be a heap of trouble in every way, first as soon as the school was built they wanted the tonne of gold, they wouldn't allow the school to start until they got their gold. Li refused to pay until the two year start off point as agreed was reached, so the school sat there unused for about twenty months. After that they wanted the school to pay the parents the right to teach their children, Li was indignant in her refusal and accused the Mongols of having no ethics which they thought was very funny.

Finally the school got started, and then they threatened to close it down again, so once again Li called on the tree spirits to bluff their way through for her or at least try.

'On the day designated to take the school over there, suddenly again appeared an army of troops outside the school grounds in a defensive formation'. When the Mongols arrived with 5,000 troops they were totally shocked, but that was only a small part of the shock they were going to get that day. There was a quick withdrawal, and then they were back with 100,000 cavalry troops ready for a fight, they attacked immediately.

It was almost funny every time the Mongols killed one of the tree spirits they simply popped up again, and kept fighting, soon the Mongols were completely dispirited. "What sort of enemy is this they asked we have killed 50,000 of them, but there are no bodies on the ground and no blood? There are more of them there now than when we started to fight, and they seem to be getting more, we kill one and it just goes pop, and there he is again what are we to do?"

The Mongols called for a halt to the fighting and asked to see the leader of the school forces, "What is happening he asked as soon as they arrived, the more we kill the more there are what does this all mean?"

"Well the truth is we are protected by our Gods because your leadership has been unfair, you may kill us all, but we will still all be there and able to fight, it may take us a long time, but we will kill you all in the end because you are wrong and have tried to beat the work of our, Gods so it's up to you, keep it up it doesn't bother us just know, this you cannot win"?

"Well what can we do?" asked the Mongol leader?

"Just withdraw and leave the school in peace and our troops also will leave, then in eighteen years time you will have the property back, and we will take our school somewhere else, and we will never bother you people the

Mongols again. Remember this of the low numbers we have killed of your people and the high number you have killed of ours, the blood out there is only the blood of your dead not ours, because ours aren't dead. Now the choice is yours let us know because we want to go home, not stay here protecting a school set up for your children!"

Without further hesitation the Mongol leader said, "Yes we will withdraw, you are right and we have been unfair so your Gods are protecting you goodbye"

The victory was complete and as agreed there were no more problems from the Mongols, and neither the Romans nor anyone else for the balance of the years that had been agreed, would clear the Orbsey debt to Earth. When the time was due to finish up with the schools, at the request of the various leaders the Orbseyns stayed for another twenty years.

After that it was left up to the teachers to decide what they wanted to do, but transport was provided for many years whenever there was a five year repatriation of staff home to Orbsey, and another team going out. The whole program was an entire success thanks once again to the little Chinese girl Li, and her fellow ambassadors Orlos and Coreum.

The tree spirits were delighted that is a wonderful success they told Li even if it only advances Earth by six months it will help to improve the lot of the poor people. One of the older spirits predicted Earth would be in two millennia equal to most of her peers except those at the level of Orbsey. Meanwhile for the present as another put it, Earthlings will continue to kill each other in big numbers, even if only with sticks and stones, best they not have all of this modern technology, they would wipe out their entire civilization very quickly.

Li decided to take one more trip to Earth to visit the tree spirits to see if there was anymore Orbsey could do for Earth, but they were all very happy. You have done a great job for your home planet they all chorused in unison, but Earth needs to stand alone now all you need do is ensure a proper accounting of any products taken and any credits Orbsey has due to it in the future, this way a future will grow as Earth develops. They will never know how much help they have had but so what? The future will tell the story, but don't forget to visit us now and again for the sake of what we have done together, and we would like to know how the Kauri plantation on Cordiance is getting along.

CHAPTER 13/

POLITICS ON THE PLANETS

The politics are a mixture throughout the planets countries, but in Coordeloo 'there is a central govt; which controls any disputes within the different countries. It seems to outsiders to be rather cumbersome, but for their people's works fine'? In spite of being so big there is an air of goodwill among the inhabitants, and they have no fear of priests, and other often malevolent forces such as on some of the other planets.

There is a huge unused land mass, not because it's poor quality, but there are just not enough people to get out and develop it, for this reason there is plenty of opportunity. Many have advocated an increase in population by all means possible, but most Corrdeloons like their planet just as it is, and see no reason for change.

This was especially before they were in danger of attack, but now they had a 'fleet of 150 nuclear war craft closing in for the attack; their self confidence were being badly shaken'. But when it was 'announced the attack fleet had been destroyed by defense missiles from Orbsey the effect was dramatic, the whole population were in strong support of the Federation' that had been the vehicle that had saved them from takeover.

The omnipresent Eye in the sky is here too but because of the huge land mass doesn't have quite so much influence as it has on most of the other planets.

The planet TeKahanui: This planet had been waiting for Li's attention until after the five year break was over, but now it was time to move ahead again, it had been a nice break with no interplanetary travel, and the team all well rested.

This planet named by its peoples TeKahanui was bigger than Orbsey and had been evenly populated, it would take about three months to reach, and from appearances was highly developed with all the evidence of nuclear energy being used but not for weapons.

The persons were rather squat in appearance with big trunk very short legs and arms with quite a large head. The head looked strange with a fish like appearance of the mouth and eyes and they appeared to breathe through their very large ears, because they had no nostrils. Although they had strong antennae protruding from their heads straight up, so perhaps that was the source of their breathing?

The planet seemed to be quite heavily populated and there was an abundance of obviously farmed animals that look similar to some of the animals seen on planet Earth.

It appeared the first planet for Li to go to would be TeKahanui mainly because of its nuclear capacity; the Plebiscite of Orbsey wanted an extensive report as quickly as Li could travel, there and back. She had decided to take the biggest freighter in the fleet because she was going to bring back a full load, even if only to get a true picture of their planet, but if it worked out then they would set up a colony just as they had already done with the three other planets.

They had a cruiser in the load out bay plus two aerocars so they were well set up for exploration, and could use their devices to move from place to place. Orlos and Coreum were of course going as security for Li, but they were hoping to find products that they could sell, just as they had from planet Earth, for them it was just business as usual for Li it was her job, and she would do it to the best of her ability as usual.

It had been a long boring trip, but finally they were there and Li and her two escorts were ready to be beamed down to the planet, they were floating really high in the sky because this was a nuclear powered planet, and they must be careful, they had to be sure not to upset anybody just yet anyhow.

As soon as they had been beamed down the three of them noticed the big difference, the air was clearer than any of the other planets, they had been on including Orbsey, Li's first thought was how is this done it's like a clear spring morning on earth. They quickly found some of the locals, and changed themselves as well as getting some quick practice with the language.

They had landed in a paddock just outside of what seemed to be a medium sized city, and they were quickly right in the hub of the busy area which seemed to be a business one, of which they were highly intrigued. These were certainly the ugliest of the persons on any of the planets so far with their fish like features, and strong antennae on their heads looking very different. As they looked at each other in their changed form it was hard for them not to laugh, Li thought ugh but said nothing. Orlos and Coreum were not so polite they both burst out laughing and Coreum said, "My goodness thank the gods we won't look like this for very long!"

Orlos pointed at Coreum and said, "gosh you are so ugly mate have you had a nightmare?" Li decided they should go to another country, and into the centre of a major city to get a real look. 'They had arrived within seconds, and found the situation there the same as in the smaller city, persons bustling to and fro, but not seeming to achieve much', so again they left and went to a farming community.

This was far more interesting the animals were much like those found on earth it was obvious they were used for domestic purposes, and also killed for eating. There was what appeared to be cows and horses as well as sheep and goats, there were even chickens and turkeys, they were all different in shape and look than the animals on earth, but the similarity was very plain for all to see, Li was delighted by her memories of home?

From there they went to an industrial complex, from which they soon learned the prime source of power was solar and nuclear energy, all of which they were able to walk around quite freely there were no locked gates.

Li wanted to go back to one of the cities because she hadn't noticed the solar complexes in the high rise buildings, but they were later able to see that every building had its own power source, and when they had a look in the suburbs they found every home was solar powered.

'Li had made up her mind she just wanted to take a freighter full of the local persons find out more and then decide if they should set up a colony, but these people sure were ugly and may have trouble in their world, but who knew only time would tell, maybe they would fit in just fine'?

They signaled to the freighter they wanted to come aboard, then they simply beamed up from a military establishment 1200 men sedated them, and started the long trip home immediately. The men were kept unconscious all of the way, they looked too ferocious to take any risks with until they were back in Orbsey, if nothing else they could question the men, and if necessary send them home again, Li was in for a few surprises with this lot they weren't at all of a difficult temperament in spite of their looks. She was about to realize they had stolen some of the most intelligent persons ever, and the most versatile.

When they finally touched down and the first few new comers had been revived, the first thing they did was change their appearance to those around them. The next thing was to listen to the thought language of the Orbseyns and they immediately started to communicate with them fluently. Then they listened to Li as she deliberately spoke to them in her Chinese mother tongue, they easily understood and replied in the same way, it was all very exciting.

Li then asked if it was safe to bring the other back to consciousness, this was greeted with hilarity by the TeKahanuins, "we are a peaceful people we may look ugly to you but to us we are beautiful, they will all change immediately to look like you, why don't you try?" Just as they had said as soon as the rest had been bought to consciousness they changed and started to communicate using the thought language of the Orbseyns. Every person present at that awakening was truly amazed, it was as if a new happening had arrived, and the new arrivals really charmed everybody.

Li for her part was very happy but at the same time disappointed, there would be no way she thought any of these new persons would want to stay on Orbsey, she was pleasantly wrong. When the blaze of notoriety they had started had calmed down, Li had a meeting with them all at the govt; facility. It turned out that before they made up their minds they wanted to know more about this planet, which wanted nothing but peace, because the politics of their own planet was exactly the same.

If this was true they wanted to be ambassadors to their own world, because for many years a philosophy of peace to all peoples no matter where they lived had been taught, and the belief in 'eradicating all war was a professed aim of all countries within their planet' and it was all starting to work. They had been given the information they wanted and within 32 hours had asked for another meeting with Li.

They were they said very impressed with Orbsey it was obvious this planet was far ahead of their own, and they wanted to know how they could work with Li and her dept; to forge a mutual agreement between their two planets. The first thing however was to bring back to Orbsey their families, and while there try to start initial talks between the two planets, they could barely contain the feelings of excitement that pervaded them all.

Li decided to start her discussions with the Orbsey Plebiscite, and get permission to start discussions at top level with the govt; in TeKahanui when they went back to collect the families. She had been warned their own govt; would want to have a colony of Orbseyns settle in their planet, but that would be at this stage only a supposition on their part. Li had the full permission to speak for Orbsey, and accept an exchange of colonies if that was required, but naturally they weren't to offer the exchange unless asked for. It was also stressed that first she must be certain that the planet TeKahanui was a peaceful one that would be a good partner in a future league of planets; as it was now being considered by the Plebiscite that controlled the central govt; of Orbsey.

Before she left to go to TeKahanui, the members of the Plebiscite asked for a meeting with Li, they wanted to make it plain to her what they were starting to see as a possibility. First they thanked her for the wonderful work she had done then they asked if she was happy with her job, after all they knew she could earn three times as much in private industry. 'They were happy when she replied that credits were of no interest to her, she worked because she loved her new country Cordiance and her Planet Orbsey, even if they paid her nothing, she would still want to do her job to the best ability she had.

Having been reassured by Li's answer they proceeded to tell her, 'they now had ambition of setting up a league of planets to ensure peace for all, not just talk about it'. They believed theirs was the most advanced planet, as such were in a position to negotiate with others and to be the lead promoters of such a program.

They wanted to have a league with ten different planets, and Li was to be in the forefront of their initial approach to the leaders of all of the other planets, but another two were to be appointed to work under her management while she and her fellow workers were negotiating for Orbsey.

Li's answer was that she had two business persons who she would like to work with her, Orlos and Coreum, she pointed out that these two persons had been to every planet, and understood them just as well as she did, whereas others would have to be trained from the start. She also guaranteed they would do the work for the planet not for the credits they could earn, that would never be important to any of them.

After three days Li got a letter from the Plebiscite agreeing to the appointments as she had requested, but seeking guarantees that any commercial profit opportunities would be allocated to the govt; treasury. This was agreed to by Orlos and Coreum and contracts were signed with the Cordiance govt; ensuring that any commercial profits that could be earned from any planetary activity would be owned by the state. In return Cordiance would finance their work including the supply of the space freighters when needed, the interplanetary ones were owned by the Orbseyn govt, and had to be leased on each trip.

And so it came about that the three originals that had started out as a trio in that long ago trip to Earth, were now joint ambassadors for the planet Orbsey. Before they left the two families celebrated together their future work for the betterment of all citizens of the planets, they all expressed the hope their work would be good for all peoples of any race, on all planets.

Before they left the trio met with the TeKahanuins the ambassador's asked if they would all like to be taken back to their homes, because they were quite happy to take them, but much to their surprise all expressed a preference to stay on Orbsey. The group offered to send with the trip, some representatives of the group, who would happily introduce the Orbseyns to their govt; representatives and help find their families to bring them back to Orbsey, when they returned.

They took with them a group of four TeKahanuins who would first make the introductions, then while the trio settled down to negotiate a peace and cooperation treaty, the four would arrange the families to be ready to go when they left. As soon as they arrived over TeKahanui the seven were all beamed down, and now the reverse happened they all became as if they were TeKahanuins both in appearance and speech. They went immediately to the govt; buildings in the biggest country and asked to be allowed to meet with the senior politicians because they were aliens from outer space, but the four locals introduced themselves as citizens of the planet TeKahanui.

A quorum of officials was quickly assembled, and was very keen for extended talks with the trio from Orbsey, but they wanted the top govt; officials to be in the meeting. For that reason they asked if the strangers would partake of their hospitality for two days while the leaders were bought from other countries, to ensure all were in agreement.

Li had presented their official papers from the Plebiscite of Orbsey so the officials of any and every planet they visited, would know they were authorized to speak on behalf of the planet as a whole. While this was happening the four locals had gone to arrange the families of the men already in Orbsey to prepare to leave.

They were given two guides and were also given the best complimentary accommodation for as long as they stayed, and because the guides couldn't be beamed everywhere as the trio could they were also supplied with govt. vehicles that were similar to the aerocars of Orbsey. For the next two days they had a wonderful time travelling through each country they were in, quickly and efficiently, and anything they asked to look at they were welcome, there appeared to be no secrets even from aliens such as themselves.

They were impressed with how developed the country appeared to be, they had nuclear, and a lot of solar power that was sourced from two suns that appeared to be in the sky almost perpetually. Like Orbsey they had a 32 hour day, but only 6 hours of night which was very well lit up by the number of moons that circled the planet all and every day.

The cities had plenty of light and there was lots of entertainment for which the persons all seemed to be addicted, so that even when the suns were down for short periods only, there were lights the entire city was all lit up. They visited farms, art galleries, museums and lots of industrial complexes including the ones generating nuclear power, which according to the guides they had had for several hundred years. But all too soon the call came to attend the Parliament the next day and so it was time for work, the lovely but too short holiday was over.

They were greeted in the hall of assemblies very formally by the prime minister and introduced to all of the senior politicians of the country. They were given the respect they were entitled to as representing the Plebiscite controlling the planet Orbsey, and then they all got down to serious discussion.

Li was the first speaker as leader of the trio from Orbsey, and she stressed they came in peace; theirs was a peaceful planet looking for partners who also wanted to develop peace in the various galactic spheres. Li spoke of the high level of development on Orbsey, but that the big advantage they had gained over the last millennia was to defeat the tyranny of distance. They stressed that TeKahanui was millions of light years distant from Orbsey, and even travelling at the speed of light it would take thousands of years to travel the distance between the two planets, they had just done the trip in three months, as their own citizens could attest, if and when questioned?

There were gasps of astonishment when Li made that statement, but smiles of encouragement when she outlined the truth that Orbsey, had no weapons of war, not even hand guns were produced anymore on Orbsey, only relics from a bygone age were still around. After Li had spoken for about two hours, Orlos took over and explained the agricultural economy and then Coreum spoke of the industrial achievements of their planet.

All told the trio from Orbsey spoke for about five hours by which time it was time to break for lunch, and they would resume in two hours time. The food on TeKahanui was very palatable to the Orbseyns so the trio ate heartily and well, they were at the table of the prime minister and his deputy, and a most convivial pair they were. The thoughts of the trio was all complimentary to their hosts, but they had forgotten all at that table had the capacity to read minds, and their companions were just as complimentary to them, so it was a well satisfied group that reentered the assembly hall after the meal, and drinks had been enjoyed.

The minister for the economy spoke first he outlined the country's economy, but then also outlined the planets products, and how well the countries worked together for the common good. Then the minister for the interior spoke and he gave a detailed outline of the different continents, and island countries on the planet, the total population was the same as Orbsey just a little over 16 billion, but the planet was a little bigger with a greater mass of saline oceans, and plenty of fresh water.

The minister of finance spoke as well as several other important ministers, and at the end of the meeting the trio was given literature, setting out what they had heard. They in turn had to beam up to the freighter to get as much data on Orbsey they had with them, but they promised that next time they came back they would bring details the same as they had received. The meeting was then adjourned until the next day at the same time.

The following day Li led off by being again the first speaker, this time she asked to be allowed to set up a colony of TeKahanuins on Orbsey, and offered to set up a colony of Orbseyns on their planet, this was greeted with enthusiastic applause. But when she offered to take some high ranking officials to Orbsey show them the entire planet, and then return them home, her words were greeted with hearty acclamation. She finished up by saying they would be glad to take their officials anytime, and asked for the right to set up a colony of 50,000 TeKahanuins, and to return with a colony of 50,000 Orbseyns within twelve months. Orlos and Coreum merely confirmed Li's offer, and thanked the assembly for their kind attention.

The prime minister then stood and accepted the offer to set up a colony on their planet, and also one on Orbsey, as he said this would cement the ties of friendship. He further pledged that the next time they came back a tour party would return with them to Orbsey, and in so doing confirm the first Inter Galactic peace treaty that had been agreed to in the last two days. He then wished the Orbseyns well, and hoped radio communications could be set up by the scientific experts of both planets as quickly as possible. Finally he pledged they wanted only peace, and would work with Orbsey to ensure those aims could be achieved.

For Li it was a major triumph she had led the first such meeting of the type ever known on two galaxies, and she was so pleased to be taking home such good news.

The persons to be taken back to Orbsey were ready for loading the next day, so they were all beamed up and within a few hours they were ready to leave. At the last meeting was with the PM and his deputy, Li assured them both they would start to set up radio communications immediately, and they would be back within twelve months excluding travelling time, which meant in reality about 18 months. They would be bringing with them a full fleet and would have on board 50,000 new colonists for TeKahanui and would want to take back 50,000 to Orbsey or a few less say 48,000 to take back. They would also be ready to take the official visitors and return them.

CHAPTER 14/

THE NEW COLONISTS

The trip back to Orbsey was uneventful and boring for all on board, but the Trio tried as much as possible to keep their new colonists happy. The children in particular had to be catered for with games, with all sorts of ways to keep them quiet, they had hundreds of movies that were constantly playing, but with almost 2,500 aboard it wasn't easy. The trio then agreed it was better to sedate the travelers because the trip was so long and boring, but eventually it did come to an end, and they were being greeted by a lot of men, happy to have their families with them once again.

The trio had a week off then reported in detail to the Plebiscite of rulers of Orbsey, but they had been joined by over one hundred politicians from Cordiance, who were all excited to hear details of this latest inter galactic trip. They had already read the thoughts of the trio, so they knew what a big success there had been. When the data from TeKahanui had been copied, and also flashed onto a screen Li started to give her thought report. She was followed by Orlos and Coreum, and at the end there were resounding claps of acclamation for the travelers, this time there was a real breakthrough, and they all knew it was a wonderful moment in their history.

The new colonists were now given over to the charge of Li's dept; heads, and she and the trio had a month's well earned holiday. Coreum who was a single man still couldn't be bothered with a holiday.

Li and Orlos enjoyed themselves immensely they stayed in bed practicing to make their first baby. They only had another five years to wait, and then Li would be made fertile so that the big day was now very near. Their physical attraction for each other was as strong as ever, even after 85 years of constant practice, they only had to be alone for a little while to be looking for a bed or table or anything on which they could come together it was still as good as at the end of their first week so long ago.

Back at work the TeKahanuins were more popular than even the earth colony, their happy disposition made them the most lovable of persons, and Li could never get over that those who were naturally so ugly could be of such a happy disposition. The govt; psychologists said it was because their home planet was so abundant in good things, that the persons were all so open with each other this made the general demeanor of its large population one of being always cheerful.

She was told that if she had a good look at the native Orbseyns they were of a similar attitude, and that was because their planet had it all, they had good reason to be happy. Li's reaction was yes and open minds, she agreed that the psychologist was right this in general was a happy planet with the right intentions. There was a lot of crime, but that was fairly natural with the size of the planet, and the number of people living on it.

The radio communication network between Orbsey and TeKahanui was now in place, and closer relations were being established daily. 'The scientific communities of both planets were in mutual agreement about how clever they all were, so much more intelligent than ordinary folk'. A group of one hundred was going to visit as offered by Li. A mixture of scientists, academics, politicians, beauracrats, and others would be coming, and there was a hum of excitement, this was going to be the first meeting of two planetary leaderships, and all only possible because Orbsey had beaten the travel problems.

The trio was at this stage setting up the colony to go the TeKahanui, this time it was real, and even though the Orbseyns thought the TeKahanuins were very ugly, they had been rushed by potential colonists. Most however wanted to keep their looks as Orbseyns, the trio thought it very funny, the TeKahanuins had also preferred to look like Orbseyns, they must realize how bloody ugly they are the trio laughed together in private.

Apart from checking up on the new colony of Earthlings the job for the trio was now complete, and it was almost time to leave for TeKahanui to take a colony of Orbseyns, pick up a colony and bring back the visitors. A cruiser that had been designated to carry the visitors; had been especially equipped with radio communications, and entertainment especially for them; this included a lot of information about Orbsey and its countries.

There was also information about the colonies settled on Orbsey from Earth, Xalafeu and Coordeloo, everything possible was done to make the VIPs comfortable.

The cruiser was a lot faster than the freighters so the VIPs would be leaving one month after the freighter, because they would make the trip in two months not the three months that would be taken by the heavily laden freighters. The travel plan of the cruiser was timed to arrive at about the same time as the freighters, and the VIPs would be on board with Li as their companion. Orlos and Coreum would stay to ensure the Orbseyn colonists were well settled, and then load up the TeKahanuins for the journey back to Orbsey. By the time the freighters arrived in Orbsey it was intended the VIPs would be there to greet and reassure the colonists of the goodwill between the two planets.

Everything had worked as planned and Li on board the cruiser had arrived one day earlier than the fleet of heavily loaded freighters. There had been a round of VIP greetings with Li as the host, and every courtesy possible had been extended to the visitors, so that there was a strong feeling of goodwill between the two groups. There were representatives from the various disciplines that had come such as politicians etc; all was going very well by the time the newcomers had been beamed down from the fleet of freighters.

The newcomers were assembled in the great palladium at the terminal and were officially greeted by the politicians of both planets. The persons that were already there were happily greeting their kin and others; it was a great day the first one when two planets welcomed the citizens that had come to settle as representatives of their own planet. The both sets of leaders expressed the hope this day would be the first of many in the efforts to bring together a league of planets, for the good of all of the different planets, their countries and all of their populations of whatever color or creed.

Li was to be the host for all of the different events that had been prepared for the visitors, as such received a great many tributes and thanks from the many dignitaries from both planets. This was especially so when one of the members of the plebiscite explained she was an Earthling who had come to Orbsey very young and whose mate was an Orbseyn.

The visitors stayed for a month during which time they were shown around the entire planet of Orbsey, and peace pledges were signed between the two planets. It had been a very useful visit especially for the politicians, and scientists of the two groups, the future for a close relationship looked very secure, but both planetary members recognized there may be harder times ahead as the more warlike planets became involved.

The two planets were well advanced with their nuclear technology, and agreed that they wouldn't pass on any scientific information, to planets that had a bias towards war. The two planets agreed to set up a trade delegation within each other's main states and would also set up mutual ambassadors. But since Orbsey was the only planet that had the technology to defeat distance, until that position changed Orbsey would be paid for all intergalactic freight, between the two planets. Li was among the party seeing the visitors off at the intergalactic terminal as were thousand of Orbseyns, and a few of the newly arrived TeKahanuins, it was a gala event appreciated by the dignitaries of both planets.

The planet Kanuitepai: The next planet Li had looked at had been named Kanuitepai and was almost as far away as Xalafeu was, appeared from the probes photos to be about earth size and heavily populated. There appeared to be a lot of military activity, but there was no nuclear capacity apparent, although such weapons may have been hidden the photos were unclear.

Close up photos of the citizens showed nothing unusual they were just two legged two arms etc; differences were merely facial or that's how it seemed, and their bodies may have had some extra parts that weren't obvious from so far away. Its size was almost identical to Earth with similar land and sea areas.

This was to be about six months return trip, but Li had decided to take the biggest cruiser in the fleet, and bring back only 250 persons on the first trip, this would reduce the time to about four months. The cost in time had now become too much for Li who had so many other duties at home as well as the approaching time for the right to have their first baby.

Li and Orlos had agreed they would settle what had to be done with the two planets as yet unexplored by Orbseyns then Li would stop working to have the baby while Orlos and Coreum carried on. They would be given an extra person to work with them, either setting up political agreements or just taking colonists and looking for agreements later on when Li was back at work.

The flight was as usual uneventful and boring, but it was worth the trip for on arrival all agreed that this was by far the most beautiful of the planets so far seen, and now to be explored. The two men went down first while Li waited on board for their initial report which would indicate, if they were just going to abduct a few persons easily, or try to have discussions with some parliamentarians.

The first thoughts coming back from Orlos was 'that this was just like planet Earth and the people were identical, but Earth was undeveloped, his thoughts were that this was what Earth would be like about two thousand years into the future. They had a world govt. controlled by a plebiscite as on Orbsey, and it was obvious that Li needed to talk to the leaders, and try to set up a radio connection back to Orbsey. Orlos was thinking he and Coreum should try to open the way for Li, only after talks had been arranged should there be further thought communication to decide what to do.

Li agreed but warned her assistants to be careful, because if they were a fully armed nuclear planet talks may not be feasible. If there appeared to be any danger at all the two of them should just suddenly beam themselves up to the cruiser, and they would decide from there what to do, maybe they would just leave?

Later the same day the thoughts from Orlos again indicated a meeting had been arranged for the morrow, but these people aren't as hospitable as the TeKahanuins had been, and they would need to be careful. However they were friendly enough and seemed interested to talk about anything to do with space travel, they had nuclear power for industry and for weapons, but were aware of the destructive power, and they weren't disposed towards nuclear war.

Orlos and Coreum then beamed themselves up to the cruiser, after confirming the meeting the next day with their planetary ambassador and themselves. Orlos was all smiles as he thought about the meeting on the morrow, but Coreum was far more conservative, these persons he predicted are real hard heads, and won't come to the table for serious debate quickly or easily.

Coreum proved to be correct, the meeting the next day started off rather coldly, as Li introduced themselves and their planet to her silent audience, the only thing that caused a small ripple was when she explained how they had defeated the tyranny of distance and time. They were also interested when Li spoke of the exchange of colonies, but their main interest was how to conquer travel times the rest to them was uninteresting.

Then Orlos and Coreum spoke, again with little reaction, so much so that the trio all had their fingers on their beamers ready to leave, and were watching for any aggressive signs. Suddenly when Coreum stopped speaking there was huge burst of applause, the trio were confused what does that mean they asked each other, they soon found out.

A speaker from the audience then came to the podium and offered a vote of thanks to the trio from Orbsey; he then proceeded to reply to the delight of the trio. They were all he said very impressed, and grateful that they had been included in a visit from representatives of a planet so far away. Overnight their scientists had briefed him it would take them at least a million light years to reach the region around Orbsey, if in fact they could even find that planet, so the enormity of what their visitors had said was well understood.

He explained that he was the leader of their planets controlling plebiscite, as such they all welcomed the trio to their world if however briefly. They were invited to accept their hospitality while they were there, instead of sleeping in a space craft, no matter how comfortable that craft may be. He agreed to the exchange of colonists, but stressed that since they had not defeated tyranny of distance the transport would have to be left to the Orbseyns.

Further he asked if a small number of politicians could be given transport to Orbsey, and back so as the further cement a possible league of planets as Li had outlined because they would certainly like to be a foundation member of such a league.

He then said that Orlos and Coreum had outlined what Li wanted the day before, which is why they had met the night before, and now he was able to reply in such a positive manner. He finished by asking for travel for twenty, ten politicians and ten scientists, and they would have a total as requested of 50,000 colonists, and they would be ready to accept 50,000 Orbseyns and they would set them up fully as a self contained colony. Another two speakers stood and welcomed the trio; they were both members of the plebiscite, and would be happy to visit Orbsey, at any time possible.

Li was the final speaker and she suggested first they could take up to 100 visitors perhaps of different disciplines, she promised to return them all well fed and happy. The meeting broke up with much courteous hand clapping! The trio as offered stayed at the best hotel in the city, and really enjoyed the hospitality of the ten members of the plebiscite that night, and for another week. An immediate radio connection was set up with Orbsey that got the scientists happy; and working together and then Li gave the trio and staff, all an agenda to work too for the comfort of the VIPs when they left.

The cruiser floating in the heavens above would be loaded only with the visitors Li and Orlos, they would return to Orbsey, just as soon as the Kanutapai visitors were ready to leave, arriving two months later she hoped. Meanwhile Coreum would stay back and arrange the new colonists that would be going to settle in Orbsey, and have them ready to load as soon as the freighters arrived.

When the fleet was ready in Orbsey, Orlos would help load, and prepare the colonists that were to settle in Kanuitepai, and travel with them back. The order had already been sent to arrange the colonists, so they should be ready by time Li arrived with her visitors. The fleet booking for 40 freighters had been made, but there were many complaints from the space freighters dept. Li was keeping them working to tight schedules, and the full fleet had to be constantly fully serviced, to be able to cater for this enormous increase in planetary travel.

A strong complaint had been received personally by Li, the director of the fleet construction program had been quite belligerent, "Do you think your program is all we have to cater for we are on a 24 hour shifts and still we are falling behind, I am going to put in my complaints direct to the Presidium such excessive pressure can be very dangerous, and you are one of the main ones at risk. I am very sorry but you are putting too much strain on my dept!"

"Yes well I am sorry to the pressure on my dept; is also excessive! Why don't we present our fears together that way we may be listened to better?"

The reaction of the Presidium was very positive, "We will reduce the space program for the present, but we will increase the funds available so that the construction industry can catch up and then stay ahead how that sound does to you both?"

The construction budget was doubled which made their Director very happy because he was able to double the size of his team, while Li could carry on with her program, but slow down her flights a little for 12 months. Li would now return with the visitors from Kanuitepai when they were bought home, and wait with Coreum until the fleet arrived, this would fulfill all of their obligations at all times as the ambassadors for Orbsey. Orlos would travel back to Kanuitepai with the space freighters, taking the Orbseyn colony for settlement.

The visitor from Orbsey had been well catered too, and VIP visitors were ready to leave to go to Orbsey in a week. The cruiser was landed to take them all aboard as VIPs, with Li and Orlos as their hosts. Nothing one can do avoids the boredom of space travel hard as they may try. This was the same cruiser that had been specially set up for the previous group of VIPs, but two months with little to do is tough unless the passengers are used to that life and these VIPs certainly weren't. By the time they had landed at the intergalactic terminal at Orbsey Li and Orlos were exhausted, but their passengers were now all smiles, obviously excited.

The visitors were given time in the best hotels to recover and then it was down to meetings and discussions! The scientists and politicians were hard at work within a few days, very interested in reach others work! Li opened the meeting in the great palladium that allowed media as well as all others with vested interests, to be able to listen to the discussions from the gallery. Li introduced the gatherings of VIPs from both planets, expressing her hope that the discussions would be fruitful then left them to their talks; so she and Orlos could enjoy a well earned rest.

The meetings and trips around Orbsey too many parts of the planet took four weeks, and then it was almost time to leave again. In the meantime there were millions of applications to emigrate, and the process was almost ready to select by ballot, another week and they were ready to leave the fleet was loaded and left a week before the VIP cruiser.

The much faster VIP cruiser arrived back in Kanuitepai three weeks before the fully loaded fleet, so Li stayed in a hotel until they arrived. She had inspected the lists of colonists going to Orbsey; so that all were ready to leave as soon as the fleet arrived. Coreum looked a bit flustered he had been under pressure all of the time Li had been away and was happy to see her back, but he would be even happier to see Orlos.

The fleet arrived and the colonists were all beamed down to the air terminal which wasn't big enough to hold any of the giant freighters, but it was all dealt with efficiently. The arriving Orbseyns were beamed down, and within two hours the fleet was ready to receive the Kanuitepai'ns on board so they were all beamed up in groups, over twelve hundred per freighter.

The arriving colonists from Orbsey were all settled into their new compound quickly and their new homes were well up to the standard they were used to back home. A few had a few minor complaints but these were dealt with quickly and efficiently, within a few days they were all happy to express satisfaction with their new homes.

There had been an agreement reached to send a load of dehydrated meat back on the cruiser as a trial shipment of protein, and the first planet to planet, actual sales at govt level. Because no killing of animals for food was allowed on Orbsey they had to manufacture protein, the Orbseyns had products the Kanuitepai'ns wanted, and they were happy to send those products in payment for the meat was a for trial shipment of ten tonnes. The entire visit was almost an exact duplicate as the visitors from TeKahanui including the departure celebrations, the Kanuitepai'ns were far more reserved, but in the end the program had been just as successful.

The members of the Orbseyn plebiscite invited the trio in for a meeting and congratulated them on another new local colony on both planets, and a great job well done. There were now at least five members of the hoped for league of planets that included Orbsey; and the three ambassadors were recognized for their major efforts. When the fleet had arrived back in Orbsey Li left all of the program details to Orlos and Coreum, she wanted to plan her last trip before she was medically treated to become fertile, but she thought it quite funny at 118 YOA to be preparing for their first baby.

The load of dried meat had been a good success, and a repeat order for 250,000 tonnes had been placed by radio ready to be picked up within 12 months, and an order for five space freighters had been accepted with delivery of the first one within 12 months. There would have to be a team of pilots sent to Orbsey for training of at least three months, and a team of buyers would be sent to Kanuitepai to investigate any other protein or supplies that the Orbseyns could buy. This planet was to become a major supplier to Orbsey in the future, a little like planet Earth but in this case there was no problem with the inter trade payments system, it was meant to be quid pro quo; but left to the trade missions to settle any differences. These differences were political usually and couldn't be left to business men to resolve!

Orbsey of course had the technology to supply what all of the planets needed, in return there were a lot of products that could be bought for processing or retailing within their entire consumer base, which was very large but evenly spread. Looking at the future for trade between the planets, the plebiscite on Orbsey had every reason to be pleased; with what Li and her team were achieving for their home planet.

The planet Tepakeha: The last of the three to be developed was the planet named Tepakeha and was really a long way off it would take at least 6 months to reach, the probes had returned with quite clear photos, and this planet looked very nice. It was smaller than Earth, but heavily populated with over 8 billion inhabitants so that even though small they had a far bigger population, but in parts looked terribly over crowded.

There appeared to be a strong well disciplined military, and the beginnings of nuclear power, but industrial power not weapons of mass destruction. The people looked to be exactly the same as earthlings and even the homes seemed similar, this was primarily an agricultural society, but the beginnings of heavy industry was starting to show in several of the countries.

The same technique was to be used the trio would go on a very fast cruiser, and should arrive in four months, then Orlos and Coreum would make contact, and try to arrange for Li to meet with their govt. In the meantime they would all catch up with their reports during the trip ahead. They were travelling in the VIP cruiser so they had all of the luxuries, but privately they all wondered if one day they could just beam across space, and be on these far off planets in seconds, it was a lovely dream especially when contemplating 4-6 boring months in space just filling in time. The three of them had bought their reports up to date, and radioed them home within a week now there was still a mighty lot of time to fill in, as they travelled through the vastness of the universe.

Li and Orlos were ok they were still busy practicing for that baby that was now only two years away, but Coreum was soon bored silly as he put it. There were hundreds of movies on board, a pool table and plenty of booze, and music, but no females on the crew. Li had agreed to ensure that female attendants on the crew for dancing partners were a part of future facilities to help break the tedium.

They finally arrived at their destination and once again this was a beautiful planet, they circled around it once then the two males beamed themselves down to the surface, a matter of seconds was all it took. Keeping their thoughts on contact all on the cruiser, could tell straight away that it was a very pleasant city they were in, but they still didn't know if it was the capital, or even if the planet had a controlling parliament.

The first need was to find the seat of planetary power; the next was to try and arrange a meeting for Li to address. Within minutes they were at the parliament for the entire planet, and soon after they were in discussions with a member of the parliament. He was startled but soon recovered his poise, and very quickly had arranged a top level meeting for these two self claimed aliens. Both Orlos and Coreum at this point had their beamer devices firmly in the hands ready to leave, but after two hours they were becoming comfortable again.

The people here were very much like earthlings, although suspicious were friendly, and gave no signs of being aggressive. The meeting was recorded and the two aliens were asked to explain exactly what they wanted, and why they had come?

Once their listeners were satisfied they understood what their visitors wanted the two Orbseyns were invited for another preliminary meeting in two days, after which their members of the parliament would decide if they wanted to talk. It was now obvious these persons were only beauracrats, and could make no decisions plenty of talk, but no answers so as requested Orlos and Coreum agreed to come back at the appointed time. Just to ensure they were being taken seriously, the two Orbseyns said they would beam themselves up to their space cruiser immediately, and return exactly on time in two days.

When they returned as promised, there was a full group of about twenty persons waiting to receive them, and the procedure was gone over again just explaining what they had come for. The apparent leader thanked them for their patience, but asked if they could return in another two days while their leader was properly briefed, and then he would meet with Li.

Orlos and Coreum declined this invitation by saying their leader wouldn't come unless an agenda had been first approved, it was pointless without that. Orlos and Coreum offered to set up radio contact with their scientists, and just leave it at that if they preferred. They thought about that then decided that no they would like to meet the ambassador from Orbsey. It was just that their leaders were away on holiday, and had to be brought home for the meeting, but first they had to find them. Orlos then said it was just as easy to come down to see how it was going in another two days, but he stressed they would be considering leaving, it had been a long trip, and they didn't need to waste anymore time. He didn't say they would be taking over 200 of their citizens away with them.

Back on the cruiser the trio discussed the situation, and then decided they would next time at the parliament building, advise the reps that they had to leave in seven days, without failure then if they weren't ready just pick up some men sedate them and start on the trip back to Orbsey. They would simply set up a colony the old way and to hell with their govt! The next time

Orlos and Coreum they went down there was still no leaders so the message was given they would be leaving in seven days and they wouldn't be back, well not legally.

On the sixth day Orlos and Coreum went back and the leader was there but didn't seem all that interested, so he was told they were leaving the next day. That sparked a change in attitude, and they were invited to return the next day for a meeting of the top leaders only, they would then decide their interest if any. Orlos felt a bit insulted by the comment 'if any', but kept his always volatile temper under control, and agreed they would to come back for a meeting the ambassador the next day.

Promptly on time the Orbseyn trio was there ready, but the Planet leaders were ten minutes late which boded badly for any good results with this planet. But they duly arrived and with full courtesy invited the trio into the board room, and then settled down to listen to what these strangers had to say. Li wasn't at all fazed by the long period of messing around and expressed why they were there beautifully, then Orlos and Coreum spoke as usual then the trio sat down and waited.

After seeming to be thinking about what had been said their main speaker stood up and said 'that he was surprised they had come so far, was there any ulterior motive such as a takeover of their planet'?

Li was surprised but stood and said, "No we are not a warlike planet we want to set up an alliance of peaceful planets war isn't on our agenda, but if that's on your mind its useless to talk more, we might as well leave and visit another planet on our way?

This finally bought a spark of interest, "do you they ask know of another planet close to us?"

"Of course we do I have already told you we have beaten the tyranny of long distance travel and know of several planets we can visit, why should we waste more time with you"? Li said with a chuckle in her voice.

"But we haven't asked you to leave you decided that yourself, we are happy to have you here you cannot blame us for being suspicious. You arrive here from a big planet over a million light years away, and then wonder why we are being careful, be reasonable, if what you say is true you are living miracles," he said now with a slight smile.

"We have offered to give your scientist the coordinates to find our planet and speak to our scientists by radio they can explain all of this, but all you have done is mess us around?" Li answered him now very sharply.

"This isn't correct at all we have been trying to check out your credentials nothing more if we didn't do that we should be sacked from our jobs, and I am surprised at your attitude. We are interested but if you have the technology to beat the distance then you must have the ability to beat us up very easy and I think that's fair comment don't you?" he said now with a real smile.

"That's true but you will find no weapons of war not even hand guns on our planet, but what we can do is lock any invaders out with a nuclear shield over our entire planet, and neutralize the enemies weapons, we are for peace not war so if your philosophy is war then yes we are wasting our time?" Li said but still sharply.

"And how do we know what you say is true?" He asked.

"Simple if you want we can take you back it's a six month trip in our fastest space freighters, but we have a luxury cruiser up there that can do the trip in four months, you can see it all for yourself and bring one hundred with you, the trip costs will be on us there and back," Li said with a laugh.

"What and you will show us your whole planet with nothing hidden?" he said again but now with a disbelieving look on his face.

"What Li asked do we have to hide you don't have the ability to beat distance it would take you a million years to attack us and then you would only bounce of the shield anyhow, so of course we won't be teaching you any of that really high tech stuff we aren't that silly," Li said now with a soft smile.

"Ok we are interested and when do we go?" he asked.

"Tomorrow" Li said now with a smile.

"Ok" the leader said, "we will be ready in the morning do I need to bring a shaver?" Now it was his turn to laugh. "What do you say we get a team of one hundred together and we will be ready to leave in a week is that right with you?

"That's fine and no you don't need a razor this is our VIP cruiser all set up for dignitaries like you, but remember it's a long boring trip".

And so it was that four months later the cruiser was landing at the intergalactic terminal, with one hundred VIPs from the planet Tepakeha. It was becoming standard procedure for the Terminal to be shut down and ready for the visitors, and flights for local travelers transferred to another terminal. The Orbsey leaders and scientist were waiting once again to greet the visitors, and were all very excited They had been advised these politicians were far harder to negotiate with than the other planet leaders because they were so suspicious, but at the terminal it was nothing, but friendliness, quite in contrast compared to what the trio had had to face.

Li was on hand to introduce the leaders she knew; the others introduced themselves, but she was quick to notice that there were a lot of scientists and politicians in the group. The visitors had kept themselves far more isolated during the incoming trip choosing not to mix with the trio and showing little interest in the data about Orbsey. Li had heard one of the visitors confirming how unbelievably quickly they were moving through the various galaxies, and how completely dumbfounded they were, the comment was 'we have no conception of how this is done'.

'Li had sent coded messages back to Orbsey setting out details of her suspicions, but admitting she may have been influenced by her reactions to their first meeting, and the lack of real hospitality after the trip had been arranged. She admitted that she and her fellow ambassadors where somewhat pessimistic about this group, but more than that they were highly suspicious'.

The Orbseyns where somewhat reserved at the terminal, but in true Orbseyn tradition offered full hospitality to the guests, in top hotels with guides to show them around. They were offered an open door policy to see anything except highly classified secrets such as thought power, and the neutralizing of weapons, although they were shown examples of the techniques that kept Orbsey way ahead of all other planets they were aware of at that time.

The politicians now settled down for discussions about the Orbseyn ambition to set up a league of planets, but only within certain boundaries. Beyond that the scale of time and distance was just too much even for the Orbsey fleet, and until the times could be improved the planet, Tepakeha was on the outer reaches of how far they would go.

Li sat in as an observer and noticed that the visitors were still just as ignorant now, as they had been back at that first meeting with Orlos and Coreum. She began to wonder if that was just the way they were, and now realized the trio should have just abducted some of them first and got to understand them a better. It was a mistake she would never make again during her long career in the planetary services!

The meeting were going moderately well, but making little progress on the question of their planet joining the future league, the main objection being; they didn't have the knowledge to travel so far so quickly, and until they did it was pointless. They were quite happy to set up a colony of Orbseyns in their capital state and happy to provide a colony to live in Orbsey, but suggested the colonists be changed every ten years as a gesture to the colonists that they weren't leaving home for ever. Finally the visitors suggested that perhaps a fleet of Orbsey freighters be sold to them, fully staffed and that a license be granted for them to copy the technology. The Orbseyns expressed themselves ready to sell freighters when a league of planets had been set up, but they stressed the power to move through galaxies wasn't in the freighters alone, that power source was always from Orbsey and at present that couldn't be changed.

When and if the change could be made the travel times would be reduced by at least 100%, but that technology was at least ten years away.

When the change in times were expressed there was a gasp of surprise from scientists present, that would make us almost neighbors they said, and for once there was a ripple of laughter from the visitors.

The Orbseyns said that if a league of planets were set up, the members would be sold freighters, cruisers and the nuclear covers over their planets, that couldn't be pierced by nuclear power of any type. They would also be able to buy the ability to neutralize all weapons way down to hand guns, any fighting even internally, could only be done with bows and arrows; this statement was also greeted with a laugh.

Does this mean the leader of the Tepakehas asked that all of the planets will be hostage to the Orbseyn technological superiority?

Not at all the idea is peace and trade; we will have systems to sell and we presume you will have products to sell to us. But it cannot do all of this until we really beat the problem of time and cost for space travel, we aren't there yet, we are about half way to the goal. If you have had a look around this planet you will see there are no nuclear weapons, but there is a nuclear shield that can go up in three days, that's our safety net.

There are way too many planets out there that have huge populations; our aim is to set up security against being invaded by such planets. And if one of our members is being attacked then we have the facility to quickly arm and counter attack, but we will never pursue war we don't have to its others out there we fear. We aren't the only ones with the technology we have, although we haven't found any yet we are sure they are there and we want to be safe, and with us a group of planets.

"And how many planets do you have now that may join?" they were asked.

"Two possibly five, we want to have ten and then will leave it at that, but we would want to set up agreements on a wide range of issues, trade, technological exchange, currency a wide range of issues that can be negotiated to everyone's advantage. We do have another two planets, but we want to slow down and sort out what we are doing, then carry on to ensure we have eight partners, before we start to negotiate the final agreements?" the Orbsey leader finished.

"Well provided our territorial integrity is assured and we have ten members around the table with heads of govt and their advisors, we would certainly be ready to join such a group. We would be silly if we didn't; but while we fully accept your integrity we would also have to be happy with the other members, that their integrity is indeed as stable as your own.

Now we are quite happy to sign a letter of intent with the provisos, and securities in place we would want, and may I say in closing we thank the planet of Orbsey and its representatives. You have been well represented on our planet by your ambassadors we look forward to their visits at any time. For now Orbsey will have to supply all transport, but of course we will pay our way in future. In the meantime let's set up the reciprocal colonies agreement; and the radio contact between our scientists and them, we will believe the future works out as we all hope. The discussions were then formally ended by the leader of the Orbseyn plebiscite, a ball for the guests was held that night hosted by the trio and the next day the cruiser was loaded the visit was over.

Coreum stayed behind to set up the colonists to go to Tepakeha, and the fleet would leave again when Orlos confirmed he was ready with a load to pick up in Tepakeha. Li would travel to the planet and come back immediately loaded with some of the first colonists and wait in Orbsey for the fleet to arrive home fully loaded with colonists from Tepakeha.

It was now time for Li to be treated for fertility, and when Orlos got back she would be off work for two years, with no more planets to settle in until she was back at work. The colonies in Orbsey would be slowly bought together, and the efforts of Orlos and Coreum would be towards trying to create unity between them all. They were to go to Earth, but only to bring back gold, spice and silk and to try and find Earth representatives, they could bring to Orbsey for talks.

The next need was to bring the different local colonies together in an effort to try and create unity, none of the groups had been placed too close together because the Orbseyn Dept; for the Colonists were aware there could be trouble makers among the groups, much as there had been with the Xalafeuns. Again the idea was to get the children to unite with their peers and Orbseyn children were an important part of that process.

Li had instructed her Dept; to do an individual report on all of the groups except the Earthlings, the rate of marriage or union between Orbseyns and Earthlings was very high and the settling down of the parents was now excellent, Li had no need to be involved with her own kind any longer they were settling in nicely, and nothing would be gained by further development.

Xalafeuns: The children of the Xalafeuns were very aggressive like their parents, but once they were bought into line they became quite settled. None of the age groups were as attractive the Earthling groups from the especially the Xalafeuns, but gradually they settled in with their Orbseyn peers.

The Xalafeuns were obviously a dour people with a very poor sense of humor and the tendency for verbal aggression, at the slightest provocation the children would break into verbal attack, and it was difficult to get them to desist. This was difficult when mixing with Orbseyns who were a mild happy go lucky people as were their children, the years for them of being aggressive were over centuries ago, and all they wanted now was peace. The exercise of bringing them together lacked the attraction for the marriageable aged Orbseyns, because there was little cohabitation amongst them once they left the clubs they didn't mix. It would take many years for the Xalafeuns to remove from their memories some of the atrocities they had lived through on their own planet. Even after the long period of being on Orbsey with its super abundance of food, they tended to hoard food away in the most amazing places, so it couldn't be found, because some day they may once again be starving. 'These children like their parents were very intelligent, and were way out in front with any combined schools exams'. They were diligent workers and would study any subjects given to them for hours until their results as a group were exceptional.

The small antennae that the Xalafeuns had on their forehead was simply an extra device that allowed them to know whoever was coming up behind them and if there was any danger. This didn't make them appear ugly at all, but it seemed to strengthen their innate suspicion of everything and everyone around them.

Corrdeloo: These children are a happy lot and this applied in all age groups, like their parents they didn't get upset easily and they loved having a good time, the lack of hair didn't detract from their appearance in fact for many Orbseyns it enhanced them. They mixed well and easily with all of the other groups and the Orbseyn young found them attractive, which was very important. They came from a planet that had the best of everything that life could offer, but were totally unspoilt, many were farmer's children and loved animals they particularly loved the fact that on this planet animal's weren't killed for food, but of course missed the taste of a good steak occasionally. Orbseyn food was pronounced as very good but bland especially the imitation meat, chicken and turkey. The children had heard their parents at home talking about trade agreements between the planets, and all hoped that Corrdeloo meat would one day be imported to Orbsey, quite forgetting this meant that many more animals on their own planet would die. Romance among them and the Orbseyns began to flourish among the eldest group, and in the future it was expected that marriage would be quite the norm.

The older Corrdeloons were very romantic as are their parents and as soon as they were getting close to thirty YOA; were looking for partners among the Orbseyns. The Orbseyns found the females very feminine, and the males were very virile so the future for mixed marriages was very strong.

Te Kahanui: The children of the TeKahanuins were a delight to work with their complete lack of any pretensions made them the favorites of all. Their natural linguistic abilities was a pleasure to listen to, but their changed appearance to being the same as Orbseyns may have made their integration a lot easier, no doubt if their natural ugliness were seen they might lose that popularity.

They were the most popular kids at schools, and clubs they surpassed even the earthlings in their popularity with all of the other groups, but they were newcomers, and would take quite a few years to settle in to their new home. These children loved food, and had no difficulty showing just how much they loved to eat, the Orbseyn food was a bit bland, but they didn't care they loved all food. It was when they were eating they were at their happiest, they only problem was they seemed to be hungry all of the time.

They weren't good students in the sense that they wouldn't work, but they were naturally very bright and did well without any apparent effort. The families were always happy, and quite content with their own company, but at the same time were glad to mix with all and any who were around them. These children tended not to mix romantically with any others, perhaps because they knew that in their natural state most others found them very ugly, whatever the reason it was obvious they would be little integration through marriage, within this group.

Kanuitepai'ns and Tepakehas: Although these two groups were very reserved, once their reserve was breached they became very friendly, and soon became well liked by the Orbseyn young of all age groups. They appeared to have very little sense of humor but this wasn't true it was just that they were totally pragmatic and had to see the point in everything before they would react.

As their peer groups got to know them they realized it was more that they hated to make mistakes, and in so doing make themselves appear foolish.

Trade agreements: The Orbseyn Govt had decided it was time to set up the federation of planets immediately before any more planets were invited to join, each one was asked to have a delegation ready to come to Orbsey, and they would be picked up by the special high speed cruisers, and returned home after the conference was over. They were asked to send delegates who had the authority to sign the agreement so that the federation in this early stage would be binding and all could continue on to get the program underway. The Earth by Li's suggestion would send an observer delegation with no voting rights who could speak for their planet, but wouldn't be able to vote on any of the binding agreements because they would be there as a protectorate of the Orbseyn govt; for the foreseeable future.

Because Orbsey didn't want to let the other leaders get a glimpse of earth and realize how backward it really was, Li was sent to invite the tree spirits to send a delegation and for which she would be personally responsible for their safety, and none except Li understood what a grave responsibility it was she was taking on. The tree spirits were delighted to be going as observers from earth, and promised they would do their best to be good ambassadors for planet earth.

It had been a momentous conference lasting several days and at the finish the Earth delegates were asked to speak on behalf of their planet. This was unexpected by all of the leaders of the other planets who had understood that Earth was a protectorate of Orbsey, and that any costs related to earth would be paid from the trade accounts between the two planets.

The leaders had sat as if mesmerized by the delegates from earth (three) who spoke, how they asked could this backward planet put up speakers with such powers of speech and persuasion, who had such understanding of what was being done at this conference. As the last one sat down there was a rapturous round of applause from the whole chamber!

Now that the legislative agreements had been signed it was time to set up the administrative aims, so that there could be immediate moving ahead on the actual trade agreements. Reciprocal political representation had been set up on every planet that was signatories of the trade agreement except Earth; which had only had a defacto representation at the signing. It was considered that Earth wouldn't be ready to join any such agreement for at least 2,000 years, if then. The full signatories to the agreement were, Xalafeu, Corrdeloo, TeKahanui, Kanuitepai, Tepakeha and Orbsey.

Orbsey had agreed it would supply all space craft including a license to operate the special energy resource only available through Orbsey, the technical knowledge to erect the nuclear protection screen over their planets, plus the equipment to stop the use of all and any explosive devices that could be used by outside planets to attack them. It was further agreed that Orbsey would take mainly food products in exchange for any products they supplied including the license agreement to break through the tyranny of distance.

Orbsey reserved the right to license any planets that had the productive capacity, and could assist in the production of some of the products ie she might have one of the industrialized planets build aerocars for consumption on Orbsey.

This would allow Orbsey production to concentrate on high tech products, and to help the planets to pay for their purchases without too much hardship on their budgets. The Ambassador and his trade staff were there to ensure each planet was able to produce a product that would help their budgets not drag them down. The following list was the first real orders between the planets and Orbsey.

From Earth 10 tonnes of gold per year plus spices and silk in return for education, but there was no formal agreement.

Xalafeun: I million Aerocars per year in return for 12 Space craft over 12 years fully licensed a nuclear shield over their planet, and the ability to control all explosive devices that had been built for the purpose of war. This planet was a full signatory to the agreement as were all of the others, the basis of the agreement was with Orbsey and with all of the other planets.

Corrdeloo: 250 million tonnes of dried beef per year, for a minimum term of twelve years, in return for twelve spacecraft including a license for the extra energy, a nuclear shield over their planet and the equipment to stop all explosive weapons selectively as required to prevent war.

TeKahanui this planet also was to be licensed to provide one million aerocars to Orbsey per year in return for twelve fully licensed space craft a nuclear shield and the equipment to destroy all weapons of war.

Kanuitepai and Tepakeha: had the same agreement as each other, their order was to supply dried fish, chicken and turkeys as required, in return for twelve spacecraft fully licensed. Also to be supplied was the nuclear shield over their planets, and the ability to control all weapons of war right down to handguns.

On top of these orders Orbsey had to ensure its own fleet was kept up to top quality standard, which required about five new spacecraft per year! The local population on Orbsey had started to complain because the price of joy flights had become far more expensive, interplanetary needs were now such that the spacecraft weren't available for these flights anymore. The govt; had undertaken to guarantee these special low cost flights would be restored when their fleet had been increased, and was able to do the job, but in reality it was going to take ten years if not more before that would happen. This could turn out to be a problem for the Orbseyn govt; in the near future, these flights were very popular and had been for many years, it wasn't going to be easy to dramatically cut off the availability of these space craft.

Problems ahead: The trade agreements had been working beautifully for over ten years when the Orbseyn scientists gave warning there was a fleet of spacecraft heading towards Corrdeloo, and all were heavily armed. Within days the Corrdeloons scientists were confirming what the Orbseyns had first spotted these craft, and quickly verified they were craft only suited for war and probably armed with nuclear warheads.

This fleet was still about eight months away from Coodeloo so something had to be done quickly. A notice went out from Orbsey to the member planets to notify them of their intent to produce 150 unmanned nuclear missiles, for the defense of Coordeloo, which could be completed in less than six months. This notice had been received by all, now the missiles were in full production, and a dangerous looking sight they were as they began to line up ready to be fired.

When there were one hundred of the missiles ready to fire, the scientists on Orbsey asked that the Corrdeloo military make contact with the incoming fleet to ask what their intent was, but there was no answer. Another question went out and it asked if the incoming fleet was bent on war, because if it was there were one hundred nuclear armed missiles that never miss their target being prepared to target them, this got an answer.

'Where and how they asked is this planet going to get so many nuclear armed missiles? They had none the last time they were inspected by our spies, and in a type of sneer they said, we will if necessary blow this planet to pieces. But then they stressed they didn't want to do that, all they wanted was to occupy and resettle this planet with their own people, to live side by side in peace and harmony with the present residents.'

The member planets had been kept well informed about what was happening, and were watching with awed interest what they hoped was soon to happen.

There was 150 craft coming into the attack and it looked as if Corrdeloo was quite unprotected, but the first 100 missiles on Orbsey were ready to fire they had been targeted on the attackers, and they wouldn't miss the targets. Now the attackers were twelve days out from Corrdeloo, the order was given and the missiles were all fired, while the members watched what happened with avid interest. Four hours later the second lot of fifty was fired also targeted on individual craft, so it was too late to stop now the missiles were on the way, and there was no way they would miss the target.

The attack craft were now only ten days away and almost celebrating their victory, when simultaneously throughout the fleet 100 were totally destroyed. While they now tried desperately to make peace with Corrdeloo suddenly it was too late the final 50 were destroyed, there was no more talking, the invasion fleet was destroyed and its crews were all dead.

The messages of congratulations came in very fast especially from Corrdeloo, the extent of Orbseyn power had never been demonstrated, because the agreement was she would only arm missiles in defense of her members. But now they had all seen just how effective that defense was and were happy, they were now convinced their defense was real, and any who dared to attack them would be destroyed. Corrdeloons were really grateful they had been the ones to first have the advantage of the real power of Orbsey, and they had no doubt now their future was secure, under the terms of the contracted agreement with them.

The cost of the defense was shared among all members including Orbsey as they would for any defense mounted for members, but the sleeping deadly giant that was Orbsey went back to normal, their entire population was glad to have been of service to one of the Federation members.

Lifestyles had changed on all of the member planets, they all now had spacecraft of varying sizes, and their staff had spent time in Orbsey leaning all about the operating procedures, and how to break the tyranny of distance, and all were delighted at how much more they could travel. The only problem was the cost of these machines, and how much they cost to run, while it bought all of the planets up to a far higher standard, their citizens had to pay the bill which the leaders thought reasonable, but the citizens thought expensive. But now with the easy demolition of the 150 attack craft against Corrdeloo they had other thoughts.

Suddenly the radio system came alive with a planet enquiring about its lost fleet, and whether anyone had any information about what had happened to it. The Orbseyn scientists were immediately busy trying to track where the message had come from, they were able to trace a planet many light years away from Corrdeloo, so they answered a query with a query what was your fleet doing they asked?

"It was searching for a new planet for us to shift some of our population to; we are becoming overloaded, and need a new home for some of us".

"And was the finding of a new planet supposed to be by negotiation or be conquest Orbsey asked?"

"As far as we are concerned by negotiation but they may have taken a war like stance just to bluff their way through".

"Yes their bluff was pretty strong so in the face of their threats we had no option but to destroy them, just as we would any other aggressor who entered bearing threats. We regret to inform you your fleet was destroyed before it reached the target but that it was verbally threatening. We gave your leaders fair warning, but they obviously felt we couldn't do what we said we could, now they are all destroyed and the crews dead, all killed by nuclear missiles".

An answer came back, "Who are you we don't believe our fleet could have been so easily destroyed they were all nuclear armed and expertly crewed".

"Whether you believe us or not is irrelevant to us if you can find them somewhere then good luck, but let us inform you once again every craft and their crews were all destroyed, they wouldn't take the warning, and refused to pull back so we had no choice but to destroy them".

"And who are you the aliens asked how did you get involved with this battle anyhow, and how do we find you"?

"We are one of a group of planets that work together; your team unfortunately tried to attack one of our members and so paid the consequences. We aren't a planet for war, but we have the installations in place to deal with any that think they can do what they like with one of our members. We think the price you have paid is high enough and you might be better off not to know where we are. We can tell you the planet you attacked was one of our groups, and if you persist we are quite capable of destroying your entire planet so it's best you desist".

The belligerent reply came back, "We will find and destroy you one day be sure of that, and when we do we will repay you for every one of our people you have killed".

"You had best hope we don't come searching for you, as we have already said we are for peace, but you may not come into our region, and attack one of ours just whenever you want to. Now as to your ability to destroy us let us say that you won't do it with the fleet you sent this first time they are all destroyed so you will have to build another".

'If you would like to send us your space coordinates once we confirm them we will be happy to send you ours. The communiqué was suddenly broken off and no further word was heard from the scientists of that group'.

The Orbseyn scientists had been able to track the radio signals received, and were already sending out two space probes to check them out, only thought communication no radio signals were allowed. The both probes were back within a year with full information about the planet, they only called X, it was quite far away from Orbsey, but closer to Corrdeloo. It was a medium sized planet a little bigger than planet Earth, but with a huge population for its size, this was obviously causing a lot of problems because the land mass had large arid areas, they could do nothing with so they had opted for conquest. The planet was fully nuclear armed and obviously very warlike, they were pushing ahead building a new fleet of fighter craft, they obviously hoped would be able to do what the previous fleet had not.

The Orbsey Govt now called a meeting of all planetary leaders to be held in TeKahanui in two month's time; the agenda was what to do about the war planet if anything.

The VIP; cruiser was made available, and Li was called in to do six month's work. She had her ambassadors with her, and the group including some of the leading scientists as well as some of Orbseys top politicians, but not the Presidium members. The Cruiser was armed with the devices to repel all explosive devices of war; that might be sent out aimed at the cruiser; such devices would be exploded fifty miles before they reached the target.

When the cruiser reached a high altitude over planet x a radio message was sent requesting talks of a peaceful nature to be held aboard the cruiser, any who would come would be guaranteed they would be safe, and would be beamed up and down just as quickly as they wanted. There was a moment of complete surprise on planet X where are you they wanted to know?

We are high above your planet and we are immune to any nuclear or other devices you may fire at us, we only want to talk peace for our group of planets, any others you attack is none of our business, but there are ten of us you may not attack without immediate repercussions.

There was confusion down on the planet but eventually they agreed to let the cruiser beam up ten of their people, the following day for peace talks. As agreed the following morning ten of planet x politicians, and scientist were beamed aboard the Cruiser. Li introduced all of the Orbseyns then the visitors introduced themselves.

Li started off the meeting by explaining who they were and from where, but she didn't name the member planets because that wasn't her place to do. She explained her job was as the chief ambassador for Orbsey on matters of interplanetary affairs, but her job was normally only to work with members that's why she had in the group some scientists, and politicians, all of very high regard in Orbsey. None of the other ambassadors had been included in the meeting, because the visitors may feel overwhelmed, if they had to face too many.

Li explained Orbsey will never fire weapons of war on another planet or their allies unless one of their own were under attack, but she said in the closing stages, your commander treated our threat as a joke not once, but twice and when asked to withdraw flatly refused, in the end it was either; defend our member or look weak; so what happened was inevitable under those conditions.

The politicians then took over and said, we haven't come here to talk war we only want to talk peace, we can tell for instance you have a massive overpopulation problem, if you want maybe we can help with that and try to take off your hands a couple of billion people. At this comment the people from planet x started to listen more intently, tell us more about yourselves they asked.

Well we are a very old civilization, and have stopped all wars on our planet over 2,000 years ago, we have also controlled our population problem, yet our people have a life expectancy of 300 years. This means that by time they retire at 255 YOA; they have given all they can and retire gracefully, what else would you like to know, oh yes we have beaten the tyranny of distance a long time ago, and we can travel anywhere in decent timing. For example it took us twelve weeks to reach here, and then we spent a few days travelling around your planet having a look.

One delegate from planet X then spoke up, and asked, "So what he asked does this mean to us do you consider us as being on a war footing with your group of planets?"

"Firstly they aren't our planets we work together for economic and security reasons, but we do have closed trade agreements, and we have given guarantees to defend any that come under attack from outside. We are the guarantors for that, but we don't want war we want peace, and no we don't see us as being on a war footing with your planet?"

"You say you may be able to help us and could place maybe two billion of our population, is this offer real or a speculation."

"Our group is meeting in another two weeks time then maybe then we can turn this from speculation to a firm offer, what else is there we may be able to help with?"

"No it's the population problem that's so depressingly urgent, we have a population of 10 billion and room for only six, and we are at our wits end. Something should have been done years ago, but our politicians were just too weak, now it's completely out of control and the people breed like rabbits. We have now put a maximum of one child per couple, but that should have been done fifty years ago. We went looking for a new planet that had lots of room and that's when we decided to take over Corrdeloo as you know, but that was an equally sorry disaster, that's over now and we must move on. We appreciate your mission of peace and thank you for that, be sure we won't attempt to take over any of your members in the future".

"Well if we can be of any help at all we will let you know, we will put it to our members including our own govt; to see if we can help, who knows if we can reach a none aggression pact, what ways there could be that we could help. The meeting broke up well with expressions of goodwill, and the Orbseyns promising to see what they could do to help with the population problem.

The Federation meeting in TeKahanui was one of goodwill all around, and the meeting came to order and settled down to work on the problem of planet X. the main problem overpopulation was dealt with immediately. Without any strings attached after the Orbseyns had made their points the following offers were received Xalafeu 1million, Corrdeloo 50million, TeKahanui 10 million, Orbsey 10 million, Kanuitepai 10Million and Tepakeha 10 million, a total of 91 million people to be relocated.

The terms were simple there must be a peace agreement between the planet, and the group, relocation costs would have to be paid for by the X planet, and the immigrants would have to be screened as to character etc before they left their home planet, any trouble makers would be returned home very quickly.

As far as Li's dept; of interplanetary affairs were concerned this was a mammoth task, and in fact almost impossible to achieve even with all of the fleets helping. Li had decided to leave the job to the men and had gone back to looking after her baby.

Planet X had been in touch and expressed how grateful they were for the offer to take so many, but now they were looking at the logistics, and realizing how hard the whole job was. In the letter they thanked the group and declined the offer because it was just too hard, and they had been foolish to even consider the foolish approach in the first place.

The Orbseyn politicians began to wander if there was any other way they could help, such as aid by way of food, but it was decided to leave that for the present because they had their own groups to care for first.

The shifting of over 250,000 people (colonists) in and out of Orbsey was now well underway, most of the member planets had decided to provide their own transport and save some money, but they also greatly enjoyed the sense of defeating distance, it took over twelve months but eventually the job was done, and the teams at Orbsey were delighted. Finally they were back to producing spacecraft and once again the people of Orbsey were enjoying their flights into the heavens at reasonable prices.

More and more of the work force was being retrained to work in the aerospace industry, as many were displaced by imports from the planets. The growth in that one industry was huge, but there were many in serious decline, and the period of adjustment was for some a little painful. The methods used on Orbsey of financial, industrial etc; balance worked beautifully, the pain was for those who had to start retraining, but their earnings were never at risk?

There was a lot of transport required for the products that was being bought off other planets, so the craft were still being used to their utmost level, but these type of flights didn't need to have attendants to load, and unload there were teams just for that purpose at their destinations and at home. The new orders from various planets were now being met, and there were orders in books for five hundred craft of various sizes and types.

The ambassadors were all very busy they had to ensure that there were no unsolved personal problems with any of their people wherever they were, and many were pulled of the space flights because of insubordination to the member planets. There seemed to be an unfortunate tendency to think of Orbseyns as the master race and that wasn't to be tolerated from any of the staff no matter how elevated their job, they were expected to be humble at all times.

One day at an airport in TeKahanui, Orlos came across two Orbseyns, telling a group of the locals why the Orbseyns were so superior. Orlos immediately slapped a set of laser cuffs on both men and started to tell the gathered crowd why they were all equal, he then beamed the two men up to their cruiser which was parked way up above. Then turning to the gathered crowd he said those men are now in the lock up on the ambassadors cruiser, they will be dealt with by the courts when we get home, in the meantime I hope this teaches them a bit of old fashioned humility.

There was a polite round of applause from the crowd who then all drifted of laughing at the two big mouths who had got themselves into trouble. Orlos had experienced this type of stupidity often when away from home, especially from tourists and it was always a pleasure to teach such people a lesson, but it wasn't always so helpful in the courts because of course the culprits denied the accusations, but now Orlos had taken to carrying video tapes to prove his point.

The same applied to Coreum, he also loved his planet but he hated to hear people making fools of themselves. Making scenes in front of foreigners, but mostly they both hated to hear people from home boasting about what Orbsey could do, and how they came from the greatest planet in the heavens.

New settlers galore: New colonists were arriving steadily, mainly on their own spacecraft, the Orbseyns who were leaving to settle were being sent out in the same craft. The craft from the various planets were distinctively marked, and were all beautifully maintained, but now the terminal at Orbsey was far more than just a terminal for people. Extensions had been built so that craft just carrying produce were able to go straight to their terminal for unloading, and get quick attention.

The new area was huge and could hold under cover ten spacecraft of a full size unloading at the same time. The children from Corrdeloo were so happy now they could get meat from home, and thought it was wonderful. The shops now had products from all of the different planets, and the citizens loved to just go window shopping, and see all of the new style products, but silks and spices from earth was still among the top favorites.

Li and Orlos often went out window shopping just remembering the places all of these goods were coming from, and how it had all started, Orlos would hold his wife tight and whisper. See what you started now it's just a self perpetuating avalanche, of wonderful goods from planets, we both got to know so well doing our jobs.

Li would smile enigmatically at her mate in the way of the Chinese, and would whisper, no my darling you started it all when you eloped with me from my parents home, that was the real genesis of all of this. They also often went out to the now huge park with rapidly growing Kauri trees, and remembered these giants and where they came from.

They never tried to communicate with the tree spirits that seemed all so unnecessary at present, but the day would come when they would play with the sprits once again just as they had done with their parents in New Zealand, but that was almost 100 years ago and neither felt much like dancing anymore.

Li was now almost due to get pregnant with their second child and they had decided to make sure it was a girl, and then they would settle down to work the next one hundred years until they were allowed to retire. This time both Li and Orlos had to have treatment, he was no longer as virile as when he was younger, and the medical centre had to check out that he wasn't just firing blanks, as was so often the case with the second child. He proved to still be fully able so Li was made ready to have her egg fertilized, which happened very quickly.

On Orbsey men got no special leave when their wives were pregnant, but all pregnant women got two years leave of absence no matter who they were, it was all paid for by the govt.

It seemed to them both it was only a few days until the little girl was born and named after her mother Lisa. Her brother came to see her, he was a strapping 30 YO now, and looking for a wife so he didn't stay around for long, but took off on his nightly hunting for a women.

Li settled down to mothering her baby girl, and she loved every moment of the time spent with the child, but all to soon it came to an end and it was back to work. Li no longer went out with any type of space travel, she was now the chief administrator for her dept; and only went to see official leaders if they came to Orbsey.

Orlos had now taken the senior position on the inter space flights and his orders were to bring in another four planets to the group. It was a lot different now first any newcomers had to satisfy Orbsey, but then they also had to face a full group of leaders from each and every planet except Earth, before they could get final approval.

The scientists had found four planets, and had probe reports back about all four; Li had selected the first one that was to be approached one named Zoa; and Orlos and his team was off again. The planet was three months away and they took a space freighter in case they decided to steal some of the people for observation purposes.

It was as usual a long boring trip, but the two extra ambassadors helped to break the boredom for Coreum, especially since they were both females. Sadly for him they were definitely not interested in getting too close, both had boyfriends at home so Coreum missed out again, while Orlos just slept most of the time.

When they arrived Orlos and Coreum beamed down and had a look around, the people looked like Orbseyns, but maybe a little taller and they appeared good natured in fact very friendly. When they asked where the parliament buildings were, the strangers were very happy to explain without asking any questions, although they obviously wandered why these strangers didn't know the way. Orlos and Coreum then beamed themselves directly to the parliament buildings, and asked to see someone of importance; they were aliens from another planet and would like to meet some of the leaders.

Some men came out but explained none of the main politicians would be available for two days, and if they would explain what they wanted they would pass on the message, they were sure their leaders would see them as soon as they got back to the parliament.

The two Orbseyns presented their credentials, and explained why they were there in detail, and then they said they would be back in four days, to see if there was any interest in what they had been saying. When they returned it was to be met by some men who seemed very suspicious, and not overly interested in what they had to say, "Why have you come to see us?" they asked.

"Because our Scientists had traced your planet as being quite close to us, so here we are it has only been a two month journey, Orlos replied and we wanted to see if you might like to join our group of independent planets?"

"Is the any reason why we should want to join," they were asked?

"Yes there are very good economic and security reasons to join us, after you come and visit us of course, we would like to take a group of one hundred of your top politicians, scientists economists etc; back with us then our top people can explain to you all what we are about".

"This sounds quite interesting," the leader replied. "Can you leave the coordinates of your planet and we will have our scientists check out if it is safe for us to go with you"?

After they returned in two days they were told their 'scientists had been talking to the Orbseyn scientists; and now felt it would be good to send a delegation, and they would be ready to leave in one week from that day'.

Orlos and Coreum assured them they would be free to look at anything on their planet, and they would have guides to take them anywhere they requested off the maps that they would be given, or could buy at any store. The trip back was as usual dull and boring, the ambassadors tried to keep to themselves to allow the foreign group every chance to get to know a little about Orbsey. When they reached the now enormous terminal, it was interesting for the visitors to see the different spacecraft, with the name of their planets emblazoned on their sides.

They were met by the usual big crowd, and at this point Li took over as the senior official, and welcomed all of the visitors to Orbsey. She then introduced their own VIP party, and asked the visitors to name their own individual VIPs, politicians first. The groups then started to mix together very successfully it seemed, the visitors were given a week to take any tours they wanted to, they could go anywhere except to the hub of thought power.

The conference was started with the Orbseyns speaking first, to the delighted applause of the visitors once they had finished.

Then the visitors tabled a list of question they wanted answered, how they asked, and 'Can we be sure your big planet doesn't want to swallow us up, and will we always be free? Are we able to do our own thing or will we be shackled to Orbsey?' and a hundred other questions the other Planets had asked.

In fact it was revealed the other planets would all have leadership teams arriving, within a few days in their own space craft, and they would confirm they were completely free and uncontrolled in every way.

The meeting was adjourned until the others arrived, and 'then reconvened with all of the planets represented by five of their top politicians and two scientists to each team. Once again Li was called on to open proceedings, she was the one best known to all of the different planets leaders, because she had spent so much time with them on their first journey to Orbsey'.

'They greeted her with subdued but very respectful applause, and the meeting was then underway'.

'The individual leaders of each planets group spoke, and between them answered all of the questions that the delegates from Zoa had asked, but each one asked a few questions of their own about Zoa, which were meant to find out for sure that Zoa was for peace with no warlike ambitions. The Zoan delegates were then given copies of documents setting out all of the agreements between the planetary groups, and allowed to take them away. Then they were allowed the freedom of once again go anywhere they wanted to, until they were ready to go home'. 'The Zoan group met once more with the Orbseyns before they left and advised they were keen to join the group, and would have the documents signed by their Plebiscite leaders, if the VIP cruiser could just wait for a few days, for them to get it all done'.

Meanwhile they would also arrange for a colony of their people to be sent to Orbsey, and would be happy to receive a full colony from Orbsey. In twelve months time all of the colonists were in place, plus ambassadors and trade delegations, Orlos and Coreum had completed their first assignment it was time to move on to other work..

The dept; for interplanetary affairs had become so big it was decided to split them up so that Li's dept; now only covered working with the planets for any political reason, finding new members and helping them to get settled. The other depts.; had been split off and it was time to separate them into several different depts. The entire division had become huge and needed close attention from specialized new dept's that had only one area each to work on.

Li and her fellow ambassadors were called into the parliament inner sanctum, and given awards for the services they had given to Orbsey. Li in particular was given the highest award that could be won by any individual on the planet for unique services to their county.

In her reply of thanks Li demonstrated why she had been so successful in dealing with such a wide range of people, her speech was flawless, and she was given a loud round of applause from every person present that day especially Orlos and Coreum. Both had worked with her for many years now, and had so often heard her work her verbal charm on so many high placed politicians, all there agreed she had earned her award well and truly, and they were delighted to see and hear her so honored.

The scientists had another two planets they had sent probes out to, and were satisfied they could be another two members for the group. One planet was about two months away in a different direction from present members, and was named by the inhabitants Kiora. The second one was three months away in the same direction and named Rimutaka, neither of them had shown signs of nuclear weapons, but both were well advanced with nuclear power for peaceful purposes.

The procedures were the same as the previous planet had been, meet with them explain what Orlos and his team had the authority to discuss, then invite them back to Orbsey which was all duly accepted. Orlos had taken the unprecedented step of picking up the VPs of the two planets, he was very nervous about whether he had done the right thing, but the two groups got along famously, and it was a very successful trip with two new members signed up from one round trip. And so it was down to finding only one more member, and they had the total that was wanted; ten excluding earth.

They were all busy trying to work out which planet they would invite to be that tenth member, when a radio communiqué came in from planet X. No one knew how they had become aware of the last membership being available; probably one of the scientists had explained what was happening, and suggested they should try to join because it would be to their strong advantage.

Because the first connection with this planet had been war, there was a lot of hesitation in political circles, but a lot of enthusiasm in scientific and economic circles. It was argued that there could be no harm to talk, and that if there was a chance to convert this planet to peaceful purposes then there was at least the obligation to try, but the politicians had reservation, and expressed them freely.

Planet X was sent a message asking when they could have 100 top officials ready to be picked up, because a cruiser would be sent to pick them up and return them to their planet after top level talks in Orbsey. The other older members were all notified of the request from planet X and given an approximate date to be in Orbsey for the high level talks. The timing on all counts was very accurate and on the date predicted all of the delegates were ready to meet in the great hall of the parliament.

When picking up the visitors the cruiser had beamed them up because Orlos had decided they wouldn't land, this could be a dangerous planet for their craft to land on, and he wasn't prepared to take the risk. But the visitors were very friendly a fact that he advised of to Li, back in Orbsey so she had prepared a suitable welcome, the same as for a friendly state visit.

There was the usual welcome at the terminal with the big excited crowds; the Orbseyns had become used to welcoming foreign dignitaries, and they always made visitors feel welcome. After the greetings the visitors were settled into hotels, but they weren't offered the same freedom to visit anywhere they may want to go. But perhaps later after the meetings, for the present they were given the best of hotel accommodation, and feted by their opposite number in the Orbseyn administration.

A few days after they arrived the first meeting was convened in the Parliament, and they were introduced to the other planet members, 'the Orbseyn members were surprised there was an immediate rapport with all of the leaders. Has there been some form of collusion here they asked'?

'After settling down the delegates from Planet X were asked to speak first since they had requested the meeting, and the Orbseyns didn't want it thought they had in some way been complicit in bringing this meeting together'. The planet X members spoke well, and articulated the reasons they had made the approach, but they agreed they had inside knowledge on what was happening within the group, and that there was only one spot left, so they had decided to apply in spite of the poor start they had had, with the attempted attack on Corrdeloo. They then spoke about their population desperation, and how they were having troubles with the new laws allowing only one child. It had been legislated in the parliament that only one child was allowed, and any extras that were born would be taken and raised by the state. They acknowledged that the attack on Corrdeloo was stupid in that even had it succeeded, they still couldn't have shifted their problems. The whole idea was poorly conceived and then foolishly carried out, by an egoistic general who would listen to no one, because had he contacted his home base with the threat, he would have been ordered to abort his mission, but he didn't and they all paid the price for his arrogance. The delegates from X made it plain they weren't just blaming one man they were all complicit, but now they were ready to destroy all nuclear weapons and guarantee a weapons free future.

When these delegates had finished and sat down the received a strong ovation from the leaders of the other planets, then the others began to reply to the request from Planet X. Every planet was positive towards this possible new member provided, they could live within the agreement that existed between all of them, with their contract provisions. Only Orbsey showed some hesitation they wanted first to know the nuclear stockpile had been destroyed, and that the people had really been forced to the population agenda in spite of objections that their Govt; could force the law through a possible hostile parliament.

The planet X delegates then invited 20 representatives from each member planet to come to planet X, and see the answer to the final questions the Orbseyns had submitted. The delegates all agreed they would go straight from Orbsey to Planet X, to see if the promises that had been made by their delegates could really be forced through their parliament.

On arrival all of the delegates were greeted warmly by the local VIPs it was soon obvious this was a very well developed society, but evidence of degeneration was beginning to show everywhere. Much to the surprise of the Orbseyns, the start on destroying the nuclear weapons were already underway, and the legislation had been passed through a parliament that wasn't hostile. The question was then asked how secure was the govt, and it was explained that the govt; was in power on the basis of reducing the population, and no more expenditure on nuclear weapons. The people were 100% behind leaving nuclear warfare, and the enormous cost that entailed. The group idea of one defending force meant their budget for weapons would be eliminated, and was a very popular idea.

Acquiring a fleet of vehicles for peaceful means and able to beat the tyranny of distance seemed to be the answer to a lot of their problems, especially if paid for on a quid pro quo basis. The members then met in private and all agreed it was a good move to offer planet Coresou (planet x) full membership if they wanted to bind themselves to the same contract as all of the others, it was decided they would wait until they received an answer.

The answer came back almost immediately; it was in the form of the documents completely signed with full acceptance of all the terms. The delegates all joined in a quiet celebration, knowing now they had a full group or a federation of planets that would in the years ahead prove wonderful for all of the peoples, and give political, scientific, security and economic etc; well being.

This was the policy first advocated by a scientist many years ago, when the first discovery was made planet Earth. Now it was a reality and there was a feeling of better security from future invasion. Then there was the enemy who was now a full member of the federation, and there were a few from Orbsey who couldn't help but smile, at the irony of the position.

It was ten years later and Li was almost due to be appointed to the high court as a judge when a report came in that Earth was due to be attacked by beings wanting to take them over, but they were still six months away and only lightly armed, they obviously thought Earth wasn't well defended if at all, so they were being rather careless for an invasion force.

Suddenly the radios started to squeal as an Orbseyn scientist cut into their communication, "What they were asked is your intention towards Earth because they are a protectorate of ours, and we will have to ask you to desist if you have intentions to invade".

"Who are you and why should we desist? There is no law saying you are in control of this universe?"was the reply.

Well to prove a point the Orbseyns said, "We will in ten hours blow ten of your fleet out of the skies, if you still refuse to desist we will destroy your entire fleet, now once again that is your choice we don't mind we have nuclear homing missiles aimed at you right now".

Their commander came on the radio and said, "This isn't correct you have no right to interfere with us unless you are from earth."

"We have said we are the protector of Earth and in fifteen minutes ten missiles will be fired, and once they are on the way they can't be stopped, so you have fifteen minutes, we don't want to have a battle with you, but we won't let you reach your destination under any circumstances".

The line went dead and the communication was cut off obviously they believed it was just a scam so right on time ten missiles were fired, and were on the way.

'In three days the missiles struck and there was pandemonium among the attackers, as ten of their freighters were obliterated. The radios started to really squeal now as the fleet broke into pandemonium immediately, the commander spoke' and asked, "Have you fired more missiles or do we have time to withdraw? We can see now you have the technology to back up your threat so we will withdraw".

"We will give you five hours to turn around and go home if not rest of your fleet will be targeted and destroyed, can you do that Orbsey asked"?

"Yes we will reverse course immediately and you need never worry about us ever again, we know now what you mean when you say Earth is protected goodbye".

The message was sent out to all of the ten member planets and the incident reported, but they were exhorted to watch their own heavens, we don't want some power getting through and causing havoc out in any of the member's areas. Orlos and his family heard of the latest defense work and were suitably happy, their special love was for Earth, and it was now safe and that was very important to them.

Bankers and others: Bankers had been purged from Orbsey centuries ago when they were found to be trying to manipulate money for their own ends, the Govt had taken over all money and now only Govt and private credits could be used as currency with the values tightly controlled. But in some of the other planets banks were in control of all currency, and the formation of the Federation of Planets had created for them they thought a golden opportunity.

They were busily trying to create an open market for all trade exchange and Orbsey was being attacked as the planet that was controlling all others, and therefore paying any price they chose to pay for products bought and sold. Orbsey treated these statements with contempt as just money brokers trying to destabilize the values to force big profits for themselves. They made it clear their govt; credits were a fixed value, and all other should value their own currency in line with that policy.

It was clear the Orbsey money of whatever ilk was backing all other currencies and if any weakened they would have to answer to the planets board of trade not Orbsey, but the battle with the bankers raged on, it was a standoff that only Orbsey could afford to sit back and watch. In the end Orbsey invited all of the planets to bring their bankers to a meeting to prove all of the charges of claimed corruption against Orbsey their govt; control of the money for which they never moved the value either up or down; the bankers were charged to prove their claims or leave the meeting.

The bankers first claim was the money being fixed worked in Orbseyns favor and that the other planets were held in thrall by Orbseys very superior economy.

'And what they were asked would you have us do, to which they replied float your money and let it find its own value'.

'And who would that benefit and where the profits from trading in our currency would go then they were asked'?

'Why it would find its own level of value and the other currencies would also float to their real level which would mean there would be a free and open currency market'.

'And who would decide the real levels you so avidly support'.

'Why the traders they replied'.

'And where would the profits of your such avid support for the value of our money go to they were asked'?

'Why it would be the market traders that earn that profit they would win or lose according to their skill or if you like their ability to read the markets on a given day'? They replied.

'And what else would you have these masters of finance be able to do they were asked'?

'Well a free and open stock market should be allowed so business could also find its true level of value up or down on any given day; and business should be able to borrow freely so they could develop freely without govt; interference'.

'And so you want us to free our business markets so the banks could become the masters of our economy with all the extras such as of course little things like fractional banking, and all of the cost traps that go with it. Now tell us if the value of a major company according to your stock exchange ideas was to go up what happens to the real value of the business that your experts and their bankers are so judging'?

'Why no it's the shares that are traded not the actual business that value remains constant unless something goes wrong', they replied?

'And could that something wrong have anything to do with how the investors see that company, or are encouraged by their advisors to see that companies trading results'?

'Well it does sometimes have an effect but overall there is a real open assessment of a company's true value'.

'Orbsey will shortly be reducing our prices to Planet members by 10%, so how would you suggest we do this or what should be done to ensure they all benefit equally'.

'We suggest you open your currency markets because the value of your currency will float down and have quite some impact on every member of this planetary group'.

'So if our currency floats down as you say who will be the beneficiary of such an action'?

'Why every planet will get an advantage and will be able to buy more Orbseyn products, they replied triumphantly thinking they had scored a great advantage'. These are only simple examples of the questions that the bankers were asked, in two days of solid questions, many were asked to leave the forum for making misleading statements, but at the end most remained.

In the final summing up the panel of judges said. "This planet many centuries ago was held in thrall by the bankers the most parasitic class of people we had, and our cost structures were always subject to the decisions made by bankers. We kicked them out and changed to the system to what we have now and this planet has never looked back, we have gone from success to success, but our success has been shared by our people, not monopolized by one class of privileged money grubbers who until then were in a class of their own, and all underwritten by the Govt".

"This planet will never go back to a system of banking that we know so well, is a fool's paradise and would be a world controlled by Bankers, which you want to extend that to an interplanetary system so the what others cannot do with war you will do with money, this will never happen to us again".

"Our member planets may leave behind as many economists etc; as they like to learn our system if they want to, but bankers and lawyers are barred, we have no need for bankers, and we don't need lawyers hypothecating about what is good or bad for us".

"We intend to unilaterally reduce our prices by 10% to all of our members in three months time, but if we are advised by our Ambassadors of racketeering by bankers in any planet that 10% reduction will be cancelled and full prices restored. As for gambling with our currency that's not going to happen because our treasury is well able to withstand the costs of what we are doing, but unless the benefit is going to the people, and not a class of people that discount will be cancelled. Any planet that wants to get rid of its parasitic system controlled by bankers we in Orbsey pledge our support even in a financial sense, we will help you get rid of this class of people".

"Thank you one and all and we wish you a good journey home, but you can be assured there will be no more invitations for bankers to meet with us in any capacity, ever again in the future, nor will any Orbseyn officials travel anywhere to meet with bankers".

As soon as the meeting was closed and the Orbseyns had all left the chamber, there was an immediate uproar among all of those from the planets left behind, and shocked at what they had just heard. Some mainly bankers and lawyers felt it was an imposition on their sovereign rights, others agreed but were going to work with the Orbseyns as had been offered nevertheless. 'But the bankers felt terribly threatened by the final summation, they knew now as a class they were being threatened, and Orbsey had proved they didn't need bankers in fact had done away with them many years ago, and had done very well without them'.

'The economists were amused and the politicians were confused, how they wandered can we change to a new system, we have been for so long controlled by bankers, but if Orbsey could do it surely we can do it too. The politicians decided to ask the Orbseyn politicians for a meeting; before they left just to get a better understanding of what it all meant. A meeting was convened for the next morning; all were welcome to attend except the bankers, who were left to their own devices the next day, almost secluded in their hotel rooms.

'The Orbseyns were very open as to what they wanted and that was the wiping out of the banking class, and they were willing to give advice and financial support to try and achieve their goal. Records from the past were shown to prove just how much the banks had benefited, from an economy in crisis when they had control of the money. Some countries had massive wealth others were desperately poor and millions starved to death'.

'Huge sums of money was spent on weapons for war, and the needs of the starving millions were ignored, graft and financial crimes were endemic because the people could see corruption all around them, society was degenerating rapidly as families fell apart. Then they showed graphs of how things had changed since govt; controls had been established, the changes were dramatic, and showed in every strata of Orbseyn society, but the system was unique and had taken a long time to perfect'.

'But it wasn't the govt that had succeeded so dramatically it was the systems they had gradually put in place, it took over a hundred years to complete and install it was a period of trial and error'.

'The universities started turning out brilliant young business people, and they went on to spend their first work period (45 years) as practicing apprentices, all working for the govt. Then in the second 45 year term they could choose govt; or private and about 60% chose govt; because of the rewards available to them when their second term was over. It was then and only then could they become captains of industry, and as such they were a respected, but not selfish class of people. Private business could go on and do whatever they wanted to do, they could get grants from the govt; but they couldn't borrow and no interest was charged on the govt grants'.

'The meeting lasted all day, but at the end there were a lot of far more knowledgeable politicians, who had suddenly found the desire to break the banker's yoke that held them in thrall. They also had the guarantee that Orbsey would give help in every way including credits, and the by time it was all in place bankers as a class would be finished.

Naturally after the meeting the bankers were all agog as to what was happening, and loudly declaiming that they weren't a parasitic class, but had helped build their planets up as much as anyone, but after the way they had been put down by the Orbseyns their claims suddenly sounded rather hollow.

The first planet to test the waters before getting rid of their bankers was Zoa, the politicians had on returning home made it plain that big changes were going to be made, they argued that with their big population the systems as laid out by the Orbseyns were very attractive. The bankers argued it couldn't be done so the economists were working to prove it could be done, and a lot easier than it had been for the Orbseyns to do, because they had had to create the blueprint which they were happy to share.

The govt of Zoa worked quietly until they were ready then suddenly announced the nationalization of the banking system, and the firing of all the leading bankers. Because the politicians had been very careful to cover all of the weak spots there was a minimum of disruption, and the people cheered what they considered was strong govt; they were proud to support such a move. The huge private assets held by bankers in many locations on their world were confiscated and taken by the state, and turned over to the consolidated accounts.

The bankers were put down and shut out they had no recourse to the media etc; and any mention of their woes was answered by proof of their former grand life styles, and it was stressed that had all been at the cost to the people. The banks were now fully under govt; control, and the Orbseyn systems were being implemented slowly but surely. The Zoan Govt; now extended an invitation to Orbsey to send a party of observers to see what they had done, which they were glad to accept.

When they arrived there were a few minor changes they advised, but on the whole they congratulated their hosts on how practical they had been in the ways they had used to force their legislation through, they predicted that within ten years Zoa would be a changed economy; and that in fifty years they would have beaten their overpopulation problem.

'The Zoans were ecstatic they felt so proud that they had at last moved in the right direction, and they were quick to acknowledge it was all because of the Orbseyns. The other politicians from the member planets were watching with interest and most now were slowly, but surely changing some of their legislation to allow them to make the changes that Zoa had made. Quite a bit of travel between Orbsey and Zoa by the politicians and advisors of the other planets were now underway and most of the bankers knew they were a class under siege because of the influence of Orbsey'.

'Then the cost of all products bought from Orbsey was reduced by 10%, and those that had floating currencies and large trading accounts with Orbsey found the value of their currency were at way higher levels than before. This was the final straw against the bankers, even to save their own position they were unable to control the currency movements. On the planets, all who now traded extensively with each other the bankers found themselves under siege, and quite unable to control the govts; in any way as they had done before'.

'Within ten years all of the banks on every planet had been nationalized, and the Orbsey methods were being put into practice. Business was moving ahead beautifully on all planets, and the savings were proving to be very substantial on the GDP of each and every planet. It was proved because after ten years copying the Orbseyn system that add on's; to productive costs had been reduced by a large value; and the boost to the moral of the peoples on every planet became stronger as they began to understand what had been done.

At a meeting of the leaders of all the planets, it was asked how Orbsey had got their lifespan up so high and whether it was a good move considering the need to control the high cost of the aged care.

It was explained that the aged care cost was all factored into the reality to having a highly trained workforce that could be worked for a long period, and didn't just die taking their knowledge and expertise with them. This was balanced by the tightly controlled birth rate of only two children per couple, and the people could be kept very well for the full period of their lives with no reason to suffer from any illness. All health problems could be treated including the re growth of body parts that may fail, and have to be replaced. All such problems were minor, and the maximum period needed to grow say a new set of heart and lungs would be 5-8 months. The only part of the body that still needed hospital attention was the brain and special hospitals were still operational for all diseases of the head.

The allowed retirement period of 40 years meant the old people could die in comfort or whatever they wanted to do, when they wanted to with their last years many just wanted to pass away peacefully, which they were allowed to do in spite of the medical system being well able, to keep them alive and well.

It was pointed out that the age limits could be increased if the people wanted that, but most felt that a limit of three hundred was enough, and any who wanted to go on could do so by paying moderate fees for the medical centers to keep them alive. All of the leaders left that meeting completely amazed at how health was managed on Orbsey and how well some of the oldest workers looked; to them it was a miracle. But they could see this system would be the hardest to copy, they could do it over a long period of time on average they thought 200 years, to get their own facilities up to the right standard.

Orbsey was quite willing to pass on the health secrets to all of their members, but they warned the medical professional had been hard to convince that they could still do well working for the govt. The dental and pharmaceuticals had been the hardest to bring under control, the drug companies in particular had been difficult to deal with. But as they saw the no nonsense approach to the bankers they had become more prepared to work with the govt; especially when the govt; had agreed to underwrite the cost of research by 50%, and even more.

Attention at a medical clinic was free for the first 12 minutes of consultation but any longer than that, full fees were charged. Home births were the norm and there was no charge for any service of that type. The setting up for growing new organs were free, as was the period of care needed while the new organs took over from the old.

CHAPTER 15/

FINAL YEARS, LI AND ORLOS

Orlos had completed his last work period and Li was now 245YOA, but had fifteen years to go. Both of their Youngsters were doing well in the interplanetary diplomatic core, and had taken over from their parents, they loved their jobs and Lisa especially was a gifted speaker. Their parents had actively supported their rise in the dept, as a new dept it didn't yet have many employees doing their third term, so it was still open to youngsters to be promoted quickly, if they showed true aptitude and attitude.

Li had handed back her personal spacecraft when she left the job, but they were happy to lend it to her if she wanted it for some reason, and she and Orlos was considering one last trip to their old love nest on Earth. They wanted to visit the tree spirits one last time to say goodbye, and go to where Li's home had been. Finally one last look at the schools they had founded so long ago. Li applied for and was granted twelve months leave of absence, both of their children were going with them too look after the old couple who were both rather frail, even Orlos who had once been so robust was just skin and bones.

Li because of her appearances in the courts still tried to look as strong as she could, but her diminutive frame was now so very tiny. When they left the old couple felt the thrill of space flight one more time, but they were soon finding it very tiring, and wandering if they should turn around and go home, but they persevered, and in the end had enjoyed that last trip.

The visit to the tree spirits was just so wonderful, even though the spirits could see their old friend's had almost run their life's course. One of the oldest tree spirits predicted that in the future the children of Li and Orlos would bear fruit and would come to Earth working for the govt; of Cordiance. They will have studied the records left by Li and would come to see the Kauri spirits for help and advice; this would be freely given and would be a great help in the future development of planet Earth. The spirits prophesied that it would take until the 23rd century to fully develop Earth, but their descendants would be in the vanguard of that development.

They stayed for a week and then reluctantly said goodbye for the last time. Then they went to Li's old home in central china which of course was no more the area was all rice growing paddies now. Li's memories of her childhood home were now a little blurred, but she had never forgotten the ugly old man Lei, to whom she was supposed to be married.

A visit to all of the schools which were thriving, and finally short trips to Rome, Alexandria and India, then it was time to go home. By time they arrived back in Cordiance they were both exhausted, but happy to have been able to say goodbye to the tree spirits, and the five schools which were thriving with loving care from the teachers, and money from Orbsey.

Both were too tired to talk when they got home, but their children stayed with them until they recovered which took about a month. Their entire peer group thought they were wonderfully brave to even have attempted the trip, but to them and their children it was well worth the struggle.

The final journey: On her last day as a judge of the high court, Li launched a scathing attack on the system for the aged, in Orbsey especially term five. She said that over the age of 200 it was only forced labor to keep the people working artificially by medical, means and that the state was actually using its aged population as slave labor.

This was one final speech from a once powerful orator, and the media really gave it maximum coverage, there was still a free press of a sort on Orbsey but it was always cognizant of that all Seeing Eye in the sky. Li said that 90% of the aged workers only kept going because they had to, the power in the sky demanded it and the health care ensured it, but they weren't in the least bit happy.

The additional term that had been added had been the straw that broke the spirit of all of the aged, that final extra 45 years of work took away the hope for a little comfort in retirement. Li said she had come to Orbsey at the age of 24 and had worked a total of 236 years, and she had loved every minute of it. But she and her husband now had only a few years if any to enjoy each other's company because they were both exhausted unto the point of death, and she doubted if they would have very long together.

My Darling husband she said is 15 years older than me and has been living day by day probably just to have a few final days together, and this shouldn't be. Even our two children haven't been allowed time off work to spend with their father, because that Eye in the sky says they must work.

That Eye in the sky she declared is evil it has gone over the bounds of decency every person has had their life polluted by this evil thing in the sky. The keeping of law and order by this omnipresent Eye is a great thing, but when ordinary decent people were being controlled mercilessly it was time to take another look.

People she said don't become criminals just because they take a day off work without permission, and by treating decent folk in this way it is an abuse of state power that if it isn't controlled will lead to the downfall of civil controls, and eventually to anarchy, as the young begin to understand the pressure their parents are under.

It is ludicrous for example for a child to get a lifetime criminal record for stealing some lollie's from the local candy store! It is a terrible shock to the parents of any girl to get a report that their daughter is taking part in the activities of a common prostitute, because she has been caught flamboyantly dressed in the company of a boy. Who says she is a prostitute that Evil Eye in the sky has decided all on its own that these children are guilty, and they are labeled for life by an Eye that never forgets nor misses anything.

The people are tired Li said of this control by this none living thing in the sky that just keeps getting tougher and tougher, and one day the people will revolt not because they want to, but because they will have no choice. By the time she had finished speaking the old lady was exhausted, and had to be taken home from work never more to return, it was all over and she had said her last hurrahs in the manner that only she could.

The media were very loud in their praise for a great citizen of Cordiance who had done so much for this, and the other planets during her long working life. She had been a leader; and instrumental in bringing together the Federation of Planets and was highly respected on every one of them. The farewells came in by radio thick and fast; and finally she was able to try to enjoy what time there was left, with her husband.

They passed away together in their sleep, they both simply wished for the end, and the look of relief on both of their faces when their children found them, made it so plain how pleased they were to go. Orlos was 300 YOA and Li was 285 YOA, and what a life they had both lived.

Chapter 16

A new era a new team

It was now the approx 420AD; Earth Time: there had been a quiet period after Li and Orlos, had passed away some 120 years ago, and everything from a federalist point of view had been progressing well. The planets had been working and trading together perfectly, to the advantage of them all, but the problem that was growing was the one annunciated by Li in her last message to the high court. It had started with small claims coming in and people refusing to pay fines, on the basis that they had been unfairly adjudicated by computers.

At the start there had been only a few, but the volume was growing slowly until finally the courts were being overrun with millions of small claims. But now there were a growing number of larger claims starting to join the small ones, which was what was spear heading what was becoming a revolt, and now reaching alarming proportions. There was no leaders creating trouble it was a simple peoples revolt, and they were expressing their rights in terms of the Orbseyn Constitution, which allowed all civilians and others to object to the high courts, if they felt their rights were being ignored.

The essence of the complaints was that there was nothing, but an Eye in the sky controlled by computers; that decided everything to control the way of life on Orbsey. As the volume of court challenges kept getting larger the confusion grew, the once close control of the legal system fell into disarray, and the once orderly society that had been Orbsey began to crumble. The argument quickly developed was that all control; was now vested in the all Seeing Eye. What happened to the various levels of govt; we elected the people were asking; and what about the Plebiscite which was supposed to have the casting vote on everything, but there were no replies?

It soon became obvious that any answers that were being given by the politicians were being over ruled by the all Seeing Eye, and any comments by politicians that weren't considered correct by the Eye, were simply being trashed, and in some cases serious charges brought against the politician.

Very quickly it became obvious the political class had been shut down, and any that remained were merely pawns of the all Seeing Eye. But what couldn't be shut down was the ordinary citizens, a whole new class was coming into being, and no matter how many were fined or even jailed the level of discontent was becoming huge, and would soon reach uncontrollable levels.

The people were asking, where are our leaders and what do we have to do to get answers in the courts, all we are getting are legal documents written by some computer, and that machine is controlled by the all Seeing Eye. This is no good how do we control this system that allows us no rights?

Then the special police were bought out, these were robots, and their instructions were linked to the will of the Seeing Eye, so that in theory there could be no revolt in a final threat from the people. But there was no threat from the people just billions of unpaid fines, all that could be done, was to fine them for late payment. The problem was that the courts were now so far behind in processing the original complaints; that the system was almost at the point of breakdown.

The special robot police could find no work to do since the fault was mainly with the govt; all that happened was to create fear among the population, as they suddenly saw these robots taking certain duties over that had been done by uniformed police, it was a foolish move.

Then without any notice the old people rebelled and refused to work out their final 45 year term, on the basis of it was just too hard, and they wanted the life span to be reduced to 255 years and working age reduced to 210 YOA. There were still no leaders stepping forward to lead what could have been a revolt, just individuals mainly husband and wife workers, who had decided they weren't going to work, after they had reached 210 YOA.

Once again from a few individuals the numbers grew quickly and before long there was a full class of workers at risk, because they wanted their final work term cancelled. All that could be done was to order the special police to pick up these recalcitrant's, and sue them in the courts, but there were no jails so all that could be done was to fine them, and keep fining them until again the courts got bogged down, and no letters of demand were going out.

There was little else that could be done as there were no leaders that could be charged with heavy offences, all there were was a lot of people over 210 years of age they could take action against when the courts became unblocked. But the courts were getting out of control as the elderly, and the unpaid fines were now blocking up the system. The problem was the computers couldn't handle the problems that were now developing, and there was a feeling that anarchy would soon break out, but how was this to happen?

None of the legal infrastructure was under attack and all laws except the last work term were being honored, but even here who would lead a fight against the Seeing Eye! None were coming forward because all were happy with their standard of living, they just didn't want to be controlled by computers in the sky, nor did they want to work until they could no longer walk.

As Li had predicted all of those years ago Orbsey had become rich on the tremendous work load it had inflicted on its elderly people and the system had to break one day, even the Plebiscite members found themselves as servants to the Seeing Eye.

Lisa was now 155 YOA married with a Son of her own, and due to return to work after having had her second child a Girl two years ago. Lisa was now the Managing Director of all interplanetary development work, having carried the job on after her mother, and just as successfully. She was surprised to have an urgent request to attend a Plebiscite meeting on her first day back at work, and that the need was urgent.

'Lisa was aware of her mother's last statement to the high court, and she was also aware that what Li had said was now beginning to come true, but she was also aware that her mother's words were not hers, and therefore wandered what was happening? She was soon to find out'!

After giving an outline of what was happening in Orbsey, the leader of the Plebiscite then continued to explain the problems on their planet was beginning to take a hold on the other planets, and creating problems for the Federation. Her job she was told was to visit all of the planets, and taking her brother they were to find out what needed to be done to contain the problems from getting any worse!

The Plebiscite members were all well aware that Lisa like her mother before her was held in high esteem with all of the leaders, and she was expected to calm down any discontent that may be growing in the Planets.

"I understand what is expected of me, it seems that what I really have to do is reassure the members that Orbsey is working to settle its own problems, and will do everything possible to bring our own people to understand the responsibility to retain civil and legal order, as an example to all of the other planets. I am quite happy we can do this, and at the same reassure them all that the problems will be dealt with fairly and properly; as they always have been and always would be!" Lisa had said.

'Lisa was finally told she was to try and strengthen the interplanetary ties, but also arrange a full members meeting for about twelve months after she arrived home. The trip would take over 18 months so Lisa applied to take her latest child with her, and much to her surprise the request was granted. Since her husband and brother were both official escorts, the trip was going to be bearable after all, but there were hard times ahead and she would be glad to arrive back home.

Earth was not being visited on this occasion, this planet was a special interest to Lisa's mother and father, but didn't have any special place as far as their daughter was concerned, they were being looked after anyhow, and certainly wouldn't be affected by the problems on Orbsey at present.

'The proto cols were vastly different than in the days when the travelers from Orbsey, had to work hard to get access to the leaders of each planet, now there was a full embassy plus ambassador and staff, to arrange all meetings for them, Lisa was the main speaker and leader of the deputation from Orbsey'.

The first planet the team visited was Xalafeu, and a great banquet was arranged on the cruiser, with all including the Orbsey Embassy heads invited. After the initial bonhomie of greetings all round, the first main speaker was Lisa who like her mother had been, was a truly gifted speaker able to explain the reason for the visit by the federal interplanetary team in simple terms. Lisa came straight to the point, and laid out the problems that had bought her planet to almost gridlock, with a silent, leaderless none violent revolution going on.

'The system she said has ground to a halt as people objected to the control over their lives by computers, through what was termed the all 'Seeing Eye', they wanted leaders from the people again not from the 'Eye in the sky' which they had developed a hatred for'.

'The problems with the fifth term old people were far more entrenched and were a group of people who had simply tired and treated the govt; with contempt. Lisa closed her speech by saying our job is to explain what is going on and why, she said put simply the elderly felt their working age was too long, and had downed tools, the Govt; didn't know what to do. The other was rule by the people as it had once been not through an all Seeing Eye in the sky, that had the final say on everything, and the people want that to be stopped and proper leaders be elected with real power not subservient to the State. The introduction of robot police was just the final straw and now the population was waiting to see what would happen'.

'The leader for the Xalafeuns now spoke and started by saying the federation of planets had been great for all members, and the Orbseyn economy had powered them all too great advances, but what now he asked?

What was going to be done about the problem with the people who it seemed wanted their elected parliamentarians to run the country not computers? The problem was whether this would spread to the peoples of other member planets, and create disruption everywhere'.

'What was of far more concern was what effect there would be on the Orbsey commitment to the mutual defense agreement, that is one of the key points in the overall security enjoyed by the members of the federation of planets. The other major part of the agreement is the supply of certain vital technical knowledge including the great air ships, which have made the whole interplanetary system viable including the trade that has now become such an integral part of all our economies. Of course the real health of Orbsey is vital to the whole system, and if the full cooperation of all of our group of planets was needed to back that continued health, then it is vital we all meet but maybe not in Orbsey'.

'It is a set back to us all if in truth our well being is falling into the hands of computers, and all necessary action must be taken to correct whatever has gone wrong. Maybe the truth is that Orbsey has become just so developed it as gone too far and its people have become anxious. We must help to rectify this situation because of course we cannot have computers with too much power playing games within their preset formulas and commands, and in this way running such a great planet'.

The leader then left the podium and Lisa closed the formal side of the gathering, 'firstly thanking the Xalafeuns for their strong support and also explaining the full agenda, she had been given by the Plebiscite back in Orbsey. After they had been to all of the member planets she and her fellow staff members would decide the best planet to have the meeting on, this was within the mandate they had been given before they left Orbsey'.

Lisa also pointed out that perhaps the leader of the Orbseyn Plebiscite had deliberately given her the authority within the mandate to make the decision away from Orbsey, but perhaps she also was being affected by the growing sensitivity of the population in Orbsey, and beginning to fear computers herself.

The reaction among all of the planets was much the same as Xalafeu, some with stronger opinions about different subjects, but all very supportive of the Orbseyn Plebiscite. At the end of the last meeting Lisa announced the full meeting of leaders would be held in Xalafeu in twelve months time, she had already confirmed this date with the Orbseyn leaders back home and all of the Federation leaders.

It was just over fifteen months by the time Lisa and her team had completed the full trip, and they were all glad to be home, but there seemed to have been a greater deterioration than ever among the unofficial protestors. It was estimated the courts were now over three years behind, in issuing summons to citizens who hadn't paid their initial claims. But the real problem was there was no top level class as the old people just refused to work, and openly defied the government to do anything they wanted too, but they had finished work. The courts had no senior judges, all divisions of society had lost their highest level of administration; and everyone was confused without the guidance of their most senior advisors.

If the situation hadn't been so serious it would have been funny, the last such strike action on Orbsey had been 3,000 years ago, so everyone just sat back and waited. The old people just stayed at home and made it obvious there was no way they would be returning to work, and it didn't matter what the govt; tried to do, they didn't care they were just too tired to continue, and they weren't going to be artificially stimulated by the medical systems anymore. It was amazing the historians could never recall such dramatic problems on their planet, and yet there was no violence of any type. Of course the oldies were too old for insurrection they were a minimum 210 YOA, all those who were refusing to pay fines the govt; had the problem not them.

The courts were blocked up and there were no magistrates or judges to issue the various summons so the backlog was becoming daily greater. The robot police controlled by the Seeing Eye were still wandering around scaring people, but doing nothing effective.

CHAPTER 17

THE PROBLEMS ON ORBSEY

The problems had been steadily growing worse as the effect of the Term Five workers having illegally retired, became more pronounced. That highest level of knowledge and administration, being lost to the system was having a deepening effect in all sections of society. Meeting production dates gradually lagging behind as quality control, and other finishing off, of products were being held up. As a result mass layoffs were being considered even though the sales books, especially for all sizes of space craft were full; and now lagging two years behind. The same applied to all industries, and the future of food production was looking tenuous, especially special food for the peoples who were genuinely retired.

Finally the Plebiscite came together and convened a full meeting of the Orbseyn Parliament in Cordiance. They had no sooner come into session than it was deemed an illegal meeting by the Seeing Eye, and ordered to be broken up by the robot police force. These numbered some 100,000 fully armed robots, but able to stun only their weapons weren't for killing.

Pandemonium broke loose as the members refused to leave the chambers and they were besieged by these robots controlled by the Seeing Eye. This was going to be it a show of strength, but where would the strength of the people come from, was there to be no answer to the computers that were controlling their lives, it seemed unlikely.

Suddenly to the surprise of all, a division of the army that had been set up and structured by the original Earthlings had surrounded the robots, and made it plain their mission was to destroy them. This highly trained and fit army now numbered ten million permanent members, and they were all trained to kill without mercy any target set by their generals. All of the generals were well known to be pro republic and pro federation of planets, so this was a challenge to the Seeing Eye the entire population could now see what was happening, and applauded the army generals.

'The robots stood firm and insisted this is an illegal gathering now disburse or we will force you all to leave, and we want this done immediately'. The army commander issued an order for the robots to leave immediately or they would be attacked. It really looked so funny the ancient style army threatening the ultra modern robots, but the looks were deceiving the robots only looked deadly, the army was deadly in every way'.

The robots seemed at a loss for what to do keep forcing the assembly to leave, or turn and face the army in this situation they were leaderless. The army had no such problem, the order was given to attack and the fight was on, but again no one told the robots. When the first robot was hit with a lethal spear thrust it looked all so strange, the robot seemed to fall to pieces. There followed in quick succession over a thousand robots destroyed, and in pieces everywhere. They weren't answering the attack just seemed to be lost, in this melee of strange men attacking them.

'The army commanders gave the order to completely destroy the robots so the attack was widened and over 50,000 robots were destroyed within a short time, and then the army withdrew. The general in charge then entered the assembly hall and told the delegates that order had been restored, and they could rest assured that unless there was another attempt to close them down by the robots the army would not interfere with politics again'.

The entire assembly then settled down to work to try to rectify the mistakes within their legislation that had allowed the Seeing Eye to attempt a takeover of their planet, and even their ancient style army were in a position to take over had they wished.

There was hope engendered by the actions of the military, but shock at how much control the Seeing Eye had over the entire planet, the politicians swore they would work until there had been a full investigation, and the passing of laws that would make impossible such a thing ever to happen again. It didn't matter how many laws were passed the high court was closed down for lack of staff and officials. The position was dangerous until answers could be given on some way to start raising the officials, from level four to have the responsibility of their former level five colleagues.

This was difficult because all levels right down to level one were affected, and there was no way a quick fix was possible. Then the govt asked the level five retirees to come in and negotiate a deal for early retirement, sanctioned by the govt; this they agreed to do, but wanted no pay for the period they had refused to work nor did they want to be paid to negotiate. All they wanted was to be left in peace, and to somehow alleviate the problems they had helped to start.

After a month of talks the oldies agreed to working for 15 years only on level five, in other words the work period had been reduced by 30 years, it was still going to be very difficult, but at least the govt; had a point to start from. The promotion from level four to level five would have to be carefully assessed, and a lot of the work load formerly done by five would have to be changed. The other problem the Seeing Eye had been unable to deal with was quickly rectified, when special legislation was listed that canceled all of the billions of summonses that had been built up and unissued. The assembly agreed and passed the bill, but of course now had to wait on the court to sign it all into law, over a trillion in govt credits had been forgiven.

A law was approved and passed the full vote unanimously, that said that henceforth the army was answerable only to the full assembly of the politicians and could never be used by the Seeing Eye, to achieve the takeover that it had almost done.

The army now became the heroes of the people, and their founders were posthumously honored. Since most of these men were Earthlings it was a great boost for the people from Earth, they were heroes. Even though the army was based on the ancient art of war; that was all Orbsey needed. It was just an extension of their overall defense strategy the same as the nuclear armed missiles, and the people felt good.

It was Lisa's job now to make personal contact with all of the federation leaders, and inform them all problems had been rectified on Orbsey, and the intended meeting on Xalafeu was cancelled. Lisa had had to move quickly, but had been able to reassure them all, and tell them the meeting had only been cancelled because of conditions at home having been stabilized. She did inform them all that the return to full production would take about twelve months, but the possibility of anarchy was now, but a bad dream.

The level four workers were now being asked to take over a spread of new duties, but the increase was not really that onerous, level five had been the lowest producers by far, and had always had a lot of workers just filling chairs and filling in the days. This wasn't the same now they were more active because they had only fifteen years to go, some even less and they were enthused again. The same with level 4 the change seemed to reenergize the entire system, it proved quite conclusively the last term of 45 years was just too much, and that the state could only get away with 15 years and no more. As for the silent revolutionaries they were all glad it was over, they weren't really happy to have been undermining what they knew was a great planet, with the best conditions of all, for its people of any of the federation members.

The Seeing Eye efforts to close down the parliament and rule by its own decree were never an alternative they had the laws right, and everything done was according to law, but they didn't have the versatility to deal with personal thought at such a huge level. It was estimated that the amount written off from the unissued and issued fines was in excess of two trillion govt credits, but the money would have taken five years to collect, and cost almost that amount by the time all of the arguments had been considered, and the judges had given their verdicts.

The robot police were deemed a joke because of the way they had been so easily destroyed, by weapons that on Orbsey weren't even seen in the museums. It was hard to estimate the damage that could have been done if that army hadn't been there, and so quickly come forward in support of real law and order.

The politicians of Orbsey had been stunned at how easily the Seeing Eye acting as a guardian of the law had almost seized political control, they had been equally stunned by the ease with which their archaic style army had so quickly routed the much vaunted robot police force. In theory the robots should have beaten the army easily, but no consideration had been given to the sureness of command, that had been just too much for the Seeing Eye to counteract. The high tech weapons had been of no use against the charging energy, forcefully expended by some very fit men who just loved the experience.

Orbsey now went into a period of unprecedented growth and maturity, it didn't turn to the creation of a modern military, but was proud of its powerful force so successfully built up over the many years, and elevated their status as the planets peace keepers with all of the original intentions preserved.

There followed a witch hunt amongst the computer giants that had put the whole system together. Because it was found suspicious at how the Seeing Eye had gained the power it did, and that suspicion gradually matured to a belief that the computer industry leaders were implicated, in a power takeover attempt.

The police force brightest and best, was given the job to trace the veracity of the claims, and they quickly came forward with charges of conspiracy against over one hundred of the planets leaders, in the computer industry, who had conspired to get control of Orbsey, and in so doing be able to control the federation of planets obviously to their own advantage. The movement had been instigated by ex bankers now in the computer industry?

The plan had been to get control first, then after having destroyed the elected govt; to install a puppet govt; controlled by them through the Seeing Eye. The computer systems would be upgraded to give the Seeing Eye more versatility and ability to deal with unusual situations such as had happened, and this would have given real control to the computer industry, the return of the old banking system was the real objective?

The men were all indicted as charged and found guilty of a conspiracy against the state, with the intent to usurp the rights of every citizen of Orbsey. They were all found guilty, given the death (sleep sentence) sentence then all executed within seven days. The investigations were continued, and given a broader mandate to find other conspirators.

Over the course of the investigation over five hundred more were found who had been complicit in the failed attempt at takeover. All who were found guilty were executed just as the original group had been. All Orbseyns hoped there was a lesson in their somewhere for computer Geeks, and their backers to in future be far more respectful of the system, that after all over thousands of years they had created.

Lisa and her team were ordered to go back to Earth, and plant a colony of Orbseyn immigrants there somewhere in the hope that that someday these people would be able to do for Earth, the same as Earthlings had been instrumental in doing on Orbsey.

It was also ordered that a fully equipped space station was to be set up over earth with a full set of medical equipment, and the entire crew, were to work five days off and five on so they could leave the station, and visit Earth as often as they wished. However they were not allowed to have any other than Orbseyns on board needing attention of some sort. The whole medical team would be replaced from Orbsey every twelve months, and they would never be asked to return unless they applied to go again themselves.

Trouble threatened: Lisa was surprised to receive an urgent call to attend a top level Plebiscite meeting as soon as she had landed; the message came to her cruiser when she was almost home again in Orbsey from planet Earth.

She was told the leaders had received a request from strangers from an unknown in Orbsey planet, to be received by the leaders at a meeting to discuss future relations between the two planets. The leaders had agreed to a meeting but decided they wanted their interplanetary ambassador present, since she was the one most knowledgeable on planets affairs. The meeting had been arranged with Lisa's present, and the leaders were now waiting to meet with the visitors in the parliament buildings.

The visitors didn't look any different than one of the many groups that could have been assembled from any of the Federation planets, but they did appear to exude an air of importance and confidence. The visitors were asked to be the first speakers since they had requested the meeting, so one of them the most officious looking of their group of twelve took the podium. They were he said there on behalf of their planet to offer the Federation of planets led by Orbsey an opportunity to join their own group, and by so doing peacefully avoid a war with them that could see Orbsey destroyed which would be unfortunate and not what they wanted to have to do.

The speaker went on to outline his own planet, which he claimed was in every way more advanced than Orbsey, with a superior in every way destructive capacity, which unless an agreement could be negotiated would be used to get what they wanted by force.

The leader for Orbsey then took the podium to reply, which he did with some effort to hide his feelings, but at the same time obviously more than a little annoyed at what he felt was a sheer impudence by the visitors. "I am surprised to receive a threat of war to be delivered in such a manner lacking in any respect, and it mattered not, just how important they felt they were. The sheer arrogance of what you are threatening is unbelievable; first of all they could at least indentify themselves and their planet, then they could produce proof of the authority for which they speak. Orbsey and its leaders were quite prepared to accept a declaration of war in a proper format, and would reply in the same way immediately, but in the meantime the visitors were told to leave since they were uninvited emissaries of war, and as such unwelcome."

An immediate order went out to trace the space craft that must be hovering in the stratosphere above and trace its origins if at all possible. The next orders that went out were for Orbseyn missiles to be put into full production as a matter of priority. Then Lisa was instructed to contact all of the Federation members, and to inform them of what was happening, and that Orbsey would do all that was needed to protect itself, and destroy any such planet that was declaring itself at war with not just Orbsey, but the entire Federation. Then the Plebiscite went into closed session to await further events as they unfolded.

This wasn't long in happening within one day there had been a declaration of war received from planet x, and its group a total of five associated planets the first attack was expected within six months. This would give Orbsey the chance to produce at least one thousand missiles fully nuclear armed, and to tighten up its defenses so that only nuclear arms of a high explosive capability could penetrate the defenses.

Lisa and her team had left on a trip to meet with all Federation members, including a team from Orbsey at Xalafeu as the most central point and easiest for all members to reach. Top scientists and heads of the defense dept; were included in the Orbseyn team, plus a group of hitherto unknowns who were in fact the heads of the secret service. Their sole job was to keep track of any subversive activities that could be destructive to Orbsey, but to always remain unknown to all but the very highest of officials in the govt.

Theirs had been a very passive role for many years, but they had been reactivated into top alert from the time of the problems with the Seeing Eye.

There were also the top army generals who had been bought into an area of importance, because they had now an army of almost ten million men fully trained in ancient warfare, but who could now be quickly taught the art of modern war as accurately as it was known on Orbsey, which wasn't much.

The scientists of Orbsey had been able to trace the source of their antagonists, and were now having manned probes investigate the five planets that Orbsey was now at war with. The reports were of five planets heavily armed and war ready, all with nuclear armed missiles aimed at Orbsey. Their big problem they had was they had not yet reached the degree of sophistication; that Orbsey had in defeating the tyranny of distance.

Their ability to defeat distance was only 50% of the Orbsey system, but they seemed unaware of this weakness in their attack plans which were in a high state of readiness. It appeared as if the initial attack was to be 500 nuclear armed missiles led by 20 separate ones designed to destroy the nuclear shield.

This would be followed up with a fleet of huge carrier space craft, bringing in a team of robots to follow up with a ground attack of some sort. They appeared to have a fleet of about 100 of these carriers on which they could bring 250,000 attack robots, they would be followed up by another 250,000 within 30 days of the first lot arriving, but only if they were needed.

A top commander had been appointed to be in charge of the coming defense of Orbsey, and a top secret team including Lisa had been appointed as his assistants. There of course was only the simplest of information released for public consumption; there was no intention to frighten the populace more than they had to be, but Orbsey was in full war preparation mode.

It didn't seem possible that this group of planets would declare war with such inadequate resources, so it was presumed that the information gleaned from the probes was only a fraction of what they had, and would use. The formerly very open approach of the Orbseyn defense system was now closed down knowing full well the enemy would have infiltrated the missile resources, and it was the first time for thousands of years, that an attack originating from Orbsey could be launched at any time. The thought of being attacked with 500 missiles etc was considered only a weak joke, and the 250,000 robots would be destroyed almost immediately so more information had to be found urgently. Manned probes were now sent out again, and they were warned the danger of this special mission was very high.

Then quite suddenly and causing a lot of surprise a request came in from the attackers for another meeting, after careful consideration the request was denied with the response, there was to be no meetings until the matter of war had been settled. Further it was suggested by Orbsey there was no further time for talk it was time for action, because war was anathema to Orbseyn thought; therefore needed to be dealt with immediately. If having declared war planet X didn't attack quite soon, Orbsey would feel itself justified to go on the attack without further notice. No response was received but then none was expected!

Orbsey attack Strategy: The big question that was being asked is why would the enemy announce their attack with such meager resources? The only answer there could be, was that they had a hidden attack team, but how were they going to coordinate such a strategy from five different planets. Unmanned probes had been sent out to all five planets, but the information that was returned was the same, except there was a very big fleet of pre nuclear battleships about 2,000, that seemed to be mission ready for conventional war.

There was another five hundred carrier craft also mission ready that could be used to transport in the infantry whether they be robots or attack troops. The attack order wasn't available; the men from the probes had been unable to steal such information. The initial enemy attack would have to be nuclear, because first they had to be able to destroy the nuclear shield that would be over, Orbsey and would require major force to remove. But they would have to first destroy the Orbseyn nuclear missiles, which would be aimed against their missiles or their planets. The big unknown to the enemy seemed to be, that the Orbseyn missile fleet air speed was twice the speed of their own.

The Orbseyn nuclear armed missile numbers were now over 2,000 and production had been changed over to producing flying bombs. These carried no nuclear warheads, but were just flying bombs using the same carriers as the nuclear missiles they were a lot cheaper and quicker to produce, but just as accurate.

It was then that the strategy of the enemy started to make sense! They wanted the Orbseyns to attack with nuclear missiles, and they would hope to see as many launched as possible. They would hope to intercept all of these missiles with ordinary bomb carrying craft, and thus deplete the stock of Orbseyn nuclear missiles. Stage two for them would be to attack the nuclear shield with the most powerful of their nuclear missiles to force entry, then they would attack with flying bombs in the hope that Orbsey would use up the rest of their nuclear missiles, and finally be open to invasion, after they had been softened up with a barrage of some 500 nuclear missiles directed at the major cities.

The audacity of the scheme started to become clear, the combined powers of the enemy couldn't match Orbseyn missile power, unless attacks could be provoked that would deplete those missiles, and create an opening. It also became clear the real enemy was an Interplanetary Bankers Group looking to gain financial control of the Federation of planets, put together by Orbseyn influence and power.

The weakness of the Orbseyn situation was they were not prepared for an aggressive war, their entire structure was based on one of strong defense; their newly formed war cabinet was inexperienced, but thankfully not foolish enough to fall for the enemies trap. It was decided to send out against the enemy five hundred flying bombs one hundred aimed at each of the five planets just as a challenge, to see just how well the enemy could deal with the faster missiles. The Orbseyn attack missiles would be traveling at over twice the speed of the enemy's defense missiles, and would test their capacity to even repel such a simple attack.

The beauty of this approach was the flying bombs could be quickly replaced, and thus no depletion of the Orbseyn arsenal would be created. The attack was timed to ensure the bombs arrived at the different destinations at as close as possible the same time, and probes had been placed high above all targets, to view the results of this simple strategy.

The enemy would have been aware of the attack launch immediately, but they faced a few problems. One was what type of missiles was on the way and whether they were nuclear armed. Second was they would suddenly be aware of the far greater speed of the incoming missiles, and would have to launch their own defense to adjusted intercept timing, that they had little time to calculate.

The reports coming in from the probes showed an orderly approach initially to the incoming missiles, which would take an average 12 weeks to arrive. It was when the calculations came in of the expected time of arrival that some panic started to show through, suddenly there were bombs due to arrive far more quickly than had been allowed for.

To expand the Orbseyn challenge one hundred nuclear missiles were launched twenty at each planet, these were twelve hours behind the bombs, and all aimed at the industrial heartlands of each targeted planet. To further create surprise the unmanned probes high in the stratosphere were armed with small but devastating nuclear warheads, they couldn't be stopped since they were in orbit way above the stratosphere, and remained unnoticed.

The probes missiles were targeted to hit the main govt buildings just hours before the enemy; would be ready to launch their intercept missiles. There would be some damage, but the confusion created would be immense and would again hold up the enemy for a little while.

Manned probes would by this time be ready to take over the surveillance and would by thought control now keep Orbsey aware of how their attack was progressing. The first reports were a surprise with a 30% strike rate being reported and a 70% intercept. This meant there had been one hundred and fifty flying bombs that had reached the target, twenty nuclear missiles as well as the initial small nuclear probes that had signaled the start of the attack. The damage from the flying bombs could be bought quickly under control, but the nuclear explosions had caused serious damage on the five planets. A retaliatory strike force had immediately been launched by the enemy, there appeared to be about twelve hundred none nuclear and another three hundred nuclear armed missiles.

This was exactly what the Orbseyns wanted, they immediately launched fifteen hundred flying bombs, and twelve hours behind them they launched three hundred nuclear armed missiles. The bombs had set targets which they wouldn't miss, and the nuclear attack was aimed at the major cities of the enemy. Then twelve hours behind the first nuclear missiles another three hundred were launched aimed at different cities.

The impact on the enemy was devastating; they were all now under heavy attack; and even a 20% hit would mean 60 nuclear bombs being exploded on their territories.

Orbsey meanwhile had loaded up two hundred space freighters with army personnel ready to be taken aboard; these would be the initial invasion force. The intent was to send out another three hundred nuclear missiles, just as soon as the strike rate had been confirmed for the current attack. A week behind the missiles the space freighters would take off and follow, but they would be going in for a ground invasion of the enemy, who it was hoped by then would be suffering from severe nuclear damage. The reports had now come in from the probes, the enemy was severely damaged, they had received direct nuclear hits by three hundred missiles, and their attack fleet had been totally destroyed. It was estimated they still had six hundred nuclear missiles and about one hundred flying bombs, but the five planets would be struggling to launch the missiles because they had been severely damaged by the nuclear blasts they had had to absorb from Orbseyn nuclear missile.

The Orbseyns then decided to launch a final attack, five hundred bombs and five hundred missiles all travelling together and identical if the enemy wanted to intercept, even with a 100% strike rate by their remaining missiles, three hundred of the attack craft would get through. Then straight behind the missiles the troop carriers would leave fully loaded and the full scale invasion would be underway. The enemies lead planet was the one first to be invaded, if this was a success the others would be asked for a full surrender, and if this was achieved they may not be invaded. The lead planet war capacity would be totally destroyed, and repatriation payments for the total cost of the war would be charged to them. As soon as these payments were guaranteed, and the war capacity destroyed the intent was the soldiers would come home.

As advised by the probes the incoming missiles from Orbsey had only been 50% intercepted by the enemy and the results were devastating over 250 nuclear warheads hit their target, and the devastation was just a shame to see if it could have been seen.

The damage and nuclear dust that surrounded the five planets caused the invasion forces to be held back, they all had nuclear clothing and head gear, but it was decided that first the atmosphere around the planets had to be tested. If the results were considered too deleterious to the possible health of the troops they were to be sent home. After waiting for a week the invasion was ordered to continue, the protective clothing was considered sound enough for the troops to be safe. The troop carriers couldn't land so the men had to be beamed down to the safest places that could be found, no enemy forces came forward to oppose the invasion. The damage that had been done was horrendous there were huge areas that had been completely obliterated by the missiles, but it was easy to see where the flying bombs had struck, this damage was nominal by comparasion.

After a month it became clear that the five planets had almost been destroyed, at least on average 50% of their entire structures were no more, and the people were mostly living like rats in sewers. The occupation forces from Orbsey were forced to bury millions of corpses, but millions had been disintegrated by the nuclear holocaust that had been inflicted on them.

It was clear most of the leaders had been destroyed as all of the major cities were no more, only the few who had left the cities to hide in suburbia would eventually be found and executed.

Lisa and her team had been ordered to keep the Federation members up to date with all information. Now she was able to announce the war was over, but as she reported the whole thing had been a farce from the start, and it was the would be dictators who had declared war, and had created a position whereby Orbsey had retaliated in full force, but this had been unnecessary. The result had been a holocaust beyond description, five planets almost totally destroyed, that would take hundreds of years to recover.

A full meeting of Federation members was called to be held in Xalafeu in six months time, a full report of the war would be tendered and discussed.

CHAPTER 18/

WAR AND PUNISHMENT

The meeting in Xalafeu was very low key; none of the delegates from Orbsey were keen to discuss the reasons, and outcome of the conflict. After the meeting started and the leader of the Orbseyn team rose to speak there was a noticeably hushed silence from the assembly, but he continued in an unemotional tone.

Orbsey he said hadn't wanted war, but having accepted a challenge from planet X; that definitely was a declaration of war against Orbsey, and that challenge was from the five planets not just the one. Orbsey he said had accepted the declaration of war, and had been certain there was a major challenge, which they planned to meet with all of the resources she had. The investigating probes sent out had reported the enemy was not as strong as it seemed, so under the circumstances it was assumed they had hidden resources such as other planets which would join them.

This had proved to be wrong therefore the nuclear attack had been far too heavy, and the destruction caused was reprehensible for any civilized society to inflict on another, it was for this reason 2,000,000 troops would be sent to help in repatriation, of this number 1,000,000 were already there.

While Orbsey regretted the over reaction to the war declaration, it made no apology for defending itself in the manner that was deemed appropriate at the time, but perhaps the use of nuclear strike weapons needed to be modified. The intent was to change over to flying bombs in future with the nuclear missiles always held back, as a threat to intending attackers; especially ones that had declared war on Orbseyn territorial integrity. After explaining a few more of the details of the brief war, the speaker returned to his seat, after inviting a speaker from the Federation to take the podium.

The leader of the Xalafeun delegation who was the elected Chairman of the Federation then stepped forward to speak, but again to a very silent gathering. "I think we should all remember that war was declared not only on Orbsey but on the entire Federation, and under its agreement with the Federation all were being defended under the Orbseyn umbrella. Therefore if Orbsey had over reacted then they all had, after all in a time of war there isn't the time to call meetings and procrastinate in any way only action was acceptable, and this was precisely what had happened. While everyone including the Orbseyns regretted the holocaust that had occurred; none regretted the fact that they were all safe, and the enemy of whatever caliber had been vanquished. The fact that the retaliation was over strong was a reality of war, and happens when one's own safety is threatened. There is no real obligation to the defeated territories, but there may be a moral obligation to try and help them get back on their feet, but in thinking about that we must consider what they would have done if they had been capable of winning the war. Certainly Orbsey would have been decimated, and the Federation would have received demands especially of a financial nature. They would have forced us to pay for their war, then we would have had real cause for complaint, instead we seem to be sitting in judgment on Orbsey which is totally wrong, and the truth needs to be understood. Planet X and its four associates declared war on a planet with far superior facilities, and technological knowhow. Orbsey was entitled to believe they must have superior forces to be so positive in the declaration of war, therefore they reacted in the interests of herself and the Federation. There is no legal or moral ground now to assist the former enemy, but Orbsey was doing this at its own further cost even though repatriation for war costs could never be paid. Orbsey officials have said they are considering increasing all of its prices local consumption and export, and in this way the enormous cost of the war will be recovered over 20 years. This isn't definite at this stage as inflationary pressures will have to be worked out before a final decision is made?" the chairman then sat.

After several speakers from all of the planets had expressed their concerns, but noted the future wars would be more cautious bearing in mind the real strength of the Orbseyn potential arsenal. The meeting was closed, but members urged to move freely and have free and open discussions. From that time for over eighteen hundred years there were no further upsets within the Federation of planets set up by Orbsey. Orbsey committed to and assisted with the rehabilitation of the five former enemy planets, but it took all of them two hundred years to recover, to a point of once again having stable economies.

Book two Introduction

This is the start of part two the star series! The Leading Planet is Orbsey and there is a Federation of ten planets that doesn't include Earth, which is a protectorate of the leading planet, and in the first century AD undeveloped in the technological sense.

Students have been given grants by the govt; of Cordiance through the university to do a full study of planet Earth. The students all meet young women in the early period AD; and get married, but they take their wives to live in the 20-22nd centuries, because when they go home to Orbsey they want them to be a little modern. There are many problems just settling the women down in the 20th century, and there is a lot of speculation about how they will settle in a far more modern society. Their first sight of a TV creates uproar, and the start of learning to go swimming on the local beach also creates problems.

Two great, great Grandsons Ebor and Eunos, of a famous pioneer couple had applied to the central govt; for the right to do a university degree based on the past and future of planet Earth. This they wanted to do by actually living and socializing on Earth, as well as interviewing prominent people. The application had been granted, and the students had been granted, a travel and time device which is no bigger than palm of one's hand, but is restricted to a very few users because of possible danger, of unskilled being lost in time, and space.

When travelling into the future if they wanted to take one friend they could do so by holding hands, doing this they travelled as one unit, but they could only go back to the time in which their friend had come from. The number of students who finally come to Earth is twelve.

Abuse of the system would mean they would automatically be returned to the present, and must return home to Orbsey ASAP. If there was any reason to halt the travel system because of abuse of the rules, all university credits would be cancelled, and no objections would be accepted by the courts.

This is because of the sensitive nature of the devices; they could for example be used for criminal activities. The abuse use is demonstrated graphically by one of the students, who came to Earth after Eunos and Ebor, he uses his for sexual adulterous activities and robbery. The unfettered illegal entry to homes using the device, and meetings in the homes of married women is easily facilitated with the T&T device. He is finally caught and sentenced to a long period of sleep in a govt; sleep facility.

THE STUDY OF PLANET EARTH

Planet earth: The two first students had made all arrangements to travel to earth, and their families had gathered at the space terminal to bid them farewell. There were general scenes of goodwill, but their parents were fairly emotional although they were confident their sons would be safe on earth. After all they were descended from the original settler to Orbsey, and there were still lots of family connections on earth should they be needed? The inter action between the two planets had been extensive for almost two thousand years, and earth was still protected by Orbsey, the only ones that knew that though were the tree spirits.

The two men were very excited and couldn't wait to leave! The journey to earth had become well travelled over the centuries; many Orbseyns with relations were living there, or just tourists wanting to have the personal experience of spending time within an ancient, to them culture. The actual travel time had been reduced to four days, including the time spent in the terminals. The unloading time on Earth was very quick, because there were no terminals and all passengers had to beam themselves down to the planet's surface. On arrival they would then be able to beam themselves to where ever they wanted to go. The students had agreed they would first go to New Zealand and introduce themselves to the Kauri spirits, and then move back to the first century AD; and begin their studies from the time of Julius Caesar and the Roman conquest of Egypt.

The students had been taught just what they had to do, from instructions left by their ancestress, when they went to visit the Kauri Trees. There was nothing in the instructions however about producing gold; obviously she didn't want the trees to be harassed by Orbseyns; only wanting to produce and take away gold. This had been one of the final guarantees she had given to the tree spirits on her last visit to earth to say goodbye.

On their arrival and after their five full days of tiring interplanetary travel, the men decided to rest under the shade of the trees for a few hours; then they would try to start up a dialogue with the tree spirits. The tree spirits on seeing them asleep realized they were descendants of Li and Orlos, so over two hundred of them gathered around the sleeping visitors, and waited for them to awake. A few females spirits who had the image of Li ingrained within their systems, manifested themselves and waited. Their images were exactly like Li when she had first come to visit as a young woman, they were breath takingly beautiful.

The two men finally awoke and were much surprised to see their visitors and to hear the spirits talking and laughing among themselves. The students understood every word, but to make them feel more comfortable the spirits because the two were now awake; switched to the Orbseyn language.

The students could see the spirits that looked like their ancestor when young and were astounded, "Gosh! We didn't know our ancestor was so beautiful," they said after the spirits explained who they were images of. The spirits decided that only fifty of them who had known Li and Orlos very well, would manifest because there was just so many of them; they realized the students would only become confused.

Instantly there were fifty manifested spirits standing in front of the students, but there was none that imaged Orlos; because they could only hold in their memories, Earthlings. The students stayed for a week while the spirits told them their own spirit history, but also that of the student's ancestors. There were many wonderful stories, and they could both visualize their first reports, which would be about this period of time spent with the spirits. Some of the spirits said they had been to Orbsey at Li's request for help, and it had been a wonderful experience.

The tree spirits explained they had been around for many millions of years, and like their ancestors; the young men if they ever needed help they should contact the tree spirits at any time. Several reference names were given for spirits that had been around before Julius Caesar was in his prime, and the younger spirits would be around in the future to help if needed. In other words throughout the entire period the students were going to travel on earth, they had friends among the spirits of the Kauri trees in New Zealand.

The Spirits said "this is the advantage of living for over 3,000 years; we will always be here as helpers or advisors to you both, this is because of your ancestors Li and Orlos. May they rest in peace and you both be worthy descendants, but we will wait and see!"